MARK THREE

A Thriller

John Hindmarsh

Cover
Cover Design by Damon Za
http://www.DamonZa.com

Formatting
Formatting by Polgarus Studio
http://www.polgarusstudio.com

Editing
This book was edited by Elyse Dinh-McCrillis and despite her best efforts, remaining errors are totally my responsibility.

Proofreading was by Randy Mundt who did an excellent job despite my lapses.

Newsletter

Subscribe to my newsletter if you would like updates, news, details of new releases, progress, etc. I estimate that I will send out three or four newsletters—say one every three months—in a year. Go to www.JohnHindmarsh.com to subscribe.

Reviews

Thank you for purchasing and reading my books. I'd like to hear what you thought of the book, so please add a review on Amazon, Kobo, Barnes and Noble, W. H. Smith, or other vendor site where you made your purchase. Or send me an email. Or indeed, do both! My email address is John@JohnHindmarsh.com

About John

I write Science Fiction and Thrillers, plus an occasional short story. In between, I hike, kayak and ski in the High Sierra region of California.

DEDICATION

I want to thank my wife Cathy for her continuing patience,
for providing her utmost support, and finally
for re-reading many drafts.
This book is for Cathy.

Chapter 1

Reb climbed the superstructure of *Hammer* using ridges and other protuberances as handholds until she reached the small recess she had claimed as her place of solitude. Here she was able to sit and watch the stars or the flow of marine phosphorescence. If it was daytime, she watched birds diving into the yacht's wake or enjoyed the rush of clouds across the sky, all away from prying eyes. Tonight, she planned to watch the ever-varying bioluminescence of different unseen ocean organisms. The faint flows of colors were entrancing, relaxing, almost hypnotic as they glowed in the wake of the yacht. The night was moonless and clouds were starting to gather in the south, blocking some of the stars. *Hammer's* internal and navigation lights provided soft illumination, but not enough to expose Reb in her lofty location. She was off duty for eight hours and apart from emergencies would not be needed until the morning.

Reb regarded herself as Welsh—she had spent her early years in Pwllheli, a coastal market town in north-west Wales, where she developed her love of the sea—and had been working on board motor yachts for nearly six years. Her role as *Hammer's* navigator meant she provided the course and waypoints the helmsman followed. Her fellow crewmembers were unsure whether her name was short for

Rebecca or Rebel, and some other variations were occasionally suggested, but only when she was not present. She carried two knives on her belt and had demonstrated she was prepared to use them. She kept to herself and no one—well, almost no one—bothered her.

The yacht had GPS, radar, and other electronic devices to manage and monitor its course. *Hammer* was a luxury vessel, a customized Princess 40M, and Reb enjoyed the opportunities her job provided for travel, for visiting different ports, some exotic, some boring, and some in between. Even the exotic became boring after too many visits.

While the new owners—they were the same as the old owners, just a different company, as far as she was aware—had changed the yacht's name, she still thought of her as *Hammer*. The current name, *Rascal,* just seemed inappropriate, but her opinion would not result in any change so she did not voice it, not even to the current crewmembers or the skipper. The previous crew, at least some of them, either had been dismissed or died, fatally beaten in drunken brawls. Another, an Australian, Pete, had been shot and killed, just days after he'd left *Hammer*. If she were superstitious, she would say there was a jinx on the crew.

She plotted courses from port to port, based on destinations announced at the whim of the client, the man everyone called the Chairman. Apart from her, none of the crew knew his name. She massaged the bruises on her arms, evidence of his brutality. The yacht was headed to Tangier; it had departed ten days earlier from Montenegro and the Chairman had in mind a safe haven destination. Reb's instructions had been clear: avoid jurisdictions with extradition treaties with the USA. The Chairman had given her a list of countries he would allow the yacht to visit. Both Morocco and Montenegro fell into his acceptable category. Reb did not know or care about the reasons for her instructions; her concerns included the safety and on-time arrival of the vessel. The weather was co-operating and *Hammer* would reach her destination in less than ten hours.

Reb relaxed into her shelter, huddling into her fleece jacket. The breeze, a southerly, had strengthened and the temperature was dropping, as forecast. She felt sad. She had reached a decision to resign and depart the yacht once they arrived at their next port. It was time to take her leave and explore new possibilities. She'd enjoyed some of her three years on board *Hammer*, at least the parts involving seamanship. Her initial training, her Yachtmaster Ocean certification, and over six years of accumulated experiences all meant she could apply for future navigator positions with confidence. Over the years she had prudently requested references from each of her skippers, to document her travels and responsibilities. Copies of those papers were on file with the employment agency that had found her current position. The agency people had confirmed they were eager to find her a new assignment. Reb expected the current skipper to give her a reference, too. However, she had no details of *Hammer's* owners, so she wouldn't have an owner's reference. Cerberus affairs were matters she would continue to ignore.

The motion of the yacht, smoothed by the stabilizers, had soothed and lulled her almost to sleep. Now, *Hammer's* sudden change of course, punctuated by the roar of its diesels as the helmsman engaged full reverse, came close to dislodging Reb from her hideaway. The change of direction was accompanied by a cacophony that caused her to sit up in alarm. There were gunshots, sounds of breaking glass, a burst of outboard motors, and the heavier thump-thump of commercial marine engines. A frisson of fear brought a shiver. This region, south-west of Gibraltar between Spain and Morocco, was supposed to be free of modern-day pirates.

While her location hid her from casual eyes, if she tried to edge forward to see more than her current view of the stern, she would be exposed and vulnerable. Forewarned by another burst of outboard engine noise, this time closer, Reb kept herself hidden as she watched a RIB, a rigid inflatable boat, bump up against the stern of the yacht. There was enough light for her to see it had a string of Chinese characters along the side, probably the name of a commercial vessel.

One of its crew tethered the boat to the port bollard on the aft deck, a flat area where the crew launched and recovered sailboats, water toys, and the yacht's own RIB. Two men from the strange RIB jumped onto the deck. Then, one to each set of stairs on either side of the yacht, they headed up to the main deck, leaving a third man with the RIB to protect their possible retreat. They all were carrying weapons. One of the intruders passed under a light and Reb saw he had an Asian appearance. They were shouting and replies were coming from other men who had boarded *Hammer* from her bows. Reb thought she recognized words, they were speaking Mandarin.

Reb heard more shouts, screams, and shots. The pirates—that was how she now classified these people— were attacking and killing crewmembers. The Chairman was the only guest on board for this trip and she suspected the assault was targeting him. She smiled and for a moment wondered if they would welcome her assistance.

Reb looked down at the boat moored on *Hammer's* stern. The guard was sitting on the edge of the RIB, which was bouncing with the waves, intermittently bumping against the yacht. He was facing away, relaxed, not at all interested in what was happening on board. His attitude smacked of overconfidence. She swung softly down from her perch. Any faint sound she made was covered by the clatter of the pirates themselves. The reverberating thump-thump of their diesel engine overlaid the activity on *Hammer*. She climbed down the stairs on the starboard side, away from the bollard where the RIB was moored. Her target was an anchor rope and chain that was coiled on the aft deck and attached to a fifteen-pound CQR anchor. Tim, the responsible deckhand, had not stowed it despite the skipper's instructions.

Reb reacted without further thought. The anchor rode consisted of about twenty feet of chain and another hundred feet of rope, the end of which was unattached. She moved swiftly, grabbed the looped chain, and draped it over the sailor's head, around his neck. She pulled back on the chain loops and kicked the anchor overboard. The man tumbled backward out of the RIB and was dragged into the sea. The heavy chain cut off any attempt by him to shout. The anchor rope flew off the lower deck as the pirate sunk out of sight. The RIB rocked, uncaring about its sudden loss of weight.

If I want to survive, thought Reb, *I have to get off Hammer, but if I steal their boat, they'll hear me and give chase.* Also, it might have limited fuel. She weighed her options for a moment.

Her decision made, she released the mooring line from the bollard and pushed the RIB out, away from the side of the yacht. The breeze would catch the craft and move it away from the yacht. She raised the hatch cover to access the yacht's boating toys for use by passengers and crew when the yacht was in port or moored somewhere for the guests' entertainment. The sailboard was her favorite. She cautiously pushed back against the hatch, hopeful the sounds she made were covered by the noises still resonating around the yacht. She pulled out the sailboard and then reached for and donned her wet suit. The storage area contained a range of supplies. She lifted out two one-gallon containers of water, some protein bars, and then rummaged around in the dark until she found a Personal Locator Beacon. When she was far enough away from the pirates, and if necessary, she would signal for help by activating the PLB's transmitter.

Reb fitted the mast into its gimbaled base and laid it along the sailboard. The mast, sail, and wishbone-shaped boom were tied together and she would not unfurl the sail until she was ready to leave. She had to hurry; all her instincts were screaming danger. She roped the small bundle of supplies to the base of the mast and tucked the PLB into her wetsuit top. She firmly gripped the sailboard's short mooring line, slid the sailboard over the stern, and, steadying herself against *Hammer*, stepped off the yacht onto the board. Her knees wobbled as she adjusted her balance. There was a moderate swell and the wind force was increasing—ideal sailing conditions, she thought, as she lifted the mast and unhitched the sail and boom. The sail snapped out as the wind caught it and she felt the board tremble. She bent her knees, controlled her balance, and stepped toward the mast, where she had greater control. The sailboard accepted the wind's invitation and moved off, heading away from *Hammer*. She should be out of sight by the time the pirates discovered they were missing both a RIB and a guard. If she was fortunate, they would not even know she had been on board. The wind tugged at the sail, reminding her it was eager to carry out her bidding.

Reb worked with the wind and sail to direct the sailboard, keeping the bulk of the yacht between her and whatever vessel was on the far side. She thought the wind speed was at least fifteen knots and under her direction, the sailboard soon was sizzling across the swell. In minutes she was almost a mile away from her starting point. As she looked back toward *Hammer*, a searchlight began its sweep across the water. Reb spilled air out of the sail and dropped the mast, sail, and herself along the board. The light swept the tops of the moving waves, missing her prone position. The operator continued the sweep; he hadn't seen the sail. She clung to the sailboard, glad of the protection her wetsuit provided as cold seawater slurped over the board.

Reb stayed down—her body aligned with the sailboard, salt spray against her face—for nearly five minutes. The searchlight made two more three-sixty degree sweeps, after which it was extinguished. She waited an additional two or three minutes before she stood, in case the light swept across the sea again. She lifted the sail against the weight of water and the pressure of the wind. The sailboard leapt with the wind. She pulled the sail inboard, maximizing her speed along the dip of the swell.

Twenty minutes later, a burst of light on the horizon followed by the roar of an explosion signaled the death of *Hammer*. More determined to survive, Reb set her course. She checked the stars, adjusted her heading and hoped the clouds stayed away. She had to sail north-north-east, she estimated, to reach Gibraltar.

Hammer had been near busy shipping lanes, and Reb was hopeful the pirates would not remain in the vicinity, that they would travel away from the scene, out of the Mediterranean and into the Atlantic. Reb thought she was reasonably safe; she was less than twenty miles from Gibraltar and even closer to the Spanish coast. If the wind and weather continued in her favor, she would arrive in Gibraltar just after dawn. If her strength gave out, she'd use the sailboard as a float and trigger the PLB. With luck, a vessel heading toward Gibraltar would rescue her. Once safely on land, she planned to contact government authorities to arrange a new British passport. However, if she was rescued by a vessel heading the other way, toward Tangier, the British Consulate would be equally helpful. The sailboard left a spray of salt water in its wake as she stepped aft and pulled in the boom, managing the drive of the increasing wind.

***

Chapter 2

Two drones, electronically tethered to their base, hovered at an altitude of almost a thousand feet. Their task was to monitor the small farm property, recording and transmitting all movement with their main focus on the property's boundaries. The drones' wing-mounted solar cells generated enough charge for their batteries, thus enabling the tiny crafts to remain aloft through the night. If a storm arrived, it was a different matter. When the weather was too violent for the self-charging drones, Mark launched larger, heavier drones designed to withstand almost hurricane-force winds, although those drones required refueling at regular intervals.

Winter was not yet finished with dumping snow across New Hampshire and each storm brought its unique challenges. So far, storms had blown away three of the smaller drones. Two had been irretrievably lost and Mark had recovered the third after tracking its homing signal. He had spares, of course, and other monitoring devices. He had placed video cameras around the property that transmitted standard images during the day and infrared images at night. Hopefully, as the end of winter approached, he would see calmer and clearer weather.

Mark's image-monitoring software programs were now very efficient. They readily distinguished a deer from a human, although as spring approached, wandering bears provided a challenge for the algorithms. When the software identified a human in any of the video material, it triggered alarms that became increasingly intrusive until someone— Mark or Anna, or one of the two children, Gabrielle or Niland—attended to the monitoring computer. The hour of day or night was irrelevant; the alarm was strident and would continue until it received an acknowledgment. Sometimes the image was of a hunter trespassing on their property. They had encountered four such intrusions during the winter, without reacting with force. Snowmobilers sometimes intruded as well, because they couldn't see the stone boundary fences topped with curls of razor wire when fresh snow partially buried them.

Today the software raised an alert when the program detected two vehicles stopping at the gated entrance, almost a quarter mile from the main house. The building was old, perhaps a hundred years or more, constructed of stone; it had two stories and had been renovated the year before. A smaller house provided accommodation for the married couple responsible for housekeeping and general maintenance, tasks they carried out with quiet efficiency. Heavy chains secured the gated entrance, giving an unmistakable *keep out* message.

The lead vehicle, a city police department SUV, implied this was an official law enforcement visit.

Mark responded to the intercom buzz. "Yes?" Anna, alerted by the alarm, stood next to him, listening and watching. Mark was momentarily distracted when she draped her arm across his shoulder.

One of the drones moved closer to monitor the entrance, supplementing the images provided by the static cameras at the gate. Mark reviewed the images on the workstation monitors along the wall at the back of his workbench.

"I'm Sam Cox, Redmont Police. Open the gate. We want some information from you."

"Officer Cox, this is a private property. I'm recording this conversation and you are on video. Please state your business and I'll refer your request to the owners."

"Listen—" It was almost a growl. The officer obviously was not accustomed to anyone thwarting his intentions. But someone had stopped him.

A different person spoke with a harsh though feminine voice. "My name is Bridget, Bridget McKeen. I'm a caseworker with the New Hampshire Child Protection Services. We haven't received replies to our communications addressed to the residents of this property."

That's odd, thought Mark, *I don't recall any official mail.* He initiated a search for the visitors' vehicle license plate number on the New Hampshire vehicle database. Both speakers had soft foreign accents, Eastern European or perhaps Russian. "Ms. McKeen, as I said to Officer Cox, please state your business and I will refer your request to the owners. And I'd point out there have been no communications received here in the last three months from any state government department."

"Stop stalling," said Cox. "Come and unlock this gate, now."

"As I said, this is private property. Unless you have a warrant or the owners allow you to enter, I'm sorry, I can't open the gate." The vehicle search program confirmed their license plates were valid.

McKeen said, "We can obtain a court order."

"To do what?"

"To enter the property and check the identification, status, and well-being of any child residing at this address." Mark heard the woman's smugness and wondered about her source of information.

"If you formally communicate your request, I'll forward it to the owners." The property was held in the name of a Panama-based foundation and Mark was confident the trail of ownership ended there.

"I'll do that."

"When I have the order, your ass will be grass," threatened Cox. "Our SWAT team will make short work of this gate."

Mark directed the drone closer to the gate, ensuring it was visible to the officer. "As long as you realize your entry will be videoed and made available to the news channels."

The putative visitors stood back from the entry and conferred briefly, after which McKeen returned to the intercom. "I'll be here in seven days with a court order. I'm leaving my card here"—she held it up to the video camera—"and you can make your life simpler by providing access as I've requested. Call me when you're ready to cooperate"

As the two vehicles reversed out of the entryway and drove off, Mark sat back, wondering how to proceed. He did not wish to expose the Cerberus children to the state's Child Protection Services. The children had no documents to say who they were, nothing to establish their legal residence, nothing to rationalize their presence in the farmhouse with Mark and Anna. A casual, uninformed observer would assess Gabrielle and Niland's ages to be somewhere near seven years, while Anna appeared twenty or older. The visitors might raise reasonable questions about the schooling and well-being of at least the two children, more so if they were aware of their chronological ages. Gabrielle and Niland were five. One of the side effects of the Cerberus processes was accelerated maturity.

In the fall, when they first arrived at the farmhouse, Mark and Anna had discussed briefly how Gabrielle and Niland, and herself, should be educated, and the decision was to obtain materials from the Internet. Mark contacted a research, manufacturing, and IT company that produced a wide range of computer-based and online training courses. He'd helped the founder survive attacks against him and his daughter, so Mark had no trouble obtaining copies of all their training materials. Anna commenced an off-campus, college degree course. She was tutoring the two younger children and they were following along with her college material. Although Mark had experienced a comprehensive, if oddly structured education at his parents' research lab, he considered the three to be surprisingly advanced.

Mark turned to Anna.

"What do you think?" he asked.

"We can't allow them to enter, or we can't be here when they arrive with their SWAT team." She shuddered. "Imagine if Gabrielle and Niland and me were caught up in the system. Besides, the exposure would generate publicity, which would be inimical to Cerberus overall."

"I wonder what prompted their attention." Mark thought for a moment. "It might be a trawling effort by someone trying to discover where we are."

"It helps to be paranoid. You never know when someone might be after you." Anna smiled to soften her words. "You'll need to stop them, somehow."

"We have limited alternatives. We can leave here or we can ask Schmidt for help. We'd be able to hack the state's records and remove any data containing references to us. There'd still be paper files so I'm not sure it would be a good step to take."

"Schmidt!" cried two little voices. They had entered the workroom undetected. Gabrielle's cloaking ability had improved, Mark realized.

"We don't want to leave here. It's too much fun. Besides, it's our home," stated Gabrielle, brushing her hair back from her face.

Niland said, "I agree."

Gabrielle was dressed as an eighteenth-century French noblewoman, wearing a long dress with lace cuffs and collar, while Niland wore what appeared to be peasant clothing smeared liberally with red paint. Mark recognized the now torn and stained shirt and realized he wouldn't see it again in his shirt drawer. The little girl carried a reed basket.

Mark looked at Anna and back at the two children. "What—"

"The French Revolution," Anna said.

"And the basket?"

"We need a container to catch my head when the guillotine cuts it off."

"The blade is cardboard," Niland rushed to explain. "I made sure it's safe. The peasants were angry and violent and cut off lots of heads. Their victims included young children, too."

"The peasants hated the nobility," Gabrielle said, "and were poor, without money, they had none at all. Sometimes they starved because of taxes and bad harvests. I don't think it justified them killing children, though."

Mark brought the discussion back to their current concerns. "What about Schmidt?"

Anna said, "Let's see what he can do."

Mark sighed. They purposely had not made contact with Schmidt since last year when they fled Washington, DC. "Okay. It means I'll be caught up in his machinations. Again."

"We can be evasive. He can't force us to get involved in Cerberus's activities," Anna said.

"Well, no more than we have been." At the beginning of winter Mark had accessed all Cerberus cloud storage facilities to download copies of their research records. He and Anna altered details and results in the original files, in the hope the changes would mislead future researchers reviewing the papers. The changes were subtle and the file contents were now filled with hidden flaws. It would take a team of researchers months, if not years, to discover the errors and re-run experiments and trials to establish the necessary corrections. Mark and Anna's objective was to sidetrack and, if possible, disrupt Cerberus's genetic engineering research. Mark hoped, one day, to stop it completely.

Of course, Mark did not inform Schmidt of those efforts. Nor had he told Schmidt he'd discovered Cerberus's financial reserves in Europe. From a revenue perspective, the organization's European activities were almost as valuable as the American operations. It seemed contracting out genetically modified humans with military training to governments and private enterprises was a major growth area. Mark used the financial information including banks, account numbers, authorized users, and passwords—to take control of bank accounts previously operated by Cerberus executives, two of whom were now deceased and the third was working with the Chinese in Beijing. He had not utilized those funds; rather, he hoped to use the money to support his efforts to curtail Cerberus's activities. He'd been kidnapped twice by that organization and wanted leverage against future threats.

Mark continued. "I think by now Schmidt's gained control of all the Cerberus operations in this country."

"That's frightening," mused Anna. "It's too much power for one man."

"Schmidt's got a balanced approach." He paused. "I know, I know, power corrupts. But we'll just have to take the risk."

"We need to establish some safeguards first," Anna said.

"We've originals of the research files we've modified. They're possible bargaining points. Or we might simply refuse to involve ourselves in any Cerberus activities. We have other pressure points. There's the ALPR data and traffic camera images that establish Schmidt was in MayAnn's neighborhood at the time of her death. Before Oliver died, he'd suggested that her apparent accidental death was staged. No one has proof, of course. If Schmidt becomes adversarial, we could anonymously release our information to the press; however, he would regard that as a declaration of war. We need to recognize that challenging him will be a last resort."

"I'm certain both MayAnn and Oliver's deaths are linked. They're far too coincidental."

"I suspect Schmidt was cleaning house. Removing obstacles to his takeover of Cerberus," Mark said.

"The President saw value in maintaining the organization. It's not surprising he agreed to Schmidt's controlling it."

"Okay, we know the risks. Schmidt is capable of forcing us to help—or join—Cerberus US. Let's see what his reaction is first."

It didn't take long for Mark to connect to Schmidt's computer using encrypted VoIP via ISP cut-outs and false IP addresses. His link included a cryptographic key-agreement protocol that he'd used previously to communicate with Schmidt and MayAnn. Schmidt answered within seconds.

"There aren't many people who know this address, but it'd be helpful if you showed caller details, at least more than a dummy IP address. What can I do for you?"

"Good afternoon, Schmidt."

"Ah. You've been quiet over the last, what, five months?"

"I'd still be on your no Christmas cards list except someone from Child Protection Services wants to visit and is threatening a court order. The accompanying police officer said he'd arrange a SWAT team to help gain entrance. If they raid us, there's a high probability of wider Cerberus exposure and publicity."

"I understand. You checked them?"

"The vehicles were legit. I've a video, of course. The only odd thing was that both officials had foreign accents. I suspect Eastern European, although otherwise they seemed American."

"Interesting. Options—you move house, allow them entry with or without the children present, or I could do something. What are you thinking?"

15

"The vote here is to stay—this is our home. Hiding the children and their presence would be a temporary solution. If we expose them to these people, we'll all have more to deal with than we need."

"What type of property do you have?"

"I'll send you a Google Map link. It's a solid stone farmhouse with a small cottage and some work sheds located on fifty acres. Wooded except in front. Hilly. High stone fence along the road, topped with razor wire. Video and motion detectors. The house is about a quarter of a mile from the gated entrance. The buildings were strengthened and reinforced last year, before we moved in. The SWAT team might have difficulties cutting through the gate but the stone fence can be easily circumvented. There's a hidden back road out and we'd be gone before they got to the house. Anna and the children would still lack ID documents, though."

"I agree we don't want any publicity for the children. I'll help you. I'd prefer to stop the process before the SWAT team tries to break in. Do you have contact details for this Child Protection Services person?"

Mark provided information from the woman's business card, which he had captured by video. He added, "This might be a trawl by the Russians, or even by the Chinese." He knew Dr. White, who'd disappeared from the Cerberus labs, was now leading a Chinese genetic engineering research team and would delight in obtaining three Cerberus children to support her activities.

Schmidt said, "I'll talk with some of my legal people here and get back to you tomorrow. What method should I use to contact you?"

Mark gave Schmidt his VoIP address.

"We'll have a long discussion once we resolve this. I'd like to know your plans and how the children are faring. New documents for you all won't be a problem. We can discuss details for those, as well."

"When this is out of the way," Mark said and ended the call.

He turned to his three eager listeners. "Schmidt can be creative, so let's see what he comes up with." He was about to say more when he was interrupted by a loud banging on the front door accompanied by what sounded like rifle shots.

"Go! Go!" Mark commanded.

Anna and the two children ran, their reactions well rehearsed. They would hide at the entrance of the underground exit, waiting for Mark to announce either a stand-down or instructions to leave the farmhouse.

***

Chapter 3

Mark sought the source of the shots while trying to identify who was at the door. He maneuvered drones, cameras, and video displays. Somehow, someone had reached the house without triggering alarms. Another someone, he surmised, was attempting to shoot the intruder.

The camera at the front showed someone huddled down against the stone wall that protected the door. Mark moved the camera position to obtain a more detailed image, but the angle was too sharp and he was unable to see details of the person at the door. He didn't even know whether the intruder was male or female. The color image showed pools of red that seemed to be blood on the stone tiles. Mark activated a steel shield, which dropped down in front of the entryway to provide protection if there were any more gunshots, while he assessed what was happening and the risks posed by the intruder.

While he worked, he spoke with Anna using the intercom. "It seems we have someone at the front door, bleeding all over the place. I'm checking for the source of the gunshots. Stay protected, just in case."

Mark checked the drones. To his consternation, someone had stopped them from sending files to the server running his monitoring software. He re-booted the drone processors, video images re-commenced their flow to his computer system, and he soon identified the source of the gunshots. A white SUV was parked just outside the property perimeter, a hundred yards away from the chained gate. The vehicle remained in position and Mark suspected the shooter was planning further attacks.

Just over a year ago, a paramilitary group attacked the laboratory complex where Mark lived with his adoptive parents, Drs. Weinek and Shutov. The attackers killed everyone at the complex, including lab workers, a security guard, and the two doctors. They destroyed the lab contents, including the genetically engineered embryos. Mark had been on the attackers' capture-or-kill list and he had retaliated, killing seven of the eight attackers and severely wounding the survivor. At that time, Mark, who was in the early days of his relationship with Archimedes Schmidt, had been testing an experimental projectile weapon for Schmidt. It was a computer controlled, servo-mounted, heavy-caliber rifle. The system was code-named Cutter, and he had used the weapon to destroy the paramilitary group's three SUVs and an experimental CIA drone flying above the complex.

This current winter he had worked with the Cutter manufacturer, RDEz, to improve the software controls of the weapon system and as a result, he had acquired and installed two of the weapons on the rooftops of his barns, where they covered most of the property. He switched on both Cutter systems and waited for the software to boot up, a process that consumed less than twenty seconds.

He used the command software and keyed in the location coordinates of the SUV. The servomechanisms adjusted both barrels until they were aligned approximately with the vehicle. Mark fine-tuned the focus of each weapon's camera on the rear window of the SUV and the Cutter software directed the servos to match his movement. The cameras provided exceptionally clear pictures, displayed side by side on a large monitor. He keyed in weather conditions including wind speed and direction, and temperature. The targeting system made small adjusting movements.

He counted three occupants. One of his drones was circling behind the vehicle, sending details of the vehicle's make, model, and license plate—information he planned to forward to Schmidt. He zoomed the camera until he identified a rifle barrel protruding from a rear side window. As he watched, someone fired the weapon. Their target seemed to be the farmhouse doorway, the shot intended to engender movement from their victim, or perhaps to set up a subsequent, more effective shot. Mark used the Cutter system positioned closer to the gate, and fired at the SUV.

He monitored the images, both Cutter and drone. Shattering glass announced the arrival of the Cutter's .50-caliber bullet. It pierced the vehicle's rear window and traveled through the driver's seat, the driver, and the dashboard, continuing on to bury itself somewhere in the engine compartment. His shot was followed by a flurry of activity as the vehicle's passengers hurriedly exited and dragged the driver to the back seat. One of the passengers climbed into the driver's seat while the other sat with the wounded man. Within seconds the vehicle roared away, skidding in overfast acceleration as the new driver tried to adapt to the snow conditions.

Mark hit the intercom button. "Anna, you can come on out. The shooters have left, in a hurry. I'm going to see who our visitor is."

"Wait, I'll help you," she said.

While he waited for Anna, Mark checked the image data from the drones. He enlarged the vehicle's license plate. "I may have started an international incident," Mark said to Anna as she and the two younger children joined him in the workroom. Anna leaned against him as she looked at the camera view of their front door.

"Why do you think that?" Anna asked.

"I shot out the back window of a foreign embassy vehicle and I think I hit an embassy employee." He indicated the still frames from the video files. "See, it reads DIPLOMAT across the top of the license plate and I think CY stands for China. That's worrying, if the Chinese have found us."

Anna said, "We'd better see to the intruder. Then you should update Schmidt. He's going to be very interested in all of this."

Mark headed to the front door, with the others following closely. Anna was carrying a Glock—she had adopted Mark's favorite handgun—in case their visitor was unfriendly. He gestured for them to stand back as he unlocked and opened the heavy door. The newcomer was curled up in the far corner of the entrance lobby. Mark reached down and pulled back the their visitor's parka hood. His movement released a fall of long wavy hair that hid most of the visitor's face. Their visitor was a young woman. Her eyes were closed and blood was seeping through her parka from her shoulder. He wondered why the Chinese Embassy would send a killer after her. As he knelt to check, she stirred, moaning softly. Mark cleared the woman's hair from her face.

He froze. Except for her long hair, it was like seeing his reflection in a mirror. The woman opened her eyes and looked into his. She began a smile.

"What—who the hell are you?" Mark asked.

The intruder managed to complete her smile. She attempted to sit up and flinched with pain. "That's not a friendly welcome to give your sister."

***

21

Chapter 4

Mark didn't reply to his visitor's comment. As far as he was aware he didn't have any sisters. On reflection, it would be an odd coincidence for someone to look so similar to him—same eye color, hair color, facial shape. Any observer would think they were siblings, perhaps even twins. He maintained a calm expression, while inside, his mind clamored for certainty.

He carefully lifted the young woman and carried her to their living room, where he settled her on a long settee.

"What's your name?" asked Anna as she attempted to remove the blood-stained parka.

"Reb," the visitor replied, grimacing as she fought a wave of pain. "Just cut it off."

Anna carried out quick introductions. "This is Niland, Gabrielle, I'm Anna, and obviously you know Mark. Niland, get me the first-aid box, quickly, and hand me the scissors. Gabrielle, get me a towel and some hot water in a bowl." When Niland returned, Anna said, "Thanks. Now I want a warm blanket."

Mark helped Anna cut through the heavy parka, exposing a bloodstained blouse.

Anna said, "Mark, turn your head while I cut this blouse off and dress Reb's wound."

Anna's efficient ministrations soon had their visitor wrapped in a large, warm blanket and her wound cleaned and bandaged. The two children stood beside Anna and the stranger, anxious to carry out whatever task was required of them. Reb's face was pale. Mark sat on a chair next to the settee and restrained his reactions and questions. He would wait until their visitor could cope with them.

Reb looked up at him and smiled.

"You look like twins," Anna said, looking from Mark to the newcomer. She was sitting on the edge of the settee, ensuring her patient was comfortable. "Now, you must tell us everything, otherwise no one will be able to relax or sleep tonight. Of course, unless you have too much pain?"

"No," replied Reb, "I'm alright. It's good to be here at last, even if I did get shot. It's a long story." She flinched as she adjusted her position.

"We can wait," Mark said, "if you're not ready?"

"No, I'm alright." She struggled to sit up and Anna helped. She looked around at the four faces. "My, what an avid audience. Mark, we're from the same parents. I'm not sure whether we're twins or simply from embryos developed at the same time. I was…sold, I suppose, when I was only a year old, to a small, private genetic research lab near Pwllheli in Wales."

"Wales? Where's that?" Niland asked.

"It's part of the United Kingdom, next to England. The researchers raised me. They monitored my development, my mental and physical growth, educated me, acted *in loco parentis*. This was all done in secret, of course."

"Do you know who sold you? Who the donors were?" Mark asked.

"No. I have some suspicions but I haven't been able to obtain enough supportive information." She tried to re-position herself and this time ignored the pain.

23

"What happened? How did you get away from them? How did you know about Mark? How did you get here?" Gabrielle rushed out her questions.

"Wow, Gabrielle, I'll try to answer all your questions. I wasn't their only, ah, lab specimen. When I was almost four chrono years old, about eight in maturity years, the lab either developed or acquired—I was too young to know which—four more embryos. Three survived the birthing process. Some time later the owner of the laboratory—it was a large corporation—well, its senior managers discovered their genetic engineering experiments were illegal, given the laws in the United Kingdom and the fact they were buying embryos or, in my case, a live person. I don't think they had ethical issues; they were simply worried about their reputation. They abandoned their research and reduced the lab staff to three employees, barely enough to tutor and care for us. When I was seven and the other children were about three or four in chrono years, they moved us to London."

"Why did they do that?" Mark asked.

"The lab was located in a small town, a bit more than a village, I suppose. It's on the coast and has a marina with lots of boats. That's where I got my love of the sea. And the three younger children—two boys and a girl—were identical. They have blond hair, blue eyes, same build, same mannerisms, which is why I don't think their parentage is the same as ours." She looked at Mark. "Anyway, the four of us were being raised in this lab environment and being home-schooled by the remaining employees, and the locals started calling us the Cuckoos."

Niland said, "I don't understand. Why did they do that?"

"An author, John Wyndham, in the 1950s wrote a book called *The Midwich Cuckoos,* which later was made into a movie, *The Village of the Damned.* The story was about these children, all alike, who were born at the same time and who, as they grew up, started taking control of the people in the village. The children were a collective intelligence, an alien master race. Anyway, the people in the town where we were living thought we were some kind of aliens. They realized we were developing very fast and were very different, and they started objecting to our presence. Their protests were just noisy at first but soon became nasty. One of the laboratory buildings was burnt down. I was attacked and beaten even though I was young. When the adverse publicity gathered weight, the corporation decided to relocate us."

"Were you hurt?" asked Gabrielle, her face showing concern.

"I thought so at the time, but I was barely bruised. Some of the teenage boys who attacked me were far more battered. They didn't realize how strong I was, or how focused I get if someone tries to harm me. At seven chrono years, I was about fourteen or fifteen in maturity years. One boy ended up with a broken arm and another suffered a concussion. The lab people scolded me for kicking; I still don't know why. I was fighting for my survival, I thought."

"Another similarity," Anna said. No one commented.

Reb continued, "They moved us to a house in London. It was serviceable, I suppose. But the people in London, who were employed to be our tutors and caretakers, lacked any empathy. Their cruelty was casual, unintended, I suppose. Oh, we were fed, clothed, home-schooled, although the standard was mediocre, but they didn't fully comprehend our rapid development or even the level of our intelligence. I was given a small allowance that I saved. I wanted to get out, far away from that institutionalized environment.

"Somehow—it may not have been entirely coincidental—I met a member of Cerberus. She supplied me with Cerberus-developed medication that stopped those horrendous growing pains. Mark, you had those, too?"

He nodded. "Yes, and oddly, the medication was also provided by Cerberus. I'm not sure of their motivation and now, with the old management team either dead or helping the Chinese, I don't think there's any way we can find out. I suppose the Chairman is still around, somewhere. He might know if it was an intended strategy."

Reb looked startled. "You don't know? He was on his yacht when it was attacked, by the Chinese, I think. As far as I know, they killed everyone on board and blew up the yacht. It was three months ago, a week or so after New Year."

"How do you know? No, continue with your story," Mark said.

"I managed to save my money and persuaded the corporation people to pay for a series of sailing courses. I qualified as a Yachtmaster Ocean. I'm a top navigator. I can calculate courses, waypoints, distances, and fuel consumption before most people can key numbers into a computer. I talked my way into a job, first on a small sailboat that was being used for charter. Next I worked on a small motor yacht, and eventually—" Reb stopped, fighting a flash of pain.

"I can give you some painkillers," offered Anna, reaching for the first-aid box.

"No, thanks. I'll be alright. After a couple of years I got a position on a larger motor yacht, *Hammer*, as their navigator. I didn't know at the time that the yacht was owned by Cerberus."

Mark and the others were stunned by this revelation. For a moment silence reigned. At last, Niland spoke. "Cerberus? You worked for them on board their chairman's yacht? Wow!"

Reb grimaced. "Yes, it was a surprise to me when I started to realize who was who. Oh, none of the crew was supposed to know about Cerberus. A steward made a recording of a meeting of the senior American executives. I heard about it and he played it for me. Mark, you were mentioned. They wanted to get you into Cerberus. The steward was killed later, I heard, in a bar brawl of some kind. I think after that one or two new crewmembers were Cerberus.

"Toward the end of last year, the Chairman must have been fearful of arrest. He told us we were to sail only to countries without an extradition treaty with the United States. In January we were heading to Morocco from Montenegro when the yacht was attacked. I thought the attackers were pirates. There were Chinese people involved. I could hear them shouting instructions in Mandarin; I can understand a few words. I thought I got away without them realizing; we were near the Spanish coast and I sailed my sailboard to Gibraltar. I don't think anyone else managed to escape. There was a lot of shooting and the pirates blew up the yacht. As far as I know, they killed the Chairman.

"After I reached Gibraltar, I needed new documents. My passport was on *Hammer*. I got a replacement and returned to London. After some thinking about my future, I decided to search for you. I had some information but not enough, so I contacted that Cerberus lady and she accessed their records and obtained more details for me. It took me a while to find this place, though. I had some very able assistance; the three children in London are capable hackers. They discovered you had moved to this property. Then I suppose the Chinese followed me, tracked my activities, but I don't think they knew who I was trying to meet. Perhaps they realized I had survived their attack on *Hammer* and they wanted to eliminate a witness."

She stopped and looked at each of her audience. "Can I stay?"

~~~

It was late afternoon before Mark was able to connect to Schmidt. He didn't waste time on pleasantries. "Schmidt, I've a problem building here. We had an unexpected visitor. She was shot and injured by someone in a Chinese Embassy vehicle. I'll send you the video files. Our visitor's injury is relatively minor but she might need to have it checked at a hospital. As soon as we take her to a doctor—it's an obvious gunshot wound—we'll be at risk. Oh, and I may have wounded one of the vehicle's occupants. They left in a hurry."

"You're on a roll. First a visit from a child welfare visitor and now a Chinese shooter."

"I don't think the two events are connected."

"Yes, the probability is low, less than 20 percent. Send me all the images you have, including everything on the embassy vehicle. I'll task my analysts to discover who they are. What about your visitor?"

"She's private."

"Hmm. I'll explore the details with you, when we meet up."

"We're worried the police may visit again. I expect them here tomorrow. I don't think anyone will report the shots—there are always hunters out, around here. However, if the guy I shot is seriously hurt, his companions will take him to the local hospital. There'll be a report to the police of a gunshot wound and after they investigate, they'll end up here."

"Okay. I'll get back to you later this evening with a detailed plan. Expect a support team to arrive in the morning. I'll utilize Bravo Company from the 145th MP Battalion. They'll see this as a challenge. You've met Major Dempsey. He'll lead."

After ending the call, Mark turned to Reb. She was sitting next to Anna who was holding her hand. His sister's face was pale; it was clear she was suffering from the gunshot wound. He asked, "You can cope until tomorrow? If your wound gets infected or the pain is too much, we'll have to break cover."

"I—I think I can. It's only a scrape."

Anna said, "You were fortunate. Any lower and it would have made a mess."

Reb nodded.

Mark said, "I have to send off some image files to Schmidt. We can talk some more once I've done that."

**

Chapter 5

The following morning everything seemed to happen at once. The intruder detection software blasted its warning only minutes after ten a.m., when everyone was in the workroom where Mark maintained all his video equipment. He was modifying the software controlling the two drones. Now that he knew how Reb had stopped the image transfers, he wanted to ensure it was impossible for anyone to block the cameras again.

Reb held her head at the sudden sound. "Oh, do you have to make so much noise?" she complained.

"We have visitors. There are police SUVs at the front gate," replied Mark, after he checked the camera images. "I'd better call Schmidt."

The VoIP connection took less than ten seconds.

Mark said, "Schmidt, good morning. Our local police force has returned. There're three vehicles. They're waiting at the gate for some reason."

"I have them on my screen, too. We use big drones, not little ones." Schmidt smiled into his video camera. "Your police officers are about to get one helluva surprise. Bravo Company's in the air and is minutes away. You should go outside and watch. You'll be impressed."

Mark disconnected the call and looked at his companions. "I think we'll play it safe and watch from here." No one dissented.

~~~

Major Dempsey, circling below the modified Army Hercules he had exited only seconds before, watched as each group from Bravo Company dropped from the rear of the aircraft. They tumbled out ten at a time, a total of fifty, their wingsuits catching the slipstream as the Hercules flew at eight thousand feet, just above stalling speed. The major had led their exit. The pressure of the slipstream filled and solidified his wingsuit, creating a platform that would allow him to fly for miles.

Bravo Company formed up on their group leaders and the resulting V formations trailed Dempsey as he headed toward their destination. He was more than pleased with the professionalism of his Cerberus team. They were difficult to motivate and he was tested each day by their unique approach to discipline and duty. But this type of exercise appealed to their sense of adventure and they reveled in the challenge it provided.

He checked his schedule in his helmet display. At this rate his small force would reach the target in under ten minutes. He planned for his men to arrive with no advance warning to the law enforcement team waiting at the gate to the small property. There would be no aircraft in sight, no engine noises, only the sudden and simultaneous landing of fifty wingsuited soldiers. Ten men—an advance party— were already in position. They had departed the aircraft earlier and he'd checked his heads-up display for confirmation of their arrival. They had landed before the appearance of the police and were monitoring events. They were now half-buried in the snow along the road leading to the entrance to the farm property, hidden from all but the most alert eyes.

The experimental wingsuits, intended for Special Forces HALO tests, were an RDEz product. Somehow, General Schmidt had managed to divert a hundred or so of the suits to the 145th and Bravo Company had worked hard to develop a level of expertise in their use. The learning curve had been steep and for some, painful. Using the wings was far more hazardous than standard parachute jumping. The company had not experienced any fatalities in training, although three men had suffered broken limbs as a result of poorly judged landings. He expected they would make a full recovery. They were Cerberus, after all.

To Dempsey's surprise, the suits were proving to be very effective for low altitude jumps. The suit's ability to support a gliding experience of at least five miles for every mile of height at exit provided his teams an excellent flying range. The suits had an experimental camouflage pattern of white and blue in random patches to help hide the soldiers as they dropped from the sky.

Dempsey checked his helmet display. His current airspeed fluctuated around forty knots, the air temperature at ground zero was about 45 F and the temperature increased almost four degrees for every thousand feet of altitude lost as he descended into warmer air. It still felt as though it was freezing. Oxygen supply was not a problem as they dropped from the initial height of eight thousand feet.

He checked progress against the flight plan. The flight computer indicated they now had an estimated flight time of less than five minutes. His men were in their intended formations, everything was proceeding to plan.

He looked down, glorying in his near silent flight over farmlands and forests, across roads and rivers, all the while unobserved. Drifting chimney smoke outlined the wind direction. Tiny streams were frozen over, as were the small lakes. A river ribboned its way across the landscape. An occasional dog barked, seemingly aware of the fifty soldiers floating above the earth, and was chastised for raising false alarms. A cloudless, blue sky and morning sunshine promised a warm day.

Dempsey wore an experimental ARG command helmet that provided augmented reality in layered projections of images and data superimposed on the real world. His men wore similar helmets, although they lacked the command features contained in his unit.

The ARG's small computer, modem, and battery pack were nestled in the small of Dempsey's back, protected by his bulletproof jacket. The large bulbous visor covered most of his face, providing one-way vision with complete clarity, while preventing observers from seeing any projections. The complete ARG unit—visor, helmet, and computer—was controlled by the wearer's mental impulses via a skullcap built into the helmet.

The ARG units provided data feeds to the team of analysts and tacticians at Camp Brewer, Bravo Company's base, and the supporting system enabled Dempsey to tap into any of those feeds to see or hear events across his command. Personnel at Camp Brewer reviewed, in real time, uploads of every action, every step, every sound transmitted from every helmet. They fed back tactical suggestions, analytic results, identification details, and other data in support of the mission. All the material would be available for his review and assessment when he returned to his base.

RDEz had provided the ARG system for field-testing at Schmidt's request. Dempsey knew the general was involved in the organization's activities, but that involvement did not give him any cause for concern, because RDEz's research teams were proving to be excellent inventors and innovators and were providing very advanced technology to the 145th.

Almost to the second, as planned, Bravo Company started its final descent under wingsuit control; They would land without deploying parachutes. The soldiers, in a synchronized maneuver, turned into the light morning breeze, slowed to stalling speed to cancel the lift of their wings and dropped the final ten feet or so to the ground. One or two soldiers stumbled as they landed on uneven surfaces hidden under layers of snow and ice. They all had landed inside the property perimeter, with twenty soldiers on each side of the gate and the remainder at the gateway. Dempsey was in the center, facing the road.

Three two-man units carried Hornet V "fire and forget" anti-tank missiles. Schmidt had expressed his concern that the police would bring in an MRAP-equipped SWAT team and had authorized the issue of the weapons. The missiles were live and the major hoped to end the day without authorizing their use. Common sense, he hoped, would prevail. They were here to persuade the local law enforcement officers to treat Midway and the other occupants of the farmhouse with respect and caution. Their intention was not to wreak havoc on the locals.

Dempsey had landed closest to the gate. He peeled off his wingsuit to reveal his army uniform, with rank and service ribbons displayed. His soldiers copied his example, removing, folding, and placing their wingsuits to one side; they would retrieve them later. They were all dressed for the winter and snow conditions. While Dempsey was armed with a holstered pistol, his men carried short barrel UZI SMGs—not regulation military issue but a weapon they had found to be very suitable when deploying in wingsuits.

The major stepped up to the gate. As he did so, he signaled his small escort team to stand back. By this time, five law enforcement officers had gathered at the entrance to the property with expressions of astonishment as they faced the men and women of Bravo Company. The officers wore militarized camouflage uniforms, bulletproof vests, and carried holstered handguns. One officer was using his radio and Dempsey listened via his augmented system, confirming the man was reporting Bravo Company's arrival to his base.

Dempsey then focused his attention on the officers, instructing his visor-mounted camera to take an image of each face and transmit it to Camp Brewer for identification.

"Who's in charge?" asked Dempsey as he reached the small group. He did not raise his helmet's visor.

"He is," two of the younger officers replied in unison as they pointed at the man still using his radio.

"And he is?"

"Lieutenant Peter Harkness. He's waiting for Corporal Cox to arrive with our MRAP so we can take down this gate," one of the officers said.

"You have a Mine Resistant Protected Vehicle for your SWAT team?"

"A thirty-tonner."

As they spoke, Dempsey's visor displayed the young officer's identification and personal details. David Leary was twenty-eight, former US Navy, and had a Criminal Justice degree. He had been recruited by the Redmont Police Department four months prior and was a junior member of the force's Containment Team. The ARG also displayed Leary's height, weight, and naval service record, details which the major ignored. Redmont was about ten miles away and had a population of under a hundred thousand. Dempsey wondered why such a small city had need for a thirty-ton MRAP, equipment intended for aggressive warfare in Iraq and Afghanistan.

"You won't need it, David," Dempsey said. "You have my assurance."

The officer appeared startled when Dempsey addressed him by name.

Dempsey continued, "Can you ask Lt. Harkness to come talk to me? Tell him I'm Major Dempsey, 145th MP Battalion, and I'm here with my Bravo Company. We're testing some of our equipment."

"Sure." Leary walked over to Harkness. Dempsey watched as Leary interrupted his superior's radio conversation. The highly sensitive directional microphones in the major's helmet allowed him to hear every word.

"Lieutenant, he says he's an army major—they're all MPs—and would like to speak with you. He says his Bravo Ccompany is using this property for testing their equipment."

"Very well. I'll be there when I finish this call."

Harkness clicked on his radio and said, "Cox, the army is here and I'll go talk with them. Get yourself here, ASAP." He replaced the microphone, closed the door of his vehicle, and walked over to the gate. Behind him, the soldiers hidden along the snow bank, stood, dusted themselves off, and stepped onto the roadway. The police lieutenant stopped for a moment, shook his head as though in denial, and continued toward Dempsey.

"Lieutenant Harkness," Dempsey greeted the man. His helmet transmitted Harkness's image as he spoke. "I'm Major Dempsey, 145th MP Battalion. Can we help you?"

"I'm not sure. We want to enter this property and I'm waiting for our MRAP. We'll take down this gate in seconds, once it gets here."

Dempsey checked the gate and confirmed Midway had shut down its electronic locks. He reached over and loosened the chains. "I don't think your vehicle is necessary," he said as he swung the gate inward. His purpose was not for the police to enter, but for some of his unit to exit the property.

Two of his men—dog handlers—stepped aside to allow the gate to open wide and then they walked out onto the road, toward the group of police officers. The handlers and their dogs had jumped together and the animals still displayed excitement from the drop. The dogs tugged at their leads as they sniffed at each police officer.

Dempsey continued, "But I think you need more than a desire in order to enter army property." He didn't mention

Schmidt had concluded a rental arrangement, for a very short period, for the house and land the prior evening.

"We suspect someone committed a crime here yesterday," protested Harkness. "My chief has instructed me to make inquiries and arrest whoever we find."

"Perhaps you can provide me with details." Dempsey checked his helmet display; the dog handlers had made some discoveries. He heard them mention Cerberus to two of the officers. "But first—" He raised his voice, "Officer Johnson, Corporal Marchini." Two police officers appeared startled. Dempsey continued, "Would you please join my dog handlers? I think you both know why. Surrender your weapons and badges to Leary." The dogs had sniffed out the two men as Cerberus. The organization's personnel records were incomplete and the two men had been omitted from Schmidt's list of police officers with Cerberus-based genetic enhancements. "Apologies, Lieutenant. We need to have a discussion with these two. They'll be coming with us, when we leave, I'm sure."

Harkness looked bewildered as his two of his team handed over their weapons to David Leary. He turned and watched as they then stood by the dog handlers. "What's this? They're two of my most experienced officers." His voice rose. "What are you pulling?"

"Assume they tendered their resignations, without notice. No, they're not under arrest. They're innocent of any wrongdoing. As I said, we want to talk to them. Now, tell me about this crime you're investigating."

***

Chapter 6

The roar of the huge SWAT vehicle as it approached interrupted the lieutenant's attempt to answer. Dempsey watched its pace decrease and the engine noise increase as the driver down-shifted to bring the monster to a halt. It skidded on loose gravel and stopped just feet away from the now open gateway. Dempsey recognized the vehicle as a Buffalo six-wheeler, an ex-army MRAP, typical of the larger ones used in Iraq, weighing over sixty thousand pounds. It loomed, black and threatening, over the group at the gate, a prime example of the militarization of law enforcement organizations. Three heavily armed and armored SWAT team members alighted via the rear ramp, their faces reflecting astonishment at the presence of more than fifty soldiers. The driver opened his door and stuck his head out.

"What the fuck—" he began.

"Corporal Cox," said Dempsey. His heads up display confirmed the driver's name and added brief personal details. Cox had been seconded from the state capital's SWAT group only two months ago. The 145th's base team had identified Cox from files Mark had forwarded. "Please exit the vehicle. Lieutenant, I think the presence of an MRAP here is unnecessary. I suggest you have one of your men—no, not Cox, we want to speak to him—take your monster back to its garage. If something could be overkill for this morning, it would be an MRAP."

Dempsey focused on each of the newly arrived SWAT officers and sent their images to the analysts. He noted the dogs were sniffing at the newcomers.

"Who do you think you are?" spat Cox. "I'll drive this wherever I want. I don't give a damn—"

Dempsey held up his hand and signaled to one of his men. "I want Special Agent Renshaw, now."

"Yessir," snapped the soldier. He returned within seconds, accompanied by a woman wearing civilian clothes under her protective bulletproof vest. The FBI Special Agent, embedded with the 145th, had jumped from the Hercules with Bravo Company. She was also Cerberus-engineered. This was her first assignment since her graduation from the FBI Academy.

The major said, "Special Agent, this is Corporal Cox. As you were briefed, his real name is Nikita Yanovich. Please place him under arrest for falsifying his visa application records—you know the rest." Dempsey turned to the MRAP driver. "Captain Yanovich please dismount from the vehicle and hand your weapon to Lieutenant Harkness."

Three soldiers aimed their weapons at the Russian as Renshaw stepped forward. Yanovich snarled another expletive as he closed his door, locking it. The MRAP's heavy construction could withstand IEDs, other explosives-based weapons, and both handgun and rifle fire. The vehicle leapt into motion, heedless of bystanders, as Yanovich guided it through the now open gate and toward the farmhouse. Dempsey made his decision. He instructed his missile teams to fire, targeting the gap between the two rear wheels on the driver's side.

He counted down the seconds as the first missile team readied its weapon and fired. He watched the missile's rapid flight and nodded his satisfaction as it impacted the target with precision. The explosion lifted the rear end of the MRAP, just enough for Dempsey's purpose. As it rose, the second missile struck, followed almost immediately by the third. The synchronized explosive staccato flipped the vehicle onto its back. The turret dug into the roadway and the vehicle tumbled, spinning until it ran out of momentum, facing back toward the gateway. It finished on its side, its engine now silent.

Dempsey signaled two groups of soldiers forward to the MRAP as he spoke to Harkness. "Lieutenant, come with Special Agent Renshaw and me. Renshaw can complete Yanovich's arrest. You can forget everything else. There's nothing here to interest you. Let's see how he fared."

Harkness was silent for a moment but then protested again. "Shots were reportedly fired here last night, according to my corporal. That is, according to Yanovich. The local hospital admitted a man with a gunshot wound."

"You're relying on the word of a Russian spy, someone who's here illegally? You have other evidence, I trust? You have the victim under guard at a hospital?" Dempsey said as they walked over to the smoldering MRAP. The stink of high explosives seared his nostrils. He never liked the odor; it always reminded him of battlefield death and destruction. The visual relayed by the soldier who had been first to reach the wrecked vehicle showed that the driver had not fared well. The Russian was unconscious and bloodied; he had not fastened his safety harness and the explosion-induced tumbling of the vehicle had thrown him around the cabin where sharp corners and the heavy unforgiving construction had pounded him without mercy. "Speaking of hospitals, please arrange an ambulance for Yanovich. He has a broken arm and, I suspect, some broken ribs. He'll require some stitches, too."

The police officers trailed Dempsey and Harkness, seemingly as confused by events as their lieutenant. Harkness said, "Leary, contact base. Tell them we have a medical emergency and need an ambulance. According to the major, Cox—Yanovich—has a number of injuries. He's probably correct, that was a helluva crash. Don't add anything ... Say I'll report in-depth when we get back."

Leary rushed off to the nearest police SUV. He returned a few minutes later, almost breathless, and reported, "Lieutenant, they—base—said to tell you the shooting victim—the guy admitted for a gunshot wound—has gone." He took a deep breath. "He was taken from the hospital about an hour ago, by someone from the Chinese Embassy. The man's vehicle was taken as well. The ambulance should be here in fifteen minutes."

Harkness stared accusingly at Dempsey. "You expected this, didn't you?"

"I received an update when we were landing. We knew the shooting victim had diplomatic protection and the embassy would not want him to be questioned. He attempted to kill someone and the target fired back. Self-defense. I think you can close your file."

The police lieutenant shrugged. "Cox was far too aggressive, trying to get to the people in the farmhouse. I should have realized something was off. Who are they? Why are you protecting them?"

Dempsey started to reply, but paused when he heard the approach of a helicopter. He said, "That's our general arriving. He'll expect me to brief him." He didn't mention Schmidt had monitored the morning's events and did not require a briefing. "It's need to know, I'm afraid. You and your men—except Officer Johnson and Corporal Marchini who'll both come with us—can leave once Agent Renshaw has arrested Yanovich. You'll want to be able to tell your boss you saw him under FBI control. We'll see he's taken to a hospital when the ambulance arrives. The FBI will guard him while he's in hospital and take whatever legal action they think is warranted."

Dempsey and Harkness watched as soldiers extricated Yanovich from the capsized vehicle. The Russian groaned, barely conscious.

Dempsey said, "We'll replace the MRAP; this one is too damaged to repair. Also, we'll arrange its recovery and disposal. We've plenty of spares from Afghanistan and Iraq and the army's still giving them away for free. We'll get you a smaller one, more practical. Now I'm scheduled to meet with the general. Have a good one."

"Thanks. The chief won't believe half of this. We've lost two good men, three, if I include Cox—Yanovich. Damn. Even I don't believe it and I've witnessed it all." He ran his fingers across his cropped hair.

Dempsey handed the police lieutenant his business card. "If your chief gets too rough with you, have him give me a call. We can also arrange for the general to talk to him."

Harkness pocketed the card. "Thanks. I've got the message—don't mess with the people who live here." He turned away, signaling to his men to accompany him.

~~~

Schmidt and Dempsey waited at the front of the farmhouse for someone to open the door. Dempsey had instructed his men to assemble at the gate where army vehicles would arrive in less than an hour to take Bravo Company back to Camp Brewer. He planned to return with Schmidt, in the helicopter.

Anna opened the door. "General, Major. Welcome to our home. Please come in." She stepped aside to provide room.

"Thank you, Anna," Schmidt said. "You're looking well. Country life must agree with you." Dempsey nodded his greeting. He had met Anna when the Cerberus children had been located at Camp Brewer.

At Anna's direction, they moved into a large room and joined Mark, Gabrielle and Niland. Mark had asked Reb to stay out of sight until they'd decided how much to disclose about her presence.

"Thank you, Schmidt. You, too, Major. Your men made a remarkable entrance, very impressive," Mark said.

"I only hope the locals don't start tweeting that the UN is invading New Hampshire. My men will leave in the next hour, if our trucks arrive on time. We'll remove the MRAP as soon as possible, although that may take a week or two to organize. We'll need some heavy lifting gear."

Mark said, "What's your impression of the police?"

"Good. I made it clear to Lieutenant Harkness the local police should leave you alone. He seemed to get the message."

"Thank you," Mark and Anna said in unison.

Schmidt said, "We still have to deal with the Child Protection Services. We've some attorneys looking at the issue."

"Thanks for that, too," Mark said. Anna nodded.

"We have some options—to accommodate you somewhere else for a while until this social worker loses interest, or we lend you some de facto parents, a couple who can demonstrate there is a normal," Schmidt looked at the three Cerberus-modified people and back at Mark, "well, almost normal, family here. Assuming we can find the right people, it might be a good medium or longer term solution."

Anna said, "I think the parenting suggestion is very good. It should work." She ignored the frowns from Niland and Gabrielle. "We need identification papers—birth certificates, social security cards, and passports. They're most critical. For me and the children."

"Agreed," Schmidt said. "I'll arrange for documents to be issued when I have all your details." He turned to Mark. "You should have asked earlier."

"Can we interview our parents?" asked Gabrielle.

"Of course. I'd enjoy observing the process. Mark, what do you need?"

"All the usual documents. I'll revert back to Midway. Just remember, we want to keep our independence."

"Understandable, but independence may not always be possible to maintain. In this case, though, I agree it's in my interest to protect the four of you."

Mark and his three Cerberus companions looked at each other. Mark shrugged and said, "I might as well tell him now. There are five of us, here. The visitor who arrived yesterday, who was shot by the Chinese, is my sister. She wants us to help rescue three children who were also genetically engineered. Reb thinks they used a non-Cerberus process, perhaps the same one used on her and me."

***

Chapter 7

Schmidt and Dempsey waited while Niland ran to ask Reb to join the meeting. She entered the room, an anxious expression on her face.

Mark said, "Reb, this is General Archimedes Schmidt. He and I worked together at various times in the last year or so. He reports to the President. I believe he now controls Cerberus, at least the US part. He took over when the Chinese murdered its senior management executives. Well, except Dr. White, who was the key Cerberus researcher, who's now working in Beijing." He realized he had surprised Schmidt; the doctor's defection to China was confidential information.

Mark continued. "This is Major Dempsey. He's the commanding officer of an MP battalion, which consists of Cerberus genetically engineered soldiers. Bravo Company is here, today. Alpha Company was also Cerberus-resourced but was wiped out last year by an attack on their base. The members of that company, plus a number of Cerberus children, were killed—some poisoned, some shot—by a Chinese assassination team that penetrated Camp Brewer." He didn't mention that Anna had shot and killed the murderers. "Dempsey and the 145th work closely with Schmidt."

"Schmidt, Dempsey, this is Reb Llewelyn. Her name was given to her at the genetics lab in Wales where she spent her childhood. She thinks we have a common parentage and based on how similar we look, she's probably correct. We're going to arrange a DNA analysis for confirmation. In Schmidt-speak, there's a 95 percent probability we're siblings. Reb is genetically enhanced, we think to the same level as me."

The two officers exchanged greetings with Reb. Schmidt added, "It's intriguing to think Mark has a sister—most unexpected. He's been very helpful on more than one occasion. I've been trying to recruit him for the last year, so far without success. I'll include you with Mark and his companions here under my protection. I'll do my best to help you all."

Reb said, "Thank you, General. There is just one thing."

Schmidt stilled. "Yes?"

"I'm enlisting Mark's—and Anna's—yes, and Niland's and Gabrielle's assistance, too." She added the two younger children to stave off their undoubted protests if she left them out. "I want Mark to help me rescue three genetically engineered children who were in the laboratory with me. They're sixteen, seventeen or so in maturity terms."

"I don't see any difficulty. That should be straightforward," Schmidt said.

"Yes," Mark said. "Except they're located in London."

Dempsey laughed. "I'll be interested to see how this works out. Bending the rules in this country, when you have the President's ear and half the Cabinet's, might seem easy, but we're short of influence in Westminster."

"Oh," Gabrielle said, "it's not a problem. We're going to rescue them ourselves. I don't think you'd be able to land Bravo Company in England without causing a lot of publicity. I saw what you did, this morning."

Dempsey looked pained. "We can be far more subtle, if we must."

"I noticed," Anna said. She was seated next to Mark. "Our drones record voice as well as images." She did not mention they'd recorded the streams of data transmitted by the soldiers' ARG helmets; Mark had worked quickly to copy those transmissions. She continued, "What did the police lieutenant say? Oh yes, "I got the message, don't mess with the people who live here." I wonder what the Child Protection Services lady will say when she hears about this morning." Her smile took the sting out of her words.

Schmidt said, with almost a defensive tone, "We had to do something, otherwise you'd be in custody by now."

"Or more likely, they would've found no one here," corrected Mark. "We have our exit. We need very little notice. We'd be on I93 in less than five minutes and in Boston in forty. We've timed it. The disadvantage of fleeing is that we'd lose this base, our home, with all our belongings and equipment."

"Did you check out this woman—what's her name, McKeen, Bridget McKeen?" Anna asked.

"Yes. She's not Russian, at least there's no evidence suggesting that," Schmidt said.

"Can you persuade her to lose interest in us?" Mark asked. He did not wish to surrender his home with Anna and he suspected Gabrielle and Niland had similar thoughts.

"She's applied for another position, with relocation to DC, and we're accelerating the selection process. When she succeeds with her application, we'll arrange deletion of all the files, both computer and paper, that she created covering her visit here. There's a 90 percent probability she was influenced by Yanovich. Maeve and her team think Yanovich told Ms. McKeen he was acting on information obtained from confidential informants. When she hears he's a Russian spy and has been arrested, she'll more than likely discount his information."

"How is she? Maeve?" Mark asked. The last time he'd seen Maeve Donnelly, then director of the FBI, she had been kidnapped by a group of Russians. Mark had been standing near both Maeve and the leader of the kidnap gang. She had signaled her instruction for Mark to shoot the leader of the kidnappers, even though he was holding a gun to her head. When the Russian was momentarily distracted, Mark had followed her instruction, to Schmidt's consternation. Maeve resigned soon afterwards and subsequently had taken on responsibility of building and managing Schmidt's team of analysts.

"She's well, enjoying all the challenges I throw at her team. I'll pass on your regards."

"Thanks. How do we go about setting up these pseudo-parents?"

"Gilmore's available, if you agree?"

Mark turned to Anna and said, "You remember, he helped us get out of Camp Brewer."

Anna nodded.

Schmidt said, "He's freelancing. I've been trying to find suitable assignments for him. I'll check if he and his business partner are interested. Or they may know someone suitable. If he agrees to take on the assignment, he'll provide excellent protection for Niland and Gabrielle."

"Should I get new papers, too?" Reb asked.

"It seems the Chinese have identified you, so I must say yes. American, though. You'll have to develop a story to explain why you have American papers but a strong Welsh accent. Mark, send me names, ages, and appropriate birth dates. I'll check if Gilmore's available and interested, and can recruit someone to act as mother. If that works out, I'll arrange parent records for these two." He indicated Gabrielle and Niland. "If not, we'll find someone. Is there anything else you need? Before I head back to DC?"

Mark said, "No, we've covered the critical items."

Dempsey said, "We may need to refute all kinds of media reports, if the police videoed our activities."

"Oh, I wouldn't worry," Mark said. "I ran a process just before they departed—it's the software equivalent of an EMP blast. I used our drones and other equipment at the gateway. All their images are corrupted. Inexplicable, I know." He shrugged.

"I suppose you copied our data feeds as well?"

"Data feeds? What data feeds?" Mark's expression remained innocent.

Schmidt laughed. "It's time we left. We've things to do, MRAPs to dispose of, papers to arrange, plus passports for all. Come on." He led the way out of the room. Dempsey and everyone followed.

Passports for all? Mark wondered. Did Schmidt expect the two young children to travel to London, too? Perhaps it would be simpler than trying to persuade them to remain here.

~~~

Mark contacted Schmidt again when his workroom was clear. He had kept the parka Reb was wearing when she arrived. It was bloodstained and Anna had cut it almost in half when she removed it. There was a bullet hole in the front, just below the top of shoulder, with an exit hole in the back. A circle of faint brown marks—not blood, as far as he could determine—raised his suspicions. They were like almost indiscernible scorch marks, near the bullet's entry hole, which intrigued Mark.

"Yes, Mark?"

"I have a small request."

"What is it?"

"Reb's parka— she was wearing it when the Chinese shot her. Can you arrange for it to be tested? I don't know what labs you can access?"

"Military. FBI. Private. Why, what's the problem?"

"Well, Anna accuses me of being paranoid. I don't mind, because I've been attacked, more than once. I might be over reacting this time."

"Tell me more."

"I have a suspicion about the wound Reb suffered. The weapon may have been fired from up close. If so, her jacket would test positive for gunshot residue. I'd like to get it tested, if you can arrange it. I'll courier her parka to you or to a lab."

"The 145th has access to more than one lab. Send the jacket to me; I'll do the rest. I'll keep it away from FBI labs. It'll take a week or so. I'll get them to use the blood for DNA analysis, too. I think we have your DNA on file, somewhere." Schmidt provided the address. Mark folded the jacket into a courier box and printed and attached a label. The following day Anna delivered the package to the FedEx pick-up point in Redmont.

***

Chapter 8

"I trust there's no record of us using this room or meeting here?" asked FBI Executive Assistant Director for National Security, Andrew Wentworth. He was in his fifties, of medium height, and heavily built. He had a reputation in the FBI for his aggressive approach to law enforcement. He had held his current position for four months, replacing Oliver Stewart who had been killed in a hit and run accident. The killer remained at large, to Wentworth's frustration and anger.

The other person in the small anonymous meeting room was Ricardo Mercante, a senior CIA officer. He was a taller man, about the same age, with a dark complexion and a thin, humorless smile that often accompanied the quick and deadly—not only in terms of an opponent's career—insertion of a very sharp blade. The two men had known each other for a number of years and occasionally worked together.

The meeting room, located in the depths of Langley, was windowless. An air conditioning vent provided a slight draft. The room contained a metal table and four chairs. There were no papers on the table, no pens, no pencils, no telephone. Neither man carried a laptop or cell phone. The room had two doors, one at either end, exiting into different corridors, thus permitting the two men to depart when the meeting ended, with no one noticing they had met. Or at least that was their intention. They sat at opposite ends of the table.

"Anonymous, swept, electronically protected, and do not disturb. No recording or communications devices will work in here, for the next hour. Your visit has not been logged. No record will exist of our meeting here today. Of course, you may be seen and recognized by people here. That's inevitable, I'm afraid." Mercante did not mention neither man should use their names in the conversation.

"Good to know." Wentworth extracted his own electronic dampening device from an inside pocket and switched it on, adding to whatever precautions the Agency man was taking. "I assume you want to start a rebellion in some unnamed country?"

"Yes." It was more snarl than speech. "Cerberus."

"Aaaah. And Schmidt?"

"Mainly Schmidt. He presents a major threat, a potential danger to all of us."

"I believe it's an actual, not potential, danger. Extreme. Stewart's killer is still unknown. Likewise for Special Agent Freewell; the claim that her death was accidental stinks to high heaven."

"He's wreaked havoc on the Agency, on our people. Tim was a good Agency man and Schmidt screwed him." Tim Edgar-Osborne had broken the law, a point Mercante did not dwell on. The former agent had assisted an illegal group of mercenaries, which had attacked a genetic engineering laboratory, murdered the researchers, and attempted to capture Midway. "Plus, he's gathering far too much power."

"Are you confident this room is bug proof?"

"My reputation stands on it."

"So does mine, from here on. What do you propose?"

"I'm prepared to arrange—I've some contacts through cut-offs—for a small team to, er, remove Schmidt from his lofty position. I need to be confident you'll support me. For example, I need your assurance you'll do your best to ensure any evidence that might lead back to my contacts or to me is permanently lost or destroyed. I'll arrange attacks on Midway, as well."

"What happens to Cerberus?"

"We take it over and take it apart. The President should never have allowed it to continue nor for Schmidt to take control. You know we tried to stop it. Failed, abjectly so. So now we have thousands of these so-called super soldiers"— he spat out the term—"deployed throughout the government. They're in the military, in my Agency, in the FBI, Homeland Security, and other government agencies. We don't know names. We know they're reporting back to Schmidt."

"It's intolerable. I've been tearing out my hair, trying to identify who on my team might be Cerberus. Everything they see or hear goes to his analysts."

"Analysts?"

"Yes. Schmidt has a team; I think a hundred or so, employed to analyze all the data they can obtain—NSA, local LEOs, DHS—anything they can get their hands on. They tap into data sources I didn't even know existed. They're managed by Maeve Donnelly. Schmidt relies on Maeve and these people for strategic analysis and I understand they're all high achievers."

"Data failure on my part—I didn't know their size or scope. I knew she had some kind of team but not how large. If you can provide details—"

"It'll be difficult. They're distributed across the country. Most don't know they're working for Schmidt. They just know it's a quasi-government department with a military or law enforcement bias."

"Hmm. You're adding to my concerns. Well, what do you say?"

"I'm in. I've some special projects budget available, I'll set up a small team to monitor and gather information on Cerberus activities and share the results with you."

"Good. I'm doing the same. I'll need to know Schmidt's movements if we're to achieve what we both want."

The two men stood, reached across the table and shook hands. They left separately, minutes apart, exiting through the door nearest to them.

～～～

Unbeknown to either of the two men, a recording of their conversation was transmitted to an Agency-embedded Cerberus member and she forwarded it to the secure Cerberus cloud. Unfortunately most of the recording was garbled; the technical equipment used by the two men had done its job. To a large extent.

～～～

"Status reports. You first, Dempsey," Schmidt directed. He waited for the attendees to settle into their respective seats and for the ARG software to connect. Major Dempsey and his new commander for Bravo Company, Captain Helen Chouan, were in Camp Brewer. Maeve and Linda Schöner, her senior analyst, were the last to join the meeting. She and her team had previously moved out of temporary offices in Quantico to a Cerberus building in Washington D. C., on 22nd Street. Schmidt was located in another Cerberus building, on Pennsylvania Avenue, near to the IMF offices.

The attendees each wore ARG glasses. They were learning how to use the RDEz equipment. Dempsey's display showed both the physical reality of his office—Captain Chouan was seated opposite him—and the augmented details provided by the software. He checked each image provided by the glasses. As he focused on a virtual attendee, the image was supplemented with details of name and location. He knew he could modify the settings, adding or reducing the amount of data displayed.

"Good morning, everyone. I'd like to introduce Captain Helen Chouan; she's our new commander of Bravo Company." He looked through the virtual images to Chouan. "Captain, I'll arrange in-person introductions as soon as possible." She nodded, still cautious in her use of the equipment. The other attendees voiced their welcome. Dempsey displayed a virtual copy of a document.

"This is my detailed report," he said. "In summary, Exercise Blown Away was successful. Bravo Company performance was excellent. There were one or two minor injuries that occurred on landing. We persuaded the local police to depart without immediate complications. The Russian, Yanovich, is in hospital under FBI guard. We found two Cerberus resources and they're undergoing evaluation. There was no media reaction, thanks to Midway's software EMP blast, which corrupted all image and audio files recorded by the police team."

Linda Schöner provided additional details. "We understand there was quite an explosive meeting when the police returned to their headquarters. The local chief had Harkness and his entire team—of course, minus Yanovich and the two Cerberus members—on the mat for almost an hour, trying to understand what had happened. He was annoyed when they discovered all their video files were corrupted, to say nothing of his reaction when he heard you wrecked his MRAP. He regarded the vehicle as the flagship for their small force, taking them into the big time. The chief wants to protest but doesn't know to whom he should do so. We informed him—well, an anonymous source contacted him—that we'd keep silent about both the Russian and the chief's loss of the shooting victim from hospital, if he dampened down his reactions. It seems to have worked."

"They didn't need a six-wheeler Buffalo," commented Dempsey. "We've requisitioned a replacement, a smaller

MRAP, to be allocated to them. It'll take about six months to process, longer if I can drag it out. We've been asked to demonstrate the wing suits to another MP battalion, and I'm making arrangements. At the moment, nothing else except routine training."

"You omitted an important item," Schmidt said. "Colonel Dempsey has been confirmed as the commander of the 145th. Congratulations, Colonel." He displayed a copy of the announcement.

Everyone congratulated Dempsey. The newly promoted colonel smiled and produced another document. "Someone has been appointed to a two-star general. I wonder who?" There was laughter and another round of congratulations.

When the meeting settled down, Schmidt said, "I'll add comments regarding Midway and his team. He's been joined by a young lady, Reb Llewelyn, who is his sister. She's genetically enhanced, and we're trying to obtain details as well as confirmation of their relationship, the latter via DNA checks. She's persuaded Mark to travel to London to help rescue or recruit three other genetically engineered children—they're seventeen years old, in maturity terms. I intend to support this venture for two reasons. One, I want to find out more about these British genetic engineering attempts, and if we help Mark, it will create an obligation for him to help us. Two, so far our attempts to take over the Cerberus operations in Europe have failed. Our American Cerberus people don't get past UK Immigration. The Brits have assembled a comprehensive watch list—I suspect Cerberus UK is involved. We're hopeful Mark will be allowed to enter the country, and we'll use his venture as cover to allow us to contact Cerberus UK management. I'll give the task to Scott Gilmore. I'll try again to send support teams, but given our experience to date, there's a 20 percent probability of success." He paused in case there were comments or questions. After a moment, he asked, "Maeve, what's your situation?"

"We agree with both your reports. There are other topics I need to introduce. Keep in mind they might be part of a larger action we haven't yet identified. Four Russian shadows, located in New York, have gone off the grid. We can't find a trace of them, anywhere. We're experiencing a lot of chatter and suspect it's directed at Cerberus and you. We also have a recording of a meeting at the Agency—two people, senior rank, no names, not logged, extreme and effective steps were taken to ensure privacy and prevent eavesdropping. Despite those steps, we managed to record portions of the discussion. The file's corrupted; whoever was involved has some effective dampening software. The general impression we've gained is they agreed to take action against Cerberus. We're analyzing all the NSA data we can get our hands on, and will continue to do so, until we discover what these people are planning. I'd suggest you add some Cerberus guards to your escort. Colonel, I suggest you raise your security level at Camp Brewer. I'm arranging additional security for my team, just in case."

~~~

Maeve Donnelly and Schmidt were in conference. It was a personal meeting, face to face, no minutes, no other attendees. Maeve pushed away her notepad. She had discovered what Schmidt was doing and wanted to express her concern. It was not so much that she had rational objections, but because she knew the process was not always harmless.

"Archimedes," she said. "Why would you do it? The Cerberus treatment is generally effective, I know, but sometimes someone reacts adversely. You run the risk of permanent disability or even death, if your body rejects the treatment."

"They have reliable predictive tests, now. They can measure the likelihood of rejection, with 99 percent probability."

"But why are you doing this?"

"The answer is simple. At least to me. I'm trying to control thousands of Cerberus's genetically engineered people, some post-conversion, some pre-conversion. We've hundreds of pre-conversions who are still children, babies from the birthing program Dr. White started. I can't eliminate them—any of them. So I need to know, at least in part, what it's like to be Cerberus engineered. I don't see any downside. I might even talk you into participating—"

"No. I strongly doubt it, despite your ability to persuade. I do understand your motivation, but I disagree with it." She shook her head as she reached over and patted the back of Schmidt's hand. "I'll pray for you."

"Thank you. I think. Different topic. What do you propose we should do about Midway?"

"You have concerns? You've always been positive about him?"

"Not concerns so much. Well, maybe. Our Cerberus researchers are encountering major difficulties with their research. The material Dr. White left behind doesn't always seem to be accurate. The result is a lot of re-work. We're wondering if the Chinese have managed to corrupt the files. Or maybe the Russians? There are other candidates, one of whom is Mark, but I can't think of a motive."

"He's difficult to predict. We only see what he wants us to. I'll ask the team to dig deeper."

"We're missing a set of embryos. We don't know if White took them and I don't think Mark knew about them. They were in the main laboratory."

"He's not Superman."

"Sometimes I wonder. We haven't any idea of his full capabilities," Schmidt said. "I know, it's a stretch. I can't blame everything on Midway."

"Everything? You have more?"

"Cerberus UK has been difficult to bring into line. Not just because of our inability to get people into London, but some funds are missing, as well. We're talking upwards of fifty million dollars, some of which belonged to Cerberus USA. The bank accounts have either disappeared or the authorized signatories have been changed. Some of the activity we've confirmed on the accounts is legitimate disbursements. It's the larger balances that worry me. Can we blame Midway?"

"Insufficient data for evaluation, I'm afraid. Why not try again to recruit him? Have him take responsibility for Cerberus UK. He has the ability. He'd need a management team to help him while he gains more experience."

"Hmm. He'd have Anna's support, that could stabilize him. Very tempting."

***

Chapter 9

Mark, alerted by an alarm from the overhead drones, checked the vehicle's arrival and recognized the driver; it was the ex-FBI agent, Scott Gilmore. There was a second person in the small SUV and Mark assumed that she was Sera Wilkins, the person Scott had recruited to share his parenting task. According the briefing paper provided by Schmidt, she was younger than Scott, ex-FBI, and post-Cerberus.

"Good morning, Scott," he said, "and welcome." He pressed a button. The heavy gate, decked with chains, swung open under control of its hydraulic system, and when Scott drove through the gateway, it closed again, heavy steel bars sliding back into place.

Mark waited at the front door. Scott introduced his companion and Mark said, "Hi Sera. Come on in and I'll introduce you to everyone."

Scott still wore a piratical eye patch; he had almost lost the sight in one eye after being tortured by a Russian who had been trying to discover Mark's identity. Scott, himself post-Cerberus, was rescued by a Cerberus team. Later, a team sniper shot and killed the Russian and his accomplice. When Scott recovered from his injuries, he had considered taking revenge against Mark for causing his torture. When two Chinese assassins tried to shoot Mark, Scott had intervened, shooting one, and Mark shot the other. As a result, he had said, he now had a responsibility to keep Mark alive.

Niland and Gabrielle stared at the newcomers, their expressions of concern warring with curiosity.

"Are you going to be our parents?" asked Gabrielle.

"Can we play pirates?" asked Niland. "That's a nice eye patch—did you get it on a sailing ship? I've been reading about the pirates in Elizabethan times. Would you class Drake as a pirate? Overall, it was foolhardy for a small country to go to war against Spain, don't you think?"

Scott was silent, apparently unsure how to react. Mark interceded. "They like to play act history, so don't be surprised if they rope you in—maybe literally. This is Niland and Gabrielle and this is Reb—Reb's my sister. Scott, you may remember Niland, Gabrielle, and Anna from when we rescued them from Camp Brewer." He waited while they exchanged greetings and then said, "Come and sit down in here." He led the way into a more formal seating area. "Children, see if our guests would like tea or coffee, or perhaps a snack."

"Mrs. Jones will help you," Anna said as the two children headed to the kitchen. Mrs. Jones was the housekeeper. She and her husband lived in the small cottage just fifty yards away from the main house.

"Schmidt told you our problem?" asked Mark.

"He said you had some issue with the Child Protection Services? And the local police? You need two people who can act as parents to two young children, to prevent any further problems."

Mark nodded. "Has Sera received a full briefing?"

"Yes—I've provided her with lots of background details. Schmidt also said you plan on traveling to London and want us to go with you?"

"We'd have problems if we tried to take the two younger children with us, without their parents, so you're invited."

Sera spoke up. "They appear to be delightful children. I assume they won't cause problems?"

Anna answered, "They're both very advanced. I would describe them as precocious."

Mark chuckled. He said, "Scott, I know your background. Sera, can you tell us about yourself? On second thoughts, let's wait until Niland and Gabrielle return. They'll be upset if they miss this conversation."

Anna added. "They're going to interview you, or so they said." She reached out and gripped Mark's hand. They both hoped the children would not object to their acting parents.

Two hours later, both newcomers appeared exhausted, while Niland and Gabrielle were still fresh and eager to continue their interview. Mark took pity on their visitors. "Whoa, you two. Let Scott and Sera draw a breath. You'll have weeks to find out all about your new parents."

Gabrielle regarded Scott and Sera in turn. "Are you both certain you want to take on this responsibility? We're only five years old chronologically, but we're eight-plus in maturity terms. I think our intellects are actually closer to ten or older. We're a challenge, because we're both aggressive learners."

Niland chimed in. "We're both socially adept, though, and know right from wrong. We look alike, so we're classifying ourselves as twins. We gave Schmidt the same birth date for both of us for our new documents. We like to plan ahead."

Scott's eyes widened. He waited for Sera to respond. She said, "I think this is going to be an interesting assignment. I'll take on the responsibility of provoking your intellects. Scott can do the bodyguard thing."

Scott said, "Well, did we pass the interview?"

The children jumped up and down, shouting in unison, "You passed, you passed."

Mark said, "Good, I'm glad it's settled." He turned to Scott. "You came prepared to stay? You can move in now; rooms are ready for you. Mrs. Jones prepared them earlier this morning. Anna will show you."

~~~

That evening, after the two children had escorted the visitors on a tour of the house and the external buildings, and after an early dinner, they all sat in the same room as earlier. The open fire filled the room with warmth. Mark found himself focusing on Anna. He tugged his thoughts away. Everyone had settled down, although he noticed the newcomers occasionally exchanged glances that seemed to convey concerns about their task. He watched while Niland and Gabrielle played a game of chess.

"Scott," he said, when he thought the two children were otherwise occupied, "there won't be any problems. You're acting as parents for the purpose of coping with government officials and similar problems. The scope of the assignment doesn't extend to full parental responsibility."

"Oh, but we'd enjoy doing that," said Sera. "I think they're sweet."

Mark wasn't sure sweet was the word he would use.

Scott nodded. "I agree with Sera. Yes, Schmidt explained it's a need to provide parental cover, but I think this is going to be an interesting assignment. We've both encountered Cerberus children before, but I don't think we've met anyone like Gabrielle and Niland. We both signed on to Cerberus years ago. I didn't know Sera at that time, and we each participated in the post-conversion process."

A whisper tickled the back of Mark's mind: *We both like Scott and Sera. I think she'll be fun. Niland agrees.*

"As soon as Schmidt gets documents arranged, we'll head to London. I expect it will take a couple of weeks." Mark raised his voice for all to hear. "I'll let Schmidt know the response is yes to Scott and Sera, and ask him to expedite our documents. We'll make travel arrangements once we have our passports, agreed?"

No one dissented. Anna smiled her approval. Reb looked relieved.

~~~

Junior Assistant Air Attaché, Colonel Alexey Grigoryevich, currently with the Embassy of the Russian Federation, Washington, DC, was experiencing a challenging day. He didn't understand why his country's internal security service, the *Federal'naya sluzhba bezopasnosti Rossiyskoy Federatsii*, or FSB, was operating in the United States, conflicting with the rightful activities of the Foreign Intelligence Service, the *Sluzhba vneshney razvedki*. He'd been a senior officer in the SVR and hoped the Americans were still not aware of that role, and that they regarded him merely as a colonel in the Russian Air Force.

Now he had an invitation to visit the State Department, a request that worried him more than it should. It seemed another FSB sleeper had been arrested after entering the United States illegally. The man, Nikita Yanovich, had managed to gain employment in one of the many American police forces, this one located in New Hampshire. And he, Alexey Grigorevich, was being called to account.

The invitation had been brief as to its subject matter and the department was one he had not previously visited. The letter stated someone in the Office of Global Criminal Justice was "desirous of his presence." He had provided the address to his driver and sat back, ignoring the press of Washington traffic. It had taken almost an hour to reach his destination. The building was nondescript, set in a block of five almost identical buildings, surrounded by parking spaces and the occasional budding tree. The driver stopped at the building entrance and waited for him to exit the vehicle. Alexey indicated he would return in an hour, and the driver drove off to find somewhere to park.

The entry to the building was almost security-free, a most unexpected openness given the American penchant for searches, identification requests, and other indications of paranoia. Indeed, they often were almost as bad as his fellow countrymen. He was directed by a receptionist in the lobby to an elevator bank, and ascended, unescorted and as far as he knew, unheralded, to the tenth floor. There, a young intern, male, formally suited, unsmiling, greeted him at the front desk and led him to a small, glass-walled meeting room. One long wall showed an exterior view while the other glass panels were opaque. Alexey sat at the table, his back to the view. He wanted to be able to see the facial expressions of whoever had requested his presence. He waited with uncharacteristic patience. A young woman entered the room after a few minutes, with a tray laden with a coffee pot, cups, and sugars of various kinds. She placed the tray on the table and departed, without a word. He poured himself a cup of coffee, black, without sugar. He sipped, enjoying the familiar aroma.

Five minutes after his arrival, the door opened again and a stranger stepped into the room. He was unaccompanied, carried no papers, and did not have a laptop. Most unusual, in Alexey's experience.

"Colonel Grigoryevich," enthused the stranger, extending his hand. He spoke in Russian, fluent, colloquial, reflecting a Moscovian accent. "So good to meet you. I must say, you produced an excellent paper last month on the current state of American aircraft manufacturing. What was the title? Oh yes - *Stasis in the American Fighter Program*. I've said for years the corporate-based revenue burdens on our defense program are excessive. Allow me to introduce myself. I'm Robert McCarr. I'm a senior manager in Global Criminal Justice." He fumbled in his pocket. "My card." He proffered the crisp white card, which Alexey accepted. The man sat down and poured himself a cup of coffee. It also was black, without sugar.

"I trust you like the coffee? I believe it's your favorite."

"Yes, thank you." Alexey thought he concealed his surprise.

"Alexey—you don't mind if we're informal? Please call me Robert. Over the last year or so, we've had more problems than we need, with the incursions of the FSB into America. We both know the FSB is domestic and should remain that way. You, as a senior officer in the SVR, must be aware there's a need for professionalism in these matters, no?"

"Mr. McCarr—"

"Robert, please. We're being informal, here."

"Very well. Robert. I know nothing about these FSB people—"

"Surely you've identified the problem. If they weren't here, intruding into your sphere of influence, this wouldn't be an issue. I can give you a list —it may not be all, but it'll be most of these FSB sleepers—and perhaps you can arrange for them to leave the United States, say in the next month or so? They can go somewhere else. Let the Special Branch or MI5 worry about them, for a change."

"I can do nothing about people who appear to be in your country legitimately, from countries you have friendly relations with. If you permit someone from, say, the Ukraine to legally settle here, it must be your problem."

"We know, we know. But when they're Russian nationals, they become your problem, since you're the key SVR officer here."

"You're wrong—I'm not SVR."

The American pulled a bundle of papers from his inside suit coat pocket. He searched for one, found it, and dropped it on the table, aligned so Alexey could read it. He hid his surprise; the Americans had more knowledge of him than he'd realized. The sheet of paper listed his service history, with precise dates, ranks, and duties. He pushed the paper away.

"Anyone can draft a sheet of paper and photocopy it a few times," he said.

"Well, this might be more, shall we say, insightful."

The American selected and dropped another sheet of paper on the table. Alexey glanced at it, looked away and then looked again. The paper was headed REICHNING ET CIE, which was a small and secretive private bank based in Zurich. He felt the blood drain from his face. The paper listed details of his deposits over the last two years. He pushed this sheet away, too. This time his fingers were trembling.

"Yes," said Robert. "I fully understand your reactions. Now, can we get down to serious matters?"

Alexey nodded, his mouth dry, his throat clamped, his heart racing.

"Good," said Robert. "I want to discuss a troublesome organization—called Cerberus."

***

Chapter 10

They traveled as a group, and the almost tangible excitement of the two younger children gave Mark cause to reconsider the suitability of the arrangement for future trips. Fortunately, the in-flight movies held their attention once the flight was underway. It would take nearly seven hours to fly from Boston to London. A worry bubbled in the back of his mind. The UK authorities might balk at the arrival of so many genetically modified people, even if two were young children. He had discussed traveling in separate groups, a spreading-of-risk approach, but no one had identified any advantage in his suggestion.

He decided to relax and stretched out, relieved to have so much space. They were seated in the upper deck of a 747, empty of passengers apart from him and his companions, and the cabin crew was enjoying the presence of the two children—at least for now. Mark thought the novelty might wear off before the flight concluded. Anna, in the seat beside him, appeared to be sound asleep. He tucked her blanket more firmly around her shoulder. She stirred and smiled at him, immediately falling back to sleep. Reb was reading the in-flight magazine and Scott and Sera were watching Gabrielle and Niland, who had no intention whatsoever of sleeping even though the flight had departed from Boston at ten p.m. Mark sighed and closed his eyes.

The next thing he knew, one of the cabin crew gave his shoulder a gentle shake, waking him from an elusive dream. "Do you want breakfast?" the flight attendant asked. "And should I wake the others? We'll be landing at Heathrow in an hour."

"Let the two children sleep, please. The adults, yes."

Reb yawned, lifting her eye mask. "I'm awake."

Anna said, "Me, too." Sometime through the short night she had reached out for Mark's hand. There was silence from Scott and Sera.

As they ate their breakfast, Mark chatted with Anna and his sister, trying to plan the day. "We land just before ten a.m. That's local time. We should be through Immigration and Customs in about an hour, although I've heard it could take a lot longer. Another hour to get to the hotel. Another hour to sort out where we are. So lunch around one p.m., I think, if it all goes as planned."

"Sounds good," Anna said, her hand on his arm.

"When are we going to visit my friends?" asked Reb.

"Let's see how we go. Passport Control is our first hurdle. We may wait two or three days before we see them. I'd like to do some hands-on research, scout around, find out where everything is, before we knock on their door."

Reb frowned. She had stated she wanted more immediate action, but everyone in the planning meeting before they left had agreed to Mark's timeline. She sat up as she returned the airline seat to the upright position, her expression challenging. Mark frowned and his sister looked away. He suspected she wanted to revisit the group's decision but seemed to realize no one else would agree to vary their plans.

An hour later they were among the first passengers to disembark the 747. Mark led the way down the narrow stairs to the main flight deck and through the exit door, nodding his farewell to the flight attendants. He slowed his pace to ensure he didn't leave anyone behind. He searched for signs and headed in the direction indicated for Immigration. After five minutes of walking and following signs along almost empty corridors, he heard Niland complain.

"I think we're going around in circles. It must be a British challenge for new arrivals, to see if they can discover the quickest way out of Heathrow."

"Perhaps," replied Gabrielle, "we should try one of these doors marked NO EXIT?"

Unsure whether her suggestion was serious or not, Mark looked back. Sera was guiding Gabrielle away from an emergency exit, to the young girl's obvious reluctance. They arrived at a T-junction and as Mark was about to turn to the left, as indicated by the sign, two men stepped forward. They seemed to be officials of some kind, in plain clothes, and of serious mien.

"Mr. Midway?" one queried.

"Yes, that's me," Mark replied.

"I'm Sergeant Taylor, SO15. We're Special Branch. Can I see your passport, please?" Mark had no idea what organization the officer was talking about, but handed over the requested document. The sergeant examined it briefly and handed it back. "Thank you, Mr. Midway. Please follow us."

As the two men headed in the direction opposite to that indicated by the sign, Mark wondered if they were being led back to the aircraft they had just left. He kept pace with Taylor and everyone turned to follow. Mark noted another two men had closed in behind his small group.

"Where are we going?" Mark asked.

"We have a special process, sir," stated the older of the two men. "It won't take long."

The directional signs had been reduced to code numbers and warnings of improper use of emergency exits. After a few more minutes, the sergeant stopped at a door, knocked, and opened it, standing aside to permit Mark to enter, followed by the rest of his team. None of the police officers entered. At least, Mark assumed they were police officers.

The door snicked shut behind Niland who was last to enter. The room, decorated in soft, bland colors, was large enough to accommodate about fifteen people. There were comfortable-looking chairs against the walls, and a coffee percolator burbled on a corner table that also displayed milk, sugar, cups and saucers, and a plate of English biscuits. Vases, five of them on small tables, were filled with fresh flowers, and the flowers added their delicate scent to the room. A medium-sized television hung on the end wall, an image of Big Ben on its screen.

Scott broke the silence. "It looks pleasant. Come on," he directed Niland and Gabrielle, "sit down and relax."

Everyone followed his suggestion, although Anna first poured Mark a cup of coffee. Gabrielle retrieved two biscuits, one for herself and one for Niland. Mark was sipping his coffee as a woman entered the room through another doorway. She was tall, dressed smartly in a dark suit with lightweight brogues polished black and shiny, and her hair, graying slightly, was brushed back, disclosing a broad forehead. She wore minimal makeup. She smiled at everyone.

"I'm Detective Inspector Goodwin. Please help yourselves to coffee. We can make tea if you prefer. There's more milk for the children in the refrigerator, and biscuits. This won't take long. Let me see." She scanned the room and addressed the children first. "You must be Gabrielle and Niland. Welcome, my dears. Scott and Sera, likewise. Anna, Reb and Mark, of course. Welcome to the United Kingdom and to London. I thought I should give you each a personal welcome. Oh, don't worry, it will be another thirty minutes before your luggage is available. We're collecting it for you. I'll arrange for your passports to be stamped, it won't take a moment. No, it's no trouble, at all. You'll be out of here before any of the other passengers have managed to find their way through Immigration."

"Er, Detective Inspector, what is this all about?" Mark asked.

"Oh, call me Lizzie, please. Why this VIP treatment? Well, to start with, we know who you are. Yes, even you, Reb, my dear. Our resources in America are well informed. We need to understand why you're all here, though. I should mention—I'm Cerberus, too."

~~~

The last thing Mark expected on his arrival was to be chauffeured in a Rolls Royce from the airport to their London hotel. Cerberus, not the Metropolitan Police, had provided two vehicles and a van for their luggage, each with a driver. SO15, Scotland Yard's Counter Terrorism Command, were providing two officers at sergeant level to assist Mark while he visited the country. He assumed, however, that the escorts were there mainly to provide the DI and Cerberus with details of their daily, if not hourly, activities. The two younger children with their new parents were in the lead vehicle and Mark, Anna, and Reb were in the second. Reb was sitting in the front seat and Mark and Anna were in the back. Anna had gripped Mark's hand very tightly when the driver headed the vehicle away from Heathrow. The luggage van trailed behind, somewhere, surrounded by a cloud of London's black taxicabs. Mark hoped the van's driver could handle both the taxis and the drizzling rain and their luggage would arrive at their hotel.

Reb provided an ongoing travelogue as the car headed along the M4 toward the center of London. The main feature of the highway was the numerous speed cameras, supposedly to ensure a safe driving speed but, according to their driver, were mostly effective in raising revenue for the local council or borough. At Reb's suggestion, the driver detoured through Hyde Park, past Buckingham Palace, along Birdcage Walk to Westminster, along the Embankment, then finally to the Tower Bridge Hotel with its view of the Thames and Tower Bridge.

Checking into the hotel required not much more than handing over a credit card and providing identification, and with adjoining rooms, everyone would be able to keep in easy contact. The drivers informed Mark they would be available any time, as long as they had at least an hour's notice. The luggage van arrived, later. After showering and changing into clean clothes, they all headed out, following the concierge's directions to a restaurant in the St Katherine's Dock area. Over lunch they agreed that when they finished their meal, Scott and Sera and the two younger children would explore St Katherine's Dock and the marina. Mark suggested Reb and Anna join them, so he could return to the hotel to do some research.

As a result of their meeting with Detective Inspector Goodwin he had names and contact details of Cerberus senior members. The UK organization had a basic management structure in place, enough to ensure the continued operation of a skeletal European business in the absence of strategic direction from the American management team. Mark intended to research the names supplied by the DI. Mark entered the lobby of the hotel and as he headed toward the elevator bank, one of the SO15 officers intercepted him.

"Sir, may I have a minute?" The man had been introduced as Sergeant Roberts, a Cerberus resource. Mark suspected the majority of the Counter Terrorism Command was Cerberus.

"Yes," replied Mark. "What can I do for you?"

"Sir, I observed three foreign gentlemen—Americans, I believe—asking for you at the desk. I surmise they paid for information. They headed to your floor a few minutes ago. May I suggest I accompany you?"

Mark considered the officer's suggestion. "Sergeant, my friends are planning a walk around the area. They're in the Brasserie. Please ask Sergeant Lowe to let them know we may have visitors, American, presumably not friends?"

"Yes, sir. I'll let him know. I'll also inform Lizzie—I mean Detective Inspector Goodwin."

"After you do so, wait a couple of minutes and then follow me to my room. Knock on the door and announce yourself as hotel security. Here's a spare key card. When you open the door, stand well back."

"Yes, sir. I can do that. Good luck, sir."

Mark waited for a vacant elevator and when it arrived, he entered and pressed the button for his floor. He wondered why an American agency would be interested in him. The visitors' behavior indicated they were not FBI, who would contact him without subterfuge, he was sure. There were a dozen other possibilities: quasi-law enforcement departments or agencies that shouldn't be operating in a foreign country. One came to mind. The CIA had a remit, at least in American law, to operate worldwide. He exited the elevator, with no resolution to his deliberations.

He walked along the carpeted corridor to Scott's room. No one was in sight, so the visitors had either departed unobserved by Sergeant Roberts or they had entered his room. There was a possibility the strangers were not aware they had adjoining rooms. Mark opened the door with his card—the locks were all keyed to the one set of cards—and stepped quietly into Scott's room. He used the interconnecting door to enter the children's room, then entered Reb and Anna's. He listened at the door into his room and heard only a faint conversation. He opened the door, gently.

***

Chapter 11

This was Colonel Alexey Grigoryevich's second meeting with the so-called senior manager from the Office of Global Criminal Justice. Alexey now wondered if the department even existed, although his research confirmed the State Department did contain such an operation. He suspected if he returned to the location of their first meeting, the office would be vacant, the signs removed, and no one would have any recollection of the tenants. He understood that, at the very least, his career would be ruined if McCarr delivered his comprehensive and accurate information to Alexey's superiors in Moscow.

He wondered what more McCarr required of him. He understood the American wanted to take action against the Cerberus organization. He, too, and SVR, even FSB's senior officers—all would be happy to see Cerberus eliminated as a player in this oldest game in the world. Both SVR and FSB had suffered losses as a result of finding themselves in conflict with Cerberus. And the other person—he tried to remember the name—oh, yes, Midway, Mark Midway. While not a member of Cerberus, Midway was of the same ilk. Alexey wondered what McCarr had in mind to counter the threat posed by Midway.

Alexey checked the address. He walked the last half mile and it seemed his journey interested no one. The building was old, built with granite blocks, five stories. It was well-maintained, in an up-market but older part of Washington. He pushed open the heavy glass doors. According to the directory in the foyer, the tenants were dentists and doctors; the distinct odor of disinfectants permeated the entrance and stairway. He walked across the foyer and climbed the stairs. When he reached the third floor he sought the suite number from McCarr's message. The door to the suite was labeled with a doctor's name and specialization, and he wondered whether the doctor actually existed. He opened the door and stepped into a small waiting room, carpeted, clean, and with a minimum of furniture. He sat down, momentarily unsure of himself. A *Reader's Digest* over ten years old sat on the top of the pile of magazines. The suite contained a receptionist's area that appeared to be vacant. There were no sounds of occupation within the suite.

The door suddenly opened and McCarr bounded in, buoyant and smiling. He wore a white jacket over his suit, with a stethoscope looped around his neck.

"Ah, Alexey, welcome. I'm so happy you spared the time to visit me, this morning. Come with me. My consulting room is along here."

The man is mad, Alexey thought, as he followed McCarr deeper into the suite. McCarr opened the door to a typical doctor's office—medical journals weighing down the desk, even heavier reference tomes were on a small bookshelf, boxes of wipes and rubber gloves on another shelf, and a plastic skeleton stood in the corner. McCarr indicated a chair.

"Please sit. My dear fellow, what appears to be your problem?" McCarr was still smiling. He also sat down, removed the stethoscope and placed it on the desk. He frowned at Alexey. "You've told no one of our little discussion?"

Alexey tried to hide his shiver. "No, I have not."

"Good. Did you contact the people I mentioned?"

"Yes."

"Did you find the material to be helpful?"

The American had given Alexey files detailing substantial criminal activities of four Russian sleepers. Those activities included sex trafficking, extortion, and drug dealing. Public exposure would result in lengthy jail terms as well as causing their illegal status in America to be revealed. If Alexey shared the details with their FSB handlers it would result in their execution, without any trial.

Alexey said, "Yes."

"And—"

"They're willing to carry out a task for me—you." This was McCarr's operation, not Alexey's.

"Ah, very good. In that case, we're ready to go to the next stage."

Alexey sighed to himself. This hole was getting deeper. "Yes?"

"Our man flies between his base and Fort Myer every Wednesday, to attend a meeting with Army Criminal Investigation Command. He also visits an MP battalion while he's there, it's another Cerberus unit." He handed across a sheet of paper. Alexey was not surprised to see the contents printed in Russian. "This provides details of his normal route, his helicopter, call signs, radio frequencies, his schedule—everything your FSB team will need. I understand he varies his route. However, given two relatively close locations, there are not many variations he can arrange. The green machine is very structured and expects its officers to follow pre-determined schedules. Oh, by the way, the paper was acquired in Russia and we used a Russian printer, in case you're wondering. You'll understand why, of course."

Alexey said, "I do." If his superiors caught him with this paper in his possession, his career in this country would be terminated, as would be his life, on his return to Russia. He hoped McCarr sought bigger fish.

"I bet you do." The man's smile was humorless.

McCarr continued, "Now, the weapon. We've obtained, surprise, a Russian-made SAM. It's a Strela 21, one of the new ones. Very effective, I understand."

Alexey did not hide his shock. The Strela 21 represented the most recent version of one of Russia's most efficient surface to air missile systems. It was compact, designed to be fired from a lightweight launch pad, was proof against most jamming techniques, able to discriminate against flares, and contained sensitive tracking technology. Russia had not yet, as far as he knew, released this new missile system to any foreign country. He wondered how McCarr had obtained the weapon.

"I thought you'd be impressed. You can see where this is going, of course. Russia—well, these FSB sleepers—will get the blame. You'll receive a substantial increment to your Swiss bank account, in addition to the amount I deposited for you yesterday. The sleepers will be gone, one way or another. Our mutual enemy will be eliminated. Win-win, don't you think?" The cold smile returned.

"How will you get the missile to the sleepers?"

"You'll provide me with a delivery address here in Washington. A vehicle with a Russian Embassy license plate will deliver the weapon—I'll arrange the delivery schedule with you, don't worry. Your FSB people should acquire a courier truck. No one takes any notice of those."

"Very well."

"Prepare your people. I want to deliver the Strela within the week. I'll contact you tomorrow to get the delivery address. I want action, understand?"

"Yes, I understand."

"Good. I think we can conclude our consultation. Just take the tablets three times a day, the pain will soon ease."

McCarr stood, and indicated the office door. "After you, Alexey."

As he walked ahead of McCarr, Alexey could almost feel the blade in his back.

***

Chapter 12

Mark cracked open the connecting door into his room, but the conversation was still an indistinctive murmur. He pushed the door and it hit the stop with a bang. He stepped into the room. The noise caused the three men to turn in his direction.

"Shit," said one. The man had moved his hand inside his jacket. Mark suspected he was reaching for a weapon.

"Midway?" questioned another. He was older, perhaps senior to his two companions and had not been alarmed by the door opening. The third man said nothing.

"Yes. I suggest you all leave. Otherwise hotel security will ask you embarrassing questions."

"It's not going to be that easy. We want you to come with us."

"What are you? CIA? If so, you have no authority here."

"I have .45-caliber authority," stated the youngest of the three men. His hand was still inside his jacket.

Mark stepped into the room. "Your task here won't succeed. This country doesn't like foreign agents who try to shoot people. I suggest you get out while you have the opportunity."

"I've heard about you. Quite the little killer." The speaker was the previously silent third man. He stood about three inches over six feet. He was heavily built and his face was scared.

"If need be. I don't know what you think you're doing here. Bugging the room? Waiting for me? Waiting for a bus?"

There was a knock on the door. "Security!" a voice called. The door swung open and the three men turned.

Mark grabbed and swung an ice bucket at the third man, hitting his right temple. The man dropped, stunned, probably unconscious. Mark then threw the ice bucket at the older man, at the same time grabbing the arm of the young man who was reaching for his weapon. Mark gripped the young man's elbow and squeezed with all his strength, crushing the joint. His victim screamed and in a reflex action squeezed the trigger of his handgun. The weapon fired and the bullet traveled through the back of his suit coat, narrowly missing the older man, who cursed his companion's carelessness. Mark pushed the palm of his other hand up into the young man's jaw. He dropped to the floor. Mark grabbed the young man's weapon as he fell, and aimed it at the remaining intruder.

Sergeant Roberts was in the room, his weapon drawn. He considered Mark, nodded, and also aimed his weapon at the man still standing.

Scarface moaned, his eyelids fluttering. The young man was silent, unconscious or dead. The older man raised his hands.

"I'm an American," he stated. "I want to contact the US Embassy."

"Sorry, old dear," replied Roberts. "I'm Sergeant Roberts, Counter Terrorism Command, Scotland Yard. You're nicked, you and your mates. We'll do the more formal stuff later." He holstered his handgun and reached for a pair of handcuffs under his jacket. "Turn around, you know the routine."

"I'm a US citizen. I want to contact the Embassy—"

Mark addressed the sergeant. "Allow me?"

Roberts nodded.

Mark swung an uppercut, connecting with the man's jaw. He dropped to the floor, unconscious. Mark blew on his knuckles. "Damn. His jaw was bonier than I expected."

"Thank you, sir," Roberts said. "Well done."

Mark checked the three bodies. Two were unconscious. He was still unsure about the state of the young man.

"Sergeant, can I leave the clean up to you? I'm sure there are a number of offenses they can be charged with?"

"Oh, yes." Roberts sounded eager. "Breaking and entering. Assault, resisting arrest, unlawful use of a firearm. Perhaps illegal possession of firearms. Conspiracy to kidnap or to murder, we'll have to discover which. Attempted kidnap or murder or both. We might even be able to drag in a touch of terrorism." His expression became more excited. "If we do that, we can hold them for up to fourteen days without trial, under the Terrorism Act. There may be more we can do, once we get them to the station. We don't like foreign agencies working here. We've got America, Russia, China, Germany, some Middle Eastern countries, even India and Pakistan. It gets tiresome."

"If I may make a suggestion…" Mark was unsure how much direction he should give the sergeant.

"Please."

"Don't take them to a nearby police location. Or hospital. Instead, if you can, take them somewhere far from here. The longer we can keep their bosses guessing about their fate and location, the better. Oh, and you'd better call for an ambulance."

"I agree, sir. I'd better call Lizzie, too."

"Can you speak with hotel security? I don't want us to be thrown out of the hotel because of this."

"Yes sir." The sergeant reached for his cell phone. "Never you worry."

Mark half saluted and headed out of his room and down the corridor to the elevators, hoping to meet up with the other sergeant and Anna and everyone else before they reached their rooms. He was relieved they had accommodation at the far end of the building, well away from other guests. Maybe no one would report the noise to management.

He met up with his companions in the lobby, just as they were heading toward the elevator bank. Sergeant Lowe was escorting them. "Sergeant," Mark said, "I think Roberts needs your assistance up in my room. I'll take over here."

"Very good, sir. Thank you." Lowe headed off to the elevators.

Mark held up his hand to the others. "No questions. We'll go and have an English treat. Scones with strawberry jam and cream, with tea. It's the afternoon special in the lounge. I've heard it has an excellent view of both the Tower Bridge and the Thames. Well, it should be, if it's not raining too hard. Come on, follow me."

Once they settled around a table each with a serving of scones and jam, Mark quickly summarized his encounter with the three men, whom he presumed were CIA agents. "I'm sure that once Roberts gets all the details, he'll keep us informed. They'll increase our security, though."

Anna asked, "Are you okay?" Her face was pale.

Mark resisted reaching out to reassure her. Gabrielle and Niland were open-mouthed in reaction to his adventure.

"Not a scratch. The three intruders are damaged." Gabrielle and Niland looked relieved.

"Have you any idea why the Agency made this move?" Scott asked.

"No. It's another question I hope Roberts, or his boss, the DI, will ask these people. How far did you go with your sightseeing?"

"We saw some neat sailboats in the marina. Reb said to call them yachts, not sailboats. She said "sailboat" is

American. One yacht was a ketch with two masts. It's big enough to sail around the world and I think that would be exciting. I'm going to be a Yachtmaster, just like Reb," Niland said. Everyone laughed.

Gabrielle said, "Not me, there are real pirates on the oceans who kidnap you, so it's dangerous if you're a lady. I want to be a pilot and fly around the world. I'll be above all the pirates."

"Both of you will have to study some more," Anna said. "The better qualified you are, the better your employment possibilities." It was a mantra she used often on the two younger children. She smiled as Gabrielle and Niland debated which occupation was better.

Mark said to Scott, "We'll need to be alert for any further attempts by the CIA or whoever they are. I think it's me they're seeking. I doubt they know anything about Reb. They may know that you, Sera, Anna, and the children are Cerberus, but I don't think it's their motivation. I'll see if I can convince the Brits to lend us some handguns."

"I don't think you need a weapon, based on your details of the encounter. I suppose it's possible they could to use the children to get to you. Or they might consider using Anna. We—myself and Sera—will be extra cautious."

"I can lend you a couple of my knives," offered Reb, hitching up her skirt to display two knives sheathed on her right thigh. A passing waiter stumbled and almost dropped his tray of dishes. "I've got another two on my left leg. And three more—"

"I think you've shown enough detail," Mark chuckled, reaching for another half scone. He covered it with heapings of jam and cream. "I'm glad you didn't try to wear those onto the plane. We'd be still in Boston, explaining."

An hour later Mark was ready to request the bill when DI Goodwin approached. "Mark," she said. "Do you have some time?"

"Why yes, Detective Inspector," he replied. "Do you mind sitting with us?"

"No, not at all," she said, as Scott jumped up to arrange another chair. It took a minute or so for the DI to settle into place. At Mark's request a waiter brought more scones and plates.

She was far more formal today, thought Mark. The happy face Goodwin had used yesterday must be to create the impression that she's a harmless bureaucrat.

"I've heard about your run-in with some intruders," she said. "We're assuming they're Americans, although they might have false papers. I'll let you know. My men think they'll all survive. One will require some time in hospital and may require reconstructive surgery. I think you broke a jaw, as well. How are your knuckles?"

"I was in danger of being kidnapped or killed. Or both," Mark said, rubbing the back of his right hand.

"I understand. Their bosses will send real heavies next time, so you'll need to be extra careful. I can arrange for additional Cerberus people to help. Ex-SAS. Very good, inconspicuous."

"Can we carry weapons?"

"I'd prefer not, at least officially. However, someone may deliver a package to you tomorrow. Not from me, you understand."

"Of course."

"Now I have two items for you to consider. First, Cerberus management here in London wants to meet with you. Tomorrow, if you're available?"

"Yes, I can do that."

"Good. I'll confirm time and place. Second, this hotel is not the ideal place for us to protect you. You're exposed. I'd prefer to move you, perhaps to a country house. Cerberus has access to one that is ideal, comfortable, protected. Not too far from London. Once we determine who's behind this, how dangerous they are, and after we eliminate their threat, we can, if you wish, arrange for your return here."

"There's a small task we want to do, first."

"Oh?"

"As we mentioned earlier, Reb lived in London with some younger children. They're also genetically engineered. We want to—well, rescue, may be the wrong word—but we'd like to offer them a place to stay with us," Mark said.

"Do you expect any problems?"

"No. It doesn't mean there won't be, though."

"Very well. Your schedule will be as follows. Remain here tonight and tomorrow night. I'll have men on guard. Tomorrow morning you'll meet with Cerberus—just you?" Mark nodded. He noted a movement from Scott, as though the man wanted to join in the meeting, but there was no need for all to attend. Goodwin continued, "Good. The others might like to do some sightseeing. Again, I'll make sure you're all guarded. We'll help you examine the location of these other children tomorrow afternoon. All being well, you can contact them the following morning. In the afternoon, I'll provide transport and security to move you all to one of our safe house in East Sussex."

Mark assessed the group's reaction, while he used a linen serviette to wipe a drop of jam from his chin. "Let's do it."

***

Chapter 13

Reverend Barker did not serve the full two years of his prison sentence. The parole board agreed to his early release, because of his good behavior and because the officials were tired of the conflicts engendered by his preaching. He used words that readily set white against black while he stepped back to enjoy the conflagration his words had caused. When his sermons were later examined, he protested with his utmost innocence, claiming he was carrying out the work his ordainment and calling required of him and he had no ability to control the subsequent behavior of his captive congregation.

It didn't take long for him and his church's militant arm to find more work on his release, although the tasks were minor challenges. A church, for some mysterious reason, burned to the ground; a store trashed and set on fire, and other misadventures in districts where the beliefs and culture of the local people conflicted with those of Barker's congregation. On occasion he reflected on his past deeds, examining the more significant challenges God had placed in his path. He regretted the loss of life of his men, killed while attacking the Lifelong lab complex, and he regretted more the fact that the lab specimen had escaped, although he heard he'd been killed later. He experienced anger as well as regret, because that specimen had been responsible for killing seven of his men.

His visitor today reminded him of those losses and of his hatred of Mark Midway. They were sitting in the reverend's study, only the two of them, enjoying a quiet conversation over a bourbon—Woodford Reserve, the reverend's favorite. The visitor had introduced himself as Robert McCarr, a dear friend of the late Senator Boothby, a man who had involved the reverend's small militia in a number of illicit assignments.

"I know you regret your men's failure," said his visitor, "and it's unfortunate Midway is still alive. Not only alive, but adding more of those...specimens to his enclave."

The reverend spluttered, almost spilling his drink. "Still alive? I thought—I'd been informed of his death. He's an outrage against God." The minister managed to restrain himself from thumping the small table where the bottle of Woodford rested.

His visitor nodded. "I had expected action, otherwise."

"Action? I'll take action. I just need to know where his enclave is located."

"I think I can help with that information." The visitor, his hands gloved against the cold—he was preparing to leave—handed the reverend a slip of paper with a laser printed address.

The reverend's eyes widened. He emptied his glass. His hands shook as he poured another large shot from the bottle. "Has this been confirmed?"

"Absolutely. A shooting occurred there a week ago. A Chinese diplomat attempted to kill one of his companions. A sibling, I believe."

The reverend stood. He had lost weight during his incarceration and was proud of his slimmer figure. His pacing now unconsciously matched the diagonal distance of his prison cell. "A sibling? You've found more of them? God's work is endless." He stopped, almost in mid step.

"The Chinese? Why were those heathens trying to kill this— this—specimen?"

"They have their own lab and want to eliminate competing examples of genetic engineering."

"What? They're experimenting, too?" The reverend frowned. There was no immediate avenue that would allow him to launch an attack against the Chinese. He settled for Midway. "I'll talk with my...friends. We may be able to do something about this enclave." He waved the slip of paper. "It's distasteful. No, it's evil, having these devil's constructs in America."

"I can help with funding, if you need," offered the visitor. He smiled his thin smile. "My associates agree with you. They will provide financial support for destruction of Midway's property. It will be a pity if anyone's living there at the time."

The reverend smiled, his lips wet with bourbon. "How much? It's expensive, doing God's work. My friends will have to form and equip a team."

The visitor mentioned an amount. The reverend's smile deepened. He wrote on a scrap of paper. "This account. It's offshore."

The visitor nodded. "I expected no less. The funds will be there within five days. I want the action of your friends to be swift and certain. Be aware, my associates are intolerant of mistakes." The smile returned, but the reverend did not note its lack of humor. "I must leave you, now. I have other duties to attend to."

"Yes, yes." The reverend had begun to plan his next steps. "It's been a pleasure." He showed his visitor out and watched as he drove off. "God's work is always there," he muttered to himself as he closed the door.

~~~

Mark paced the floor of his room. He was jet-lagged and worried. The presence of three Americans intending to do him harm, had surprised him. The Agency had not troubled him before, although some agents had illegally supported the attack on his parents' lab. The agents had been either killed or arrested. There had been no indication from the CIA that they wanted revenge. He decided make a call, using encrypted VoIP.

"Schmidt?"

"Hello, Mark. So, the Brits let you into their country?"

"They treated us like VIPs."

"Really? As you know, we've found it difficult if not impossible to get our Cerberus people into Europe."

"Someone else was less than pleased." Mark described the intrusion of the three Americans. He concluded, "Did you or Maeve have any indication an Agency attack was pending?"

"No, none at all. You're fortunate you suffered only bruised knuckles. I'll check with Maeve's team, but she usually lets me know if her analysts detect anything. You think you're safe now?"

"We're being protected by SO15 and some Cerberus ex-SAS guys. I think there're four or five on duty tonight, to ensure we get a good night's sleep."

"SO15, their anti-terrorism force. I've heard good things about them."

"I think they're Cerberus—well, a lot of them. I'm meeting with some of the senior Cerberus team tomorrow morning. After that, we'll research the children Reb wants to recruit or rescue, I'm not sure which. Cerberus is moving us to a safe house. They claim it's more defensible than the hotel."

"Send me a copy of their report on the attack. If SO15 have IDs or details of who these people work for, I can pass them on to Maeve for further research."

"I'll let you know as soon as I get any information."

"Contact me after your meeting with Cerberus. Maeve and I have been talking about you. Our question is whether you'd be interested in taking full responsibility for the UK operations. Think about it; we can discuss it tomorrow."

"Interesting. Okay, I'll think about it. Do you mind if I discuss this with Anna?"

"It'll be good to hear her reaction."

"Have you received any lab reports yet? On the parka?"

"No. Don't worry. Maeve or I will forward results as soon as we have them. I have a meeting in less than five minutes—I have to go." Schmidt disconnected the call.

Mark closed his laptop. Schmidt had sown a seed that would ensure he remained awake for another hour or two. Should he consider involving himself more in Cerberus operations? He was involved, albeit on a minor basis, because of Anna and the two young children. He had control of Cerberus funds, or at least their non-US accounts. He could either assist or sabotage their operations. He had all his parents' research materials still had substantial value. The Cerberus files he and Anna had modified could be corrected or destroyed. Gabrielle had somehow acquired or stolen a mobile freezer filled with Cerberus embryos. The freezer unit was locked away—safely, he hoped—until he determined what to do with the contents. He knew what it was like to be genetically engineered. Did he have the motivation, the experience, the ability, to take charge? Should he? These were questions he needed to examine with care before he responded to Schmidt. Mark paced his room.

The distant thrumming of rain on the double-glass layers of the windows and the noise of the wind rattling the tiles reflected his mood. A soft knock on the door from the adjoining room interrupted his reverie. He eased open the door and Anna slipped into his room, closing the door behind her.

"Reb's asleep," she said, "and I heard you pacing. Gabrielle told me you were worried."

Mark blinked. Anna stood very close to him. He wanted to reach out—

Anna dropped her robe.

"I want you to reach out, too." She placed her hands on his shoulders.

"Are you sure?"

"Oh, yes."

Mark wrapped his arms around Anna. He kissed her, his hunger now revealed. She met his need with a hunger of her own. He led her to his bed.

***

Chapter 14

Mark entered the Cerberus UK meeting room. It was more or less a standard conference room with seating for twelve people. The table was oval, highly polished, with small name cards in place. Five attendees were already seated around the table. One, he noted, was DI Goodwin. The others were men, three of whom wore suits and the fourth wore a police uniform. Their formal dress was in sharp contrast to Mark's winter jacket, polo shirt, and casual pants. There was a card in front of one of the empty chairs. He checked the name on the card; it was his. He sat in the chair. He nodded a greeting and Goodwin returned it with a slight smile. No one else acknowledged his presence.

He had requested assistance from Maeve's analysts and their research had been comprehensive, their report a far better result than his limited efforts had achieved. He now had a detailed dossier on each of the attendees. Mark wondered whether their research had been as effective; he wondered what details they had discovered.

"Good morning," Mark said. There were only two reciprocal nods from around the table. "I'm Mark Midway. I'm not Cerberus engineered. I'd also point out you requested this meeting." He stood and walked to a small corner table where he poured a cup of coffee. He carried it back to the main table and sat, waiting while he sipped his drink.

One of the men spoke. "Now, lad, there's nowt to get feshed about." He was older than most of the other attendees, and his British accent was so strong Mark had to listen intently to understand what he was saying. "Yes, we called this meeting. But one thing I want to know—why t' bluidy 'ell have you pinched all our money?"

Mark checked the man's name card. The speaker was Andrew Jeffries. Mark said, "All Cerberus operations in Europe were set up by the American organization. The corporate structure establishes Cerberus US as the owner, whether directly or indirectly, of all Cerberus operations in Europe generally. Is that not correct?"

Jeffries didn't respond though he did grow redder in the face.

Mark waited, sipping his coffee. No one else spoke. After almost three minutes, he said, "If all you wanted me here for today was to claim I had stolen your funds, I think the meeting is now concluded?"

There was more than a modicum of truth in the claim; he *had* moved the accounts. But he had not touched the money in them. The funds provided substantial leverage, and should allow him to influence both US and UK operations. He finished his coffee, replaced the cup on the saucer, and pushed it away. He started to stand.

"Mr. Midway, please wait." Goodwin said. "I think the other members here do have things to say. Please be patient with us."

Mark sat back in his chair and waited.

At last one of the other men spoke up. William Nicholson, according to his name card. "Mr. Midway, we've been operating without direction for six months or more, ever since the executives went missing. We've heard two of the senior US managers ae dead and Dr. White turned traitor and joined the Chinese. We lost contact with the Chairman at the beginning of the year."

"I think the Chairman might be dead, as well. It's likely he was killed in January, we think by Chinese military personnel. They sank his yacht." Mark didn't mention Reb was an eyewitness.

They all nodded.

Nicholson continued, "We're not company executives or managers. I'm a soldier by training. The time I'm spending sitting at a desk takes me away from where I want to be—in the field."

"Agree with that," said one of the other men, the police officer. His name card identified him as Nelson Cobb.

Mark asked, "How many Cerberus people do you have operationally?"

Goodwin said, "We have about two thousand. We have eight hundred or so embedded in military and law enforcement, and twelve hundred on contracts covering anti-piracy and hostage rescue. Plus we have almost a thousand children of various ages. We have non-engineered lab and child-care employees. They number about five hundred."

Mark nodded. The details confirmed his assumption that the UK operation was less than half the size of Cerberus US.

Cobb said, "What can you offer us? Can you make sense out of all this and provide a strategy, a focus, for us?" Mark noticed Goodwin smiling.

"Schmidt—I assume you know of him?" Everyone nodded. "He asked me a similar question last night. I haven't answered him yet. I have a question—I understand you've managed to block most, if not all, Cerberus US representatives from visiting the UK. Why?"

Cobb said, "We were concerned the Russians, or the Chinese, or some other group, may have taken control. So we arranged a ban on all Cerberus US people. We weren't able to discriminate."

"Yet you allowed me and my group to enter? You provided VIP treatment."

Cobb said, "We decided we had to take a risk. We knew your history, we were confident you weren't part of a Chinese conspiracy, and we didn't think you were in bed with the Russians. Our contacts—we have some Cerberus, er, sources in America—told us you were more likely to keep your distance from Schmidt and unlikely to be involved in Cerberus. Your, er, removal of funds did worry us, though."

"I've tried to be independent of any group. I'm not sure I can continue to maintain my independence, though."

"Why not?" asked Goodwin.

"I have befriended, protected, three Cerberus people, two of whom are very young children. I might have to add three more genetically engineered children—young adults—to our group. It will depend on what we discover tomorrow. My sister is genetically engineered. I have an obligation to protect these people, these children, who rely on me. As of yesterday, as you undoubtedly have heard, either my life or my freedom is at risk. I've tried to maintain my independence but I think I may need to review and alter my strategy."

Nods from all around the table.

"I want to raise one major point," Mark said. "We—me, you, all Cerberus people—don't know whether we'll live to enjoy our old age. We don't know what will happen to Cerberus children as they develop. We don't know whether we can or should mate, Cerberus to Cerberus, or Cerberus to other genetically engineered people, at least those engineered in embryo. We don't know what health problems may occur. Dr. White's research program focused on producing genetically engineered embryos and nanite-based DNA proteins for adults. As far as I know, she didn't research any after affects. She wasn't emotionally concerned whether an engineered child lived or died, let alone what would happen if the child grew to become an adult. These things worry me. I don't believe any research has been done on these issues in America. What about here?"

Goodwin answered. "We've done no research here. Our laboratories focus on finding and checking potential mothers, and implanting embryos provided by Cerberus US. Our technicians monitor and help raise and support Cerberus children. We provide educational structures to match their rapid maturing process. Genetic engineering of human embryos is illegal so we haven't conducted any of those experiments. We've been skating close to the law with what we've implemented. I don't think anyone has thought seriously about the lifetime impacts. I agree there are significant gaps in our knowledge."

No one said anything as the group considered all this.

Mark broke the silence. "I think there are two areas we should consider. First, I believe Cerberus must implement an intensive research program focused on the aging impact for both pre- and post-engineered people. US and UK organizations must support this and minimize or cease further DNA research, unless the researchers encounter needs based on their aging research. I will do everything I can to ensure Schmidt implements such a program. I'll consider taking a role in Cerberus UK as long as we organize it as an independent operation, which we can discuss once I've spoken with Schmidt. Do you agree?"

There were nods—some reluctant—from the Cerberus people around the table. They all appeared to be deep in thought. Mark let the silence settle for a few minutes.

He said, "I'll discuss this meeting with Schmidt. Do you want my involvement?"

Goodwin said, "Show of hand, please. Are you interested in Midway taking a role in our operations?"

"Subject to further discussion and agreeing responsibilities, yes," Jeffries said. His strong northern accent was subdued. He looked at Mark and said. "You raised some very strong points. I agree, we've neglected the children."

Five hands were raised, one or two with apparent reluctance.

"Good," Goodwin said. "Mark, we'll continue after you've spoken with Schmidt and have his agreement."

~~~

After he returned to the hotel, Mark contacted Schmidt to report details of his meeting. He repeated his comments about the kind of research Cerberus labs needed to focus on.

Schmidt was silent for a few moments. Then he said, "I've been thinking along similar lines. I've undertaken, almost completed, the series of Cerberus post-engineering nanite medications. I decided to do this because I believe I need to understand what it means to be genetically engineered, if I'm to be responsible for Cerberus US. I think you're correct. We need to research the long term effects."

"Good. Also, we discussed future management of the Cerberus operation here. They're looking for strategic guidance and want to know what I can contribute. In other words, should I take on management of Cerberus UK? Basically the same question you asked me. I must say, I'm interested."

"Excellent. Let's schedule a meeting with me, Maeve, you, and whoever you suggest from the people you met with."

"I'll include DI Goodwin. I'll discuss with her whether anyone else should be involved."

"Send me an e-mail with the details. Schedule it for late tomorrow, my time. I have meetings most of the day, at least through mid-afternoon."

As Mark terminated the call, Anna, Reb and the two children invaded his suite through the connecting door. Reb stood back, silent, observing.

"We've been everywhere," Gabrielle said. "I think Scott and Sera are worn out."

Niland added, "The two extra security guys have sore feet, they said."

Anna gave him a soft smile. "What have you been doing, Mark?"

"I met with the UK management team. Afterwards I had a discussion with Schmidt. I'm still absorbing it all. Reb, it's time we visited your friends; we'll go there in the morning. You, Anna, and I only." Niland and Gabrielle immediately protested. Mark held up his hand. "No, not this time. Settle down. You'll stay here with Scott and Sera."

"But why?" Niland asked.

"Because I have a feeling...we should proceed with caution," Mark replied, trying to describe the flow of apprehension that entered his mind whenever he thought of Reb's three genetically engineered friends. "I don't know why. My concern has been growing stronger every day."

A flicker of worry darkened Reb's face. "Wh-what kind of concern?" she asked. "I've been getting more and more worried, too, for the past week."

"It's difficult to describe. The only solution is to visit them."

"When?" Reb asked.

"Let me check with our support team. DI Goodwin promised a package would be delivered—it should be our weapons. She also promised me a copy of their report on your friends, and I'd like to review it. Plan for ten tomorrow morning, okay?"

~~~

Alexey Grigoryevich had the cell phone on vibrate. He was halfway to his apartment, at the end of a boring day at the embassy. The phone was a throwaway provided by the American, and he would throw it away as far as possible after this. He flipped open the lid—the phone was as simple as it was cheap—and accessed the text message.

"PLAN FOR B."

Well, if McCarr's intelligence was any good, he had eliminated two of the possible three locations for their mission against Cerberus. The third building was an almost derelict warehouse.

The American had provided addresses of three properties, each under one of the likely flight paths of the target helicopter as it flew between its base and Fort Myer. Alexey, together with the senior member of the FSB sleepers, had visited the buildings, confirming their suitability, including that each building was unoccupied. The task now for Alexey was to contact his fellow Russians and inform them of the building they needed to use as the launch site for the Strela missile. He called the local leader of the four-man FSB team on McCarr's disposable cell phone. When he finished the call, he threw the phone away.

***

Chapter 15

SO15 delivered the package containing their unofficial
weapons. To Mark's delight, they were Glock 17s, four of
them, plus ammunition. The firearm was a standard issue for
the Metropolitan Police—at least, for those authorized to
carry weapons. He kept one and handed a pistol each to
Scott, Sera, and Anna. Reb was comfortable with merely her
knives. He had also received a report containing the Counter
Terrorism Command's assessment of the property that he,
Anna, and Reb were planning to visit later in the morning.
There were no red flags raised by the details. The property,
located south of the Thames, was over a hundred and fifty
years old. It had been constructed with red bricks and slate
tiles, and had been used for a range of purposes over its
lifetime. Prior to its current use it had been owned by a small
religious order that used it as a Bible study school.
According to the report, the building now housed one or two
adults and three teenagers.

Mark put the report aside and reflected on their plan for
the day. Reb thought the children from the Welsh laboratory
needed to be rescued but she had not indicated any pressing
need for this action. On the surface the three children, with a
maturity level of seventeen or so, were adequately cared for
and not in any immediate danger. There was a chance his

and Anna's involvement might bring danger to them. He shivered. There was something...no, it was too elusive: he was unable to pin it down. He read through the report again. Nothing leapt out at him. He dropped it on the table beside his chair.

Anna joined him in the small sitting room adjacent to their bedroom. She had showered and dressed, ready for the morning's activities. She smiled and placed her hand on the back of his neck.

"Still concerned about these children?" she asked.

"Yes, but I can't seem to identify why I should be worried."

Anna took the report from the table and read it. She looked at Mark when she finished. "There's nothing to worry about here. All straightforward."

"I know. I think that's the problem. Reb says she wants us to rescue the children. But from what?"

"Is it her way of wanting these...pseudo-siblings, to be with her? She was with them through part of their early childhood and then she left them, traveling for years with little contact. Perhaps she has a guilt complex?"

"A valid assumption. Well, there's only one thing to do. Visit them to see what their situation is. Breakfast first, though."

~~~

It was like a small convoy, thought Reb, as three cars stopped outside the building where her young friends lived. Two vehicles contained Cerberus guards and she, Mark, and Anna were in the middle vehicle. She hoped it all would work out. Her friends had helped her discover Mark's whereabouts in America and now she wanted to pay her debt by offering them a different home. Somewhere safer than this old religious school building.

London weather was doing its best to dampen everything and everyone, and their exit from the vehicles was hasty and rushed. Four people crowded under the overhang at the front door, while most of their Cerberus escort remained at or in the vehicles. Faded letters high along the front of the building announced its prior purpose although all that were legible now were the last two words reading BIBLE SCHOOL. Reb pressed the doorbell button and waited, concealing her impatience. After a long minute someone partially opened the door; the movement was restricted by a security chain.

"It's me, Reb," Reb said to the face revealed in the gap.

"Reb?" the voice was doubtful.

"Yes, Mrs. Grabski, it's me, Reb."

The door closed and Reb heard the rattle of the security chain. The door was then opened wide to reveal a large lobby area. It was institutional—despite the probable oak flooring underneath, the floor was covered with dark gray, almost black, linoleum, while the walls and ceiling were painted a doubtful white. The only decoration was a drooping dusty-leafed aspidistra in a large black pot, which sat on a wooden three-legged stand. The overhead lights were dim and the bulbs lacked shades. Mrs. Grabski wore a black dress, and her gray hair was bundled under a black scarf with a handful of threads escaping its boundaries. She wore no makeup and scuffed her worn slippers as she walked, leading them along the hallway. Reb, Mark, Anna and a Cerberus security guard followed.

Reb shuddered. She had developed an intense dislike of this place.

The housekeeper stopped at the end of the hall at a closed door and knocked. The response was undecipherable. She thrust open the door and announced, "Visitors." She turned and walked back along the hallway.

A head popped into the doorway. "What—" It was a young girl, blond, slim build, wearing jeans and a sloppy shirt. She looked to be a young seventeen.

"Alright, butty?" Reb said. Her Welsh accent had strengthened.

A smile broke out on the girl's face. "Reb," she cried and rushed forward, enveloping Reb in an enthusiastic hug. "It's you. You came back."

At last the young girl released Reb. She stepped back and shouted into the room, "It's totes amaze. Guess who!"

A young male voice replied, "We—and everyone in the building—heard you shout 'Reb!' so it must be the postie."

Reb turned to her companions. "This is my friend. Carys, this is Mark and Anna. The lady there is our security escort; her name is Trina." The young girl, suddenly shy, bobbed her head.

Another head appeared in the doorway. "It is Reb," the boy said to someone else in the room. He stepped forward and hugged Reb. "We weren't certain—I'm shattered."

"This is Owen," Reb said. Another face appeared and she added, "And Lewis." Both boys were also blond and slimly built. The three children were obvious siblings. Reb pointed. "Mark, Anna, and Trina Neville. Can we come in?"

"Absolutely. Quick, Owen, tidy up." Lewis turned to the visitors. "Everyone, please do come in. Reb, you're a sight to see." He led the way into a large room. It had been a classroom at one point in its life. It now contained four old settees and a scattering of chairs, there were small tables loaded with books, computer parts, and the occasional remnants of a sandwich on its wrapper or a half-empty coffee cup. A rack of computer equipment, servers, and bare processors with cables hanging untidily lined part of one wall. A coffee pot sat on a table in a corner of the room. Owen was quickly straightening pillows and removing food scraps from the tables. "This is our common room," Lewis explained. He waved his hand. "We live in here, mostly, as you can tell."

"Please sit," Carys said. "Reb, why didn't you warn us? Tell us what's happening."

Reb sat beside Carys and the two boys sat on an adjacent settee. Mark and Ann sat farther away, and Trina remained standing inside the doorway.

Reb said, "Not much, really. I was shot—" The outburst of rapid questions stopped her. She waved a hand and the noise subsided. "No, it wasn't so serious. It's just across the top of my shoulder. It's still painful, though. It was the Chinese. They were trying to kill me." The sudden hush was a marked contrast to the previous surge of shouted questions. Reb smiled. "I'm alright now. I have Mark and Anna and some other people looking after me, guarding me."

"This is the person you were searching for? Your brother? Mark Midway?" Carys was hesitant with her question, still shy with so many strangers present.

"Yes, and Anna is his friend. Mark helped her escape an attack last year. There're two young Cerberus children with us as well. They're dears. Plus—I've lots to tell you."

"Totes emoshe," Owen whispered.

"Now we want you to think about moving out of here," Reb said. "I know, it's short notice. All of us are under threat of being killed. Mark was attacked two days ago by three Americans, we think. There are people who are trying to murder anyone who's genetically engineered. That includes you as well. I—we—can protect you."

The silence stretched to a minute or more. Reb looked at each face, gauging their reactions. "I know, it's not much in the way of advance notice." She turned to her brother. "Mark?"

"I agree, currently we're all at risk. If you remain here, we can't protect you. Come with us and we'll do our best."

"We've lived here for years, now," Lewis said. "Alright, it's a bit of a drab place, but it's been our home. What will happen if we move? Will we remain together, as a family? Can we still make a mess?" He pointed around the room. "Can we do our computer experiments?"

Mark smiled. "Yes to all. You should see my computer mess."

Anna said, "His workroom is far worse than this, and he has drones, too, in pieces all over the floor."

"Drones?" the three voices were in complete unison. Lewis said, "We're totally into them. I've been trying to get money to buy one. The people here aren't interested in helping."

"But they care for you?" Anna asked. "Feed you? Give you some money?"

Lewis said, "They feed us. What's left is only enough to buy clothes and some books. And a few computer components. No luxuries. I don't think I'd class it as caring for us." The other children nodded in agreement.

Mark said, "We can take you into our care, and I mean care. We'll fund your education, through college and more, if you want. Provide protection. Whatever you need."

Carys looked at Reb. "Is he for real?"

"Definitely."

"Amaze balls," said the two boys, their Welsh accents strong. Carys smiled.

*   *   *

Chapter 16

The militia convoy, five vehicles with three men to each vehicle, halted along the road leading to the heavily chained and barred gate. It was only minutes after sunrise and the sun cast elongated shadows across the half-melted snow along the side of the road. A man exited the lead vehicle, a Dodge Ram 3500, black and threatening, and spent three or four minutes examining the gate. His breath was visible in the morning air. He walked to the rear of the Dodge and sorted through his equipment, selected a small slab of C4, a wireless detonator, and the matching transmitter. He spoke for a moment with the driver of the lead vehicle. Seconds later all the vehicles in the convoy reversed fifty yards or so. The man returned to the gate and placed the explosive in position. He inserted the detonator and backed off to stand next to the lead vehicle. He pressed the button on the transmitter.

The C4 cracked its sudden ignition and the explosion rocked the gate. Fragments of chain spun through the air, some landing close to the Dodge Ram. The man nodded his satisfaction and returned to the gate. He lifted the now scrap metal and pushed it open, far enough to permit the vehicles to drive through. As the lead vehicle moved forward, he opened the passenger door and swung himself back into the front passenger seat.

"Well done, Jay," remarked Payne, the driver.

Jay acknowledged the militia leader's praise with a hand gesture. He had gained substantial experience in managing and setting explosives as a result of his service in Afghanistan, and now utilized his knowledge for a different calling. And for better money.

The lead vehicle was two hundred yards into the property when the front tire blew. The Dodge swerved to the left and hit the bank of snow along the side of the lane. The second tire blew moments after the vehicle stopped.

"We're under fire," shouted Jay, not hiding his surprise. Their briefing had not indicated the possibility of encountering any serious opposition.

He had hardly completed his comment when the rear end of the Dodge was hit by the following vehicle, its driver caught by the unexpected stop of the lead vehicle. Jay heard more shots and assumed the tires of that vehicle had also been shredded by weapon fire. He looked back. The SUV had swerved the other way, hitting the opposite snow bank. He and the other two men in the Dodge jumped out, taking their firearms. He heard more shots and when he checked, he saw the following vehicles also had flat tires; as far as he could tell, the shooter had destroyed the two front tires of each vehicle.

The Dodge's windshield exploded and Jay heard other bullets hitting the front of the vehicle. A cloud of steam indicated the radiator had been holed. Payne cursed, removed his black Stetson, threw it onto the road, and jumped on it repeatedly. Jay was impressed by the man's command of invective.

"I purchased this damn vehicle only six months ago. I still have payments to make on it." Payne cursed again.

Jay realized the shooter was targeting the second vehicle once the driver and passengers had exited. With a measured momentum the shooter meticulously destroyed the three remaining vehicles.

"Where is he? Where's the shooter?" asked Bro, their sniper. He was younger than either Jay or Payne, although he too had done a tour of duty in Afghanistan.

"No damned idea," said Jay. He was sheltering behind the partial protection of the passenger side door. He knew the thin metal would be ineffective if the shooter selected him as the next target; it was more his subconscious reaction to a psychological need to seek safety, even if it was only apparent. "We've been suckered into this. Five vehicles immobilized in less than five minutes. He's good, whoever he is."

Some of the men, now out of their vehicles, were returning fire in the direction of the farmhouse. It was a stone building and Jay doubted their random shots would do any significant damage. He motioned to Payne, indicating the lane in front of them. "We should move closer. We can't do anything hiding here."

"It's clear space. We'll be sitting ducks," Payne protested.

Jay shrugged. "What do you think we are, standing here? Besides, the shooter hasn't hit anyone so far. He's targeting the vehicles, not people."

"He's encouraging us to leave," Bro said. "On foot."

Payne cursed again. He reached into the Dodge Ram for his CB radio. "Okay, listen up. The shooter's sending a message we should leave, but we only get paid if we complete the job. What do you all think?"

There was a confusion of replies. Most seemed to deride the shooter and his ability to hit targets that would shoot back. Jay wasn't so sure; the man had demonstrated a precision which spoke of experience. Another driver said one of his men had been hit in the arm by a ricochet, but the wound, now bandaged, was not life threatening.

Payne said, "Shoot out all the front windows of the house. We'll move forward."

Bro grabbed Jay's arm with sudden excitement. "Look, look! The gunfire's coming from those two barns. There must be two shooters. See, there's some reinforcement and protection around where the barrels are, on the roof."

Jay was impressed with the sniper's visual acuity. The buildings were a hundred yards away and the small snipers' nests were well disguised.

Bro began to return fire. He was good, thought Jay, as he watched while his companion fired three shots at each location. Jay observed the bullet impact points. Some of the other men began to follow Bro's example and soon seven or eight of his companions were returning fire as they moved toward the house. The unseen shooters weren't deterred; they fired more shots at the vehicles and Jay heard a whoosh as a gas tank exploded, followed by a second tank. Two men cursed.

Bro worked it out. "Hey," he shouted to Payne. "They can't cover the front of the house from those positions. If we move up closer, we'll be protected."

Jay watched as Payne considered his man's suggestion. Bro had moved forward fifty yards and was covering three other men as they leap-frogged ahead, firing at each of the apparent shooter locations in turn. Three others began firing in support of Bro, to protect those men who were moving ahead. At last most of the men were in a shadow zone, protected by the farmhouse from the two shooters atop the barns.

Payne said, "Jay, I want you to target the house. When it's ablaze, we'll set fire to the barns. We need to get these people out into the open."

Jay reached into his backpack and extracted a grenade. He shouted a warning and everyone dropped to the ground. Jay pulled the pin and tossed the grenade through a window, now almost glassless from gunshots. His aim was true and the small device sailed all the way into the room through the broken window. He counted the seconds. Smoke and flames followed the explosion.

"Good one," said Payne. "Lob a second one at the far window."

Jay's aim was just as precise with the subsequent grenades. Within minutes flames leapt up and smoke poured from the windows. There was a wave of heat as something inside the house, possibly a gas tank, ignited. Three of the men moved away from the house, inadvertently moving out of its protective shadow. Jay heard a shot and screams and turned to look. One of the drivers had been shot and his two passengers raced to assist him. There were two more shots and the would-be rescuers also fell, screaming.

Jay thought the shooter was using a .50-caliber weapon and knew bullets of that caliber would cause horrendous injuries. The three victims were alive, although in extreme pain. They were shouting for assistance as they clutched their legs. *The shooters are smart*, he thought. They knew their attackers would be distracted by the screams. Jay took another grenade and threw it through an upper window. He repeated the process three times and at last both floors were in flames. While the smoke was helping to cover them, it was also causing breathing difficulties. One of the still-standing militia, caught in a particularly heavy acrid cloud, began coughing and tried to get to clearer air. He fell, shot in the leg, screaming.

A section of the upper floor collapsed and the wave of heat forced another militia member back; he, too, fell to the marksman, screaming and clutching his leg. The team had now incurred six injuries, and Jay was unsure whether anyone inside has been hurt or killed. *This is a losing game*, he thought.

Payne heard the siren first and he said to Jay, "Damn, we'll have fire engines and law enforcement here in no time and we can't get away, either. At least we've completed most of our assignment, don't you think?"

Jay cursed. He'd been so focused on destroying the house and distracted by the screams that he had entirely overlooked the probable arrival of emergency services or police. This part of the country was far too heavily populated. Back home in Texas, it would have taken an hour or more for a fire engine to respond to a call from a remote location. He sighed.

Bro said, "How about we take them out?"

Jay snarled. "And what, flee on a fuckin' fire truck? Don't even think about it."

The truck was about to enter through the gateway, which he had cleared earlier, and an ambulance followed. Police cars were behind the ambulance, lights flashing.

"Payne," Jay said, "tell the men to drop their weapons. Otherwise we'll be caught in a firefight with the police."

~~~

Lieutenant Harkness was in the lead vehicle. This property and anything happening here was on his hit list. He was sure this place would haunt him for the rest of his days. He had not before experienced anything like this crime scene. He supervised as his officers handcuffed the uninjured men who had their arms raised in surrender. While this was in progress, an SUV arrived and two men alighted from the vehicle and introduced themselves.

"I'm Agent Fresner, Theo Fresner. This is Janice Mortimer." The agent held out his FBI ID.

Harkness looked at it briefly and shook each agent's hand. He said, "Peter Harkness and this is David Leary."

Fresner said, "I'm normally in Boston but I've been doing some work in Concord, so I was allocated to respond. One of our crime teams is heading here from the Boston office. It'll be an hour or so, before it get here."

"What do you think?" Harness indicated the still burning house and barns where the fire fighters were working to control the fires.

Fresner looked up and searched the sky for a second or two. A drone was circling a hundred feet or so above his head and he pointed it out to Harkness. "This helps. The property is under observation all the time. I received a video file on the way here, from one of our ex-agents. We've both worked with him on a number of assignments before he retired and can vouch for him. He provided what seems to be a very comprehensive set of video files. While I haven't viewed them all, he included a summary file that covers key points. I expect the videos contain enough close ups to confirm the activities of these guys," he indicated the group of men under police guard. "It seems they had a mission to destroy and probably even kill, I've no doubt about that." He produced his cell phone. "Watch this, it's the summary video." Fresner started the video and handed his cell phone to the police lieutenant.

Harkness and Leary watched, not hiding their surprise as the details unfolded. "It's almost unbelievable," Harkness said when the video ended. He handed back Fresner's cell phone.

"We had a similar reaction, at first," the FBI agent said. "I'll send you a copy of the file. Fortunately the house occupants were away—I believe they're in Europe and the housekeeper and her husband are on vacation."

Leary said, "So these guys attacked an empty house? I wonder if they knew that?"

"We'll find out. If you don't mind, we'll take over. We're intending to process this as a terrorist act."

"That'll be a pleasure. Can you handle these men by yourselves?" Harkness asked.

"We'll need some assistance from you until our crime team arrives."

"No argument there. My only question is how the hell did Midway shoot these people if he's currently in Europe?" Harkness said.

Fresner asked, "You were here when Bravo Company landed?"

"Oh, yeah," Harkness said. "You know about that? I can tell you, that day is seared into my soul."

"I understand the 145th was testing some advanced equipment. Same for the shootings here today—test equipment."

"They have some effective test equipment," murmured Leary.

Fresner and Harkness watched as the firemen dealt with the fires—the buildings were still ablaze. The uninjured men had been searched for weapons and were all handcuffed. The ambulance crew had requested another two vehicles to assist with the injured men.

The lead responder briefed Fresner and Harkness. "These guys have some very serious injuries. One of your prisoners said he thought the weapons firing at them were .50-caliber and I think he's correct. I've treated this kind of injury in Afghanistan. Whoever was defending this property didn't pull any punches."

Harkness said, "I'm sure they've now learned not to mess with the people here."

***

Chapter 17

Mark returned to his room. They were leaving the hotel later in the afternoon and he wanted to send Schmidt a message updating him about the genetically engineered teenagers. He also had a message to call Goodwin and he decided to do that first.

"Detective Inspector? Mark."

"Good. I wanted to update you. Your three intruders are—or at least were—Immigration and Customs Enforcement, ICE, part of Homeland Security. They were operating well outside their jurisdiction. They've been disowned and thrown to the wolves. Their presence in your room was apparently part of some unauthorized venture. I've some leverage to discover what their plan was. I'll let you know as soon as I find out more."

"I don't understand why, or who—"

"That's what I wanted to check. You've had prior contact with these people?"

"No, never, nothing with ICE or DHS. I've had an encounter with the CIA, a year ago or more, when my parents' lab was attacked."

"Yes—I recall a Cerberus US brief on that attack. Hmm. I'll see what I can discover."

"Thanks. Oh, we're heading to your safe house. We'll leave here late this afternoon."

"Good. I'll be happier when you move. We can provide better protection there. What about the people Reb wanted to meet with?"

Mark had assumed the DI had been kept informed by his Cerberus escort. He provided a synopsis. "We had a good discussion. I think they're interested in what we can offer. Reb is going to call them after we get to the safe house, to check if they have any questions. It might take a day or two before we have a decision."

"Keep me updated. I can arrange for a Cerberus guard for them, if you think it's necessary?"

"I'll see what Reb thinks. They're probably all resourceful, anyway."

Goodwin concluded the call and as Mark replaced the hotel phone, his laptop sounded an alarm, an alert from the farmhouse security system in New Hampshire. He clicked the flashing red light symbol on the screen. The sound stopped. He opened the image feed and within seconds was watching a split screen video from the two drones circling the property. He selected the feed from the camera closer to the front gate. A line of five vehicles, two trucks and three SUVs, had halted in the road leading to the gate. It was early morning, about five minutes after six a.m. on the East Coast. Mark clicked on the small plus sign on the software to see an enlarged view. A man in military style clothing was working at the gate. He walked to the first vehicle and moments later Mark saw the flare of an explosion at the gate. The man returned to the gate and pushed it open. As the lead vehicle drove through, the man swung himself aboard. The other vehicles followed, accelerating toward the farmhouse.

Mark wondered if this was an attack by either the Chinese or the CIA. The vehicles were unmarked so he assumed it was not a police raid. He was confident it was not

Cerberus. Another possibility was the Russians. He watched as the drone followed the vehicles.

He activated both Cutter weapon systems. These intruders had destroyed his front gate and presumably planned the same for his home. He decided it would be lawful for him to prevent their incursion; at least, that was a risk he was prepared to take. He targeted the lead vehicle's front wheels and fired two shots. The vehicle shuddered to a stop as its tires burst and it slipped sideways, into the snow mound on the side of the lane. The following vehicle clipped the leading vehicle's rear and it spun into the ice and snow on the other side. Mark fired again, targeting the tires of the second vehicle now stalled in the snowbank. Men jumped from both vehicles and, sheltering behind their vehicles, commenced firing at the farmhouse. The other three vehicles had stopped about fifty yards behind the two lead vehicles. Mark targeted each vehicle in turn until all five had flat tires. He focused the targeting system back at the first vehicle and fired more shots, blowing in the windshield, penetrating the radiator, and hopefully damaging the engine. He repeated the process for each vehicle. Each time one of the drone cameras focused on a face, Mark extracted a still image and forwarded it to Maeve's analysts.

The men on the ground destroyed the front windows of the house with their weapon fire, probably thinking the building was occupied. Mark realized they had discovered the source of defensive fire when they started to target the protected areas on top of the barns.

One man moved closer to the house until he was out of sight of the targeting cameras. Mark adjusted the drones and watched as the man signaled his companions. They all followed his lead and Mark counted fifteen men in total, moving closer to the house. Mark continued to pepper the SUVs, firing at those in the rear, and two burst into flames. He was confident he had damaged all the vehicles and they now were out of commission. At least the intruders wouldn't be able to use their vehicles to flee the scene. He wondered if he should alert the FBI. In normal circumstances he would contact the local police, but they may not be sympathetic to a request for assistance given their recent adventure with Bravo Company.

He checked the time. Less than fifteen minutes had passed since the alarm had sounded. Mark had not targeted any of the individuals, although he saw that one man had been hit, presumably by a ricochet. Anna entered the room as he watched the men continue to move closer to the house, trying to get out of range of the two weapon.

"What's wrong?" she asked. "What's happening?"

"Intruders at the farmhouse. It's under attack. I've shot out their vehicles. Get your laptop and see if you can get a look at the vehicle license plates, and try to identify the owners. I've sent facial images to Maeve's people but it's too early to get results back."

Anna opened her laptop. "I'll use the second drone," she said. "It will take a minute to get it into position." After a minute she said, "Well, you made a mess of their vehicles. Thank goodness the Joneses are absent. They'd be terrified by all this. Okay, I've picked up three license plates. I'll see what the ALPR system makes of them. What's happening on your end?"

"The intruders have moved up closer to the house. I think this is a revenge move of some kind. They'll destroy our home, I'm sure. We'll lose everything but at least our files and software are backed up to our cloud. I want to identify as many of these men as possible. When this is over, I'll deliver each one a message. I want to discourage them and whoever authorized this from ever attacking us again."

"Okay, I have license details. They're all privately owned vehicles with Georgia license plates. Some kind of local militia for hire, do you think?"

Mark focused on the activity showing on the monitor. "Let me see. Hold on, they're being really nasty. Someone decided to set the house on fire. I expect the barns and the housekeeper's cottage will be included in this pyromaniac's scope before he's finished. It's too bad the weapons can't cover the area close to the house. A lesson for next time."

Anna watched the house as one of the front rooms burst into flames. "That's so sad. The children will be so disappointed."

"We need to contact the FBI. There must be a local branch. See if Scott knows any of the local agents. Also, we should try the police. They may be glad to get their hands on anyone involved with us, even if they're burning down our house. Offer videos of the entire raid. I want to keep monitoring here in case I can use the Cutters."

Anna raced away while Mark continued to watch the scene from the drones. One of the intruders moved into range of a Cutter. Mark did not hesitate. He fired at the man's legs. The man fell and two of his companions rushed to his aid. Mark shot each of them in their legs, as well. The weapons were devastating. The men would require substantial medical assistance. The other intruders ignored the fallen men and continued their destruction, smashing windows and lighting fires. Before long, the entire house was aflame.

Anna returned with Scott, and Mark showed him the live images. "We have a dozen or so intruders at the farmhouse. They blew in the gate and now they've set the house on fire. The barns will be next. Do you know any local FBI agents you can contact? We can provide copies of video files showing what these men have done. We've got full facial images and license plate details."

Scott said, "Let me get my laptop. I can call one or two contacts. I'll know soon which FBI agents are in the area."

"Good. Anna, use your laptop and call the local police and emergency services and report the attack and the fire. Mention the wounded men, tell them ambulances will be required."

Mark continued to monitor the activity around the farmhouse. The plume of heavy black smoke was growing in intensity and height as the fire took hold. Heat from the burning house was pushing the men back, away from the house. He hoped for opportunities to fire more shots before the intruders fired the barns. He listened as Anna reported the fire to US authorities. The dispatcher promised to have a fire engine at the farmhouse within ten minutes. When Anna completed her call, Mark said, "Try to contact Maeve, ask if her analysts can start working on the images I sent. When you've finished, try Schmidt. They both need to know about this. I want to stay focused on the Cutters. They'll learn to leave us alone."

Scott returned. "Two FBI agents are on their way to the farmhouse. They expect to be there in twenty minutes, and an additional team is now leaving Boston. It's going to take them an hour or more to get there. They'll let me know when they arrive."

"The intruders will still be there; the vehicles are all inoperable." Mark fired another round and watched his target collapse. "I've counted five men down. The others won't aid them—they're too exposed. If they do try to help, they'll go down as well." There was an element of glee in his voice. He heard Anna make contact with Schmidt but his focus on the scenes provided by the drone cameras did not waver.

Schmidt called Maeve and conferenced in Anna, who had the call on speaker. Mark listened as Anna briefed both.

When she finished, Schmidt said, "The analysts identified a lot of chatter over the last couple of days. Perhaps it was setting this up?"

Mark said, "These are freelance. Their vehicles are all from Georgia. According to SO15, the people who broke into my hotel room are ICE and have been disowned by their bosses. There must be some connection between both operations."

Maeve said, "My team is still in analysis mode. We don't have enough data yet for precise conclusions. They say there are layers of activities, a lot from ICE, threads from the CIA, and some local Russians may be involved."

Mark fired another shot with the Cutter. "That's six injured now. Six gunshot wounds are going to require a lot of explaining. When will your analysts start working on the images I sent? It'll help to have IDs of these people as soon as possible."

"I'll get them started when we finish this call."

"Good," Schmidt said. "Scott, when do you expect the FBI to reach the site?"

"Another ten minutes. I know the two agents and briefed them. I'm sending them video files, as well"

"The fire engine has arrived," Mark said. "I can't use the Cutters anymore. Firemen won't approach a burning building if there was a risk of them getting shot."

"An ambulance and a police car just arrived, behind the fire engine," Anna added.

Schmidt said, "Okay. We'll work with the locals and the FBI. I'll keep you informed."

"Likewise," Maeve said.

"I wish the audio pickups were functioning," Mark said. "I'd like to hear what kind of story these guys are telling the local law."

"The FBI will be there soon. I sent them as many video files as I could," Scott said.

"Good. They can share with the local police. It will be difficult for the intruders to contradict the video evidence," Mark said.

He navigated the drone so it would show the house and barns. The house was engulfed in flames and the two outer buildings were smoldering. His links to the drones would fail once the barns caught fire and destroyed his equipment. The black stream of smoke was reaching farther into the sky.

Anna said, "They've destroyed our home. I hope these bastards go down."

***

Chapter 18

Schmidt could not rid himself of the concerns raised by the attack on Mark's farmhouse. It smacked of government-supported activity, yet there was no obvious motive apart from possible revenge for the CIA agents taken down a year ago when a militia team attacked Mark's home and his parents' lab. The recent chatter may be associated with the morning's attack, although it seemed a fruitless, even careless venture. Of course these attackers would not have expected Midway to counter attack using software-controlled weapon systems. Schmidt explained the situation to his traveling companion, Colonel Dempsey.

"It smacks of revenge, some kind of warning," Schmidt said. "I don't know why ICE got involved. It's perplexing."

"Their actions in London were amateurish," said Dempsey as they waited for the helicopter to lift off. They were using helmet mikes and earphones. "ICE lost three men in London, perhaps four including their controller, assuming the Brits go all out. I can't imagine them releasing these agents if ICE has disowned them. SO15 will want to make a point. They won't like ICE freelancing on their home turf."

"They *are* zealous in that regard, just as we would be, if foreign agents were prancing around here."

The helicopter lifted off, distracting the two men for a moment. The flight was routine. They were heading to Ft. Myer for their weekly meeting with CIC. Schmidt expected the meeting to be routine; nothing serious had arisen in the previous week. He and Dempsey sat back, lost in thought. Schmidt was trying to understand what was driving the increased chatter.

Finally he said, "Remind me to phone Maeve when we land. I think all these activities are some kind of feint, intended to distract us. Someone out there is planning something and he's hiding it under layers of subterfuge. He must be sacrificing his men, almost twenty so far, which is a sizable decoy. I wonder what the hell—"

"General, we've been tagged by a missile," the pilot said. "I'm firing decoy flares and descending in case it's—" The man's words were cut short by an explosion that rocked the helicopter. It went into a violent spin as the momentum of the overhead rotor took control. The pilot struggled fruitlessly with the controls. Schmidt and Dempsey braced themselves for the hard landing.

~~~

Earlier that morning Colonel Alexey Grigoryevich had driven to the location he had designated for his meeting with the leader of the FSB sleepers. He parked his car on a side street and walked around the corner. The sleeper was waiting. He was driving an old green Volkswagen, its sides rusty and dented. Alexey struggled to shut the bent passenger door.

"A cheap car," his fellow countryman explained as he accelerated into the stream of traffic. "One we can dump. Remember to wipe clean anything you touch."

The warning was unnecessary, thought Alexey, annoyed with the other Russian. "You need to burn the damn thing, otherwise there'll be DNA traces. Or dismantle it and sell the parts. At least that way you might recover some of my money." The FSB members had claimed poverty and were using Alexey as their banker. He knew he was being taken for a ride but refusal was not possible. The American would have his scalp if this plan failed. He grabbed a handhold as the driver took the corner faster than the vehicle could properly handle.

"We want to get there alive," he said.

The driver smiled. His expression was almost a sneer. "That's the problem with you *intelligentsiia*. You cannot handle a little hardship."

Alexey ignored the insult. "Is your equipment in place?"

"*Da*. We moved it last night. The team is there now, waiting for us."

"Are you confident you know how to fire this weapon?"

"One of my men is a specialist. He knows."

Alexey remained silent for the remainder of the journey, not wishing to disturb the driver's concentration or desirous of attracting any more insults. The helicopter flight was due to pass almost overhead in two hours and this car trip would take another thirty minutes. He hoped the noisy and almost unroadworthy vehicle did not attract the attention of DC police. He almost leapt from the vehicle when they arrived, and slammed the door aggressively. The driver had parked behind the warehouse building, out of the way, where casual passersby wouldn't notice the vehicle. Two other old vehicles and a courier van were parked in the same area.

"They'll all be on the roof," the driver said, leading the way to the rear entrance. Large double doors, locked and chained, barred their way. A small side door opened into the musty and dim interior. Alexey stumbled over a discarded carton.

"Watch where you're going," the other Russian admonished. "There are no lights, it's safer without them. Besides, the building has no electricity. Follow me."

Either his companion had cat's eyes or he was trying to demonstrate some kind of superiority, because he led off without hesitation across the rubble-strewn floor to a stairwell hidden in the far corner. The man pulled open a rusty fire door and began his climb. Alexey followed, not without some trepidation. He did not entirely trust his fellow Russian. When they pushed through the exit door onto the flat roof, the morning sunshine almost blinded him.

It took a moment or two for his eyes to adjust. Three other Russians stood around the Strela 21, admiring the missile mounted on its launch pad. One man was adjusting controls on the missile. They all looked at Alexey and smiled. They believed this would be some kind of masterstroke that would gain them tremendous favor with their FSB controllers. Alexey had sworn them to secrecy, claiming any leak before the weapon was fired would unravel the entire plan.

The man adjusting the Strela's controls spoke. "This is a marvelous weapon. I wish we had more here. Oh, the aircraft I would bring down with them. One day you'll have to tell me how you managed to procure this one."

"Trade secret." Alexey smiled. "Is it ready?"

"*Da, da*, she is ready, aren't you, my beauty." The man stroked the side of the missile. It was almost a loving caress.

Alexey hid his shudder. He was not a natural murderer and regretted his agreement with the American to carry out this assassination. He said, "You have the camouflage netting to hide us and the weapon? We don't want the helicopter pilot to see the Strela before we launch it."

One of the other Russians nodded. "The netting's ready. It will take only minutes to erect and we can fire the missile from beneath it. We've done it before, in the Ukraine."

The third man was holding a radio. He lifted it in Alexey's direction. "We're tuned into the frequency you provided. I can monitor the flight."

"Good," said Alexey. He checked his watch. "We need to wait for forty minutes. Did anyone bring coffee?"

Thirty-five minutes later the Russian with the radio signaled to his companions. "The pilot has clearance. If he follows the flight plan he'll be overhead in five minutes."

The men stirred from their relaxed positions and moved under the netting and Alexey followed their lead. One of the sleepers had found a vantage point and positioned himself with a pair of binoculars; he was to give an alert when the helicopter came within range. Alexey listened to the harsh sounds from the small radio, trying to follow the arcane traffic control messages.

The man with the binoculars spoke, "I can see the helicopter. It's on course and should be here in less than a minute."

Alexey heard the aircraft as it approached. The expert busied himself at the missile's launch controls. The weapon was located at the edge of the camouflage netting and would trail the helicopter as it passed overhead. The other Russians were standing to either side, waiting. Alexey was at the far corner of the netting, well away from the launch blast. As the helicopter ranged across the building, the missile leapt up with a roar of sound and a wash of heat. It accelerated, heading for the aircraft.

"It's got a lock," shouted the expert. "The pilot's firing flares but they're not working. The Strela is too smart."

Alexey heard the explosion. He grabbed the binoculars from the Russian standing beside him and focused on the falling helicopter. The tail fin had disappeared and the helicopter was spinning out of control as it descended. He watched, entranced, as it spun faster and faster until it struck a small building about half a mile away. Within seconds a dense cloud of smoke hid the view.

"Let's go," he said as he returned the binoculars to the owner. "Remove the netting. It's time we were out of here."

He could hear the discordant sounds of an emergency vehicle shrilling its way to the crash site.

Alexey did not see the man dressed in black rise from the far corner of the building. He watched in disbelief as one by one, four Russians collapsed around him. It took only seconds. He suddenly realized what was happening and looked up. The man was walking toward him, a silenced sniper rifle held across his body. Alexey's mind raced—this was not part of the scenario they had agreed.

"Thank you, Alexey, for a job well done," the shooter said.

"What—you never said—"

"I never said a lot of things," replied the man Alexey knew as McCarr. He gave his thin smile, raised the rifle, and aimed it at Alexey. "Farewell." He fired.

***

Chapter 19

Maeve Donnelly received the first notification less than ten minutes after the helicopter crashed, when one of her Cerberus FBI agents phoned her with as many details as she had been able to gather. "Maeve, there's been an accident. CNN or the other news channels will have details soon. Schmidt's helicopter crashed on the way to Ft. Myer. We're not sure yet, but we've received reports of a missile being fired from an old warehouse building. I expect it'll be chaos and mayhem out there for a while."

"What about the people on board?" Maeve asked, her hand trembling.

"No news. There're emergency responders at the location and more on the way. When I hear, I'll let you know."

"Thanks." Maeve disconnected. She sat motionless for what seemed like hours but was less than a minute. She brought her wild thoughts back under control, lifted her head, and spoke to her assistant.

"Harry?"

"Yes, ma'am."

"Emergency meeting. Five minutes. Main meeting room. The A team. B team is to listen in. I don't care what they're working on."

"Yes, ma'am." Harry had started typing the e-mail summons while Maeve was still speaking and sent it before she had finished. He reached for his phone to make follow-up calls. Maeve closed her laptop and headed for the meeting room. She might have to dispossess anyone who was using it. Her analysts straggled in one by one and at the five-minute mark the last one arrived, his hair disheveled, his expression worried.

"Sorry, ma'am," he breathed as he sat at the end of the table.

Twenty people were in the conference room, silent, apprehensive. Another ten analysts had connected by video. Thirty more were watching a live stream of the meeting on their laptops.

Maeve said, "Harry, turn on the TV. CNN." She waited for a moment as her assistant clicked the remote. As the image formed on the monitor at the end of the room, Maeve spoke.

"I want you to drop anything you're currently working on that isn't connected to this new task. We think someone blew up an army helicopter—Schmidt and Dempsey were on board."

She was interrupted by exclamations from her audience. She waited a moment before continuing. "There are rumors of a missile. I want to know everything about this—who did it, who's involved, motives, countries, and anything else you can find. I want to know if this is a domestic act or foreign. I also want to know why we didn't discover any indication this was being planned. I want facts and evidence. Guesses are acceptable if they're well supported."

"Do we know if Schmidt is alive?" Linda Schöner asked.

"I'm waiting to hear."

"The chatter we've been hearing—it must be related."

"Discover the relationships."

"The attack on Midway's property?"

"Stay on it. There must be a connection. I want identities of all those people Midway photographed."

"And the people who attacked him in London?"

"Same. Stay on it."

A CNN anchor had started reading a news report on the helicopter crash. Maeve held up her hand and said, "Listen. Though I doubt they know anything yet."

The news item was full of promise without any details. Maeve said, "Tap into all the news feeds. They may discover items we need to know. Questions?"

Schöner spoke again. "Maeve, we all hope he's okay. Come on, team, let's get on this." Almost as one, the twenty analysts rose and left the room.

Maeve stayed to watch the news even though she knew it was far too soon for the television media to have reliable information. She couldn't believe someone had tried to take out Schmidt—and perhaps had succeeded. She reminded herself that Schmidt thought he was indestructible. This time he might be wrong.

~~~

The lead medical emergency responder stood for a moment and stared at the disaster before him. The helicopter had hit the side of a three-story building and, according to eyewitnesses, slid almost in slow motion down the wall, scraping off windows as it went. No bystanders had been injured in the accident. The aircraft was now sitting on top of three cars in the parking area at the rear of the building. It was on its side and missing its tail rotor. The main rotor blades were buckled from their impact against the building and the ground. The helicopter's automatic fire extinguisher system had deployed, filling the cockpit and cabin with foam. One of the crushed cars had started to burn but a quick-witted bystander had grabbed a fire extinguisher and doused the flames. The man had not realized the danger he was in, standing so close to the wreckage.

The senior EMT watched as the fire crew evaluated the scene. They were concerned about the Jet A fuel still leaking from the helicopter's fuel tanks. The medical emergency team wanted to approach but they stayed back waiting for an all-clear signal from the fire crew. The EMT would be surprised if there were survivors. News helicopters buzzed overhead and he hoped they maintained a safe distance. Sometimes the producers encouraged their pilots to take unnecessary risks. At least the sight of the crashed helicopter would help instill some caution in the more sensible pilots.

At last the fire crew signaled the all clear. Two members of the emergency response team, wearing flame retardant gear, hastened toward the wreckage, one to the cockpit and one to the cabin. Firemen provided assistance as the paramedics struggled to gain access. The man at the cockpit signaled that the pilot showed no signs of life. The responder in the passenger cabin, after struggling with the ungainly position of the wrecked helicopter, indicated he had life signs. A swift team response followed. The senior EMT was pleased with his team's performance. His team members stretchered the injured man out to a waiting ambulance and it sped away to the nearest hospital. Other team members followed with two more stretchers, each carrying a body and they required respect rather than an urgent response.

~~~

Maeve received the second telephone call about ten minutes after the hospital had received the victim from the wreckage. Her informant said, "Schmidt survived. He's in a critical condition. The medics declared both Dempsey and the pilot dead at the scene. Military and FAA investigative teams are on the way—they should arrive in minutes. The police have sealed off the area. No details of what caused the crash, except the helicopter is missing its tail boom. So far, no one's confirmed it was caused by a missile. There are reports of a missile in flight and police are backtracking the helicopter's flight path, trying to identify a possible launch location. That's all we've got so far."

Maeve thanked her informant and disconnected the phone. She felt a wash of relief. Schmidt had survived. Now she wanted to know who had caused this disaster. Those responsible would face more than Schmidt's ire. She would bring their world to an end, she vowed. Her phone rang again. She checked the caller ID—the White House.

"Donnelly."

"Maeve, the President has been informed that Schmidt's helicopter crashed. We've also heard Schmidt is the only survivor. The President offers his thoughts. A couple of action points. He wants to meet with you tomorrow morning to discuss Cerberus. Also, if your analysts gather any information as to who was behind this, he wants to know as soon as possible."

Maeve acknowledged the action points and disconnected. The next few days were going to be hell. She looked to see if her assistant was at his desk.

She said, "Harry, please call Midway. I want to let him know about Schmidt."

Moments later Harry told her Mark was on her phone. She picked it up and said, "Good morning, Mark. I've some unfortunate news. Schmidt's helicopter was attacked at ten this morning. He's in a critical condition."

"What? That's horrifying. Damn. I hope he survives."

"Me too. I'll keep you updated with his progress and whether his condition changes. We're searching for who did it, who was behind them, for anything that will give us a lead. Talk with your DI Goodwin and see what additional information she can uncover in case there are links between the attack on you and this attack on Schmidt. The action on your property was a diversion of some kind. Or maybe to blow dust to hide their real plan. Anything you wish to do to get information, go ahead. Send me details if you uncover anything interesting."

"I'll do that. Thank you for letting me know. Please keep me informed. When you're able to talk with him, give him our wishes for a speedy recovery."

"I will. I'll be making a nuisance of myself at the hospital." Her laugh was nervous. "I'm scheduled to meet with the President tomorrow morning. He's heard about Schmidt and wants to discuss Cerberus. I surmise I'll have a responsibility to hold the organization together until Schmidt recovers. Can I add your name as head of the UK side?"

"Uh…yes, I'll do it. We can review the details when Schmidt's up and running again."

"Very well. I'll contact you after I meet with the President."

She disconnected. She wanted to call the hospital but decided not to. Instead, she contacted the senior Cerberus managers who worked with Schmidt and advised them of the morning's events. She said she wanted guards on Schmidt while he was in the hospital. There were no disagreements.

***

Chapter 20

After Maeve's call, Mark sat for a moment, deep in thought. He had accepted responsibility for Cerberus UK, without fully determining what that entailed. He called DI Goodwin.

"Yes, Mark?"

"I've some news. Maeve Donnelly called me. Schmidt's helicopter crashed and he's in critical condition."

"That's shocking. Do you have any details on his condition? Do they know what caused the crash?"

"I've no news on his condition. This happened at ten a.m., Washington time. The authorities suspect someone fired a missile at it. Maeve's meeting with the President tomorrow. She thinks he'll want her to manage Cerberus US while Schmidt's out of action."

"I hope he survives. Donnelly'll do a good job. She headed the FBI until sometime last year, if I recall?"

"Maeve was director of the FBI for a long time. She was kidnapped last year and some of her people were killed or injured. She decided she needed to do something else. She's been managing Schmidt's analytic team for nearly a year now. Maeve knows everything, and if she doesn't, she can usually find out. Before she was appointed director, she held several positions in private and public legal areas."

"I'd like to meet her some time. It sounds as though she has an interesting background."

"There's more. Maeve asked if I'd take responsibility for Cerberus UK and I said yes."

"A drastic way to make your decision."

"Yes, it is. Also, my home in New Hampshire was attacked earlier this morning. It was burned to the ground."

"Is everything happening today? Did they think you were there? You and Schmidt both, in the one day. That's not a coincidence."

"That's what we think as well. I've a video I'll send you as an FYI. Some kind of militia group was involved. Six of them will be in the hospital for some time, recovering from gunshot wounds."

"They were shot? Who did that?"

Mark decided not to disclose details. "I have some security, just in case. While the attackers were arrested, we don't know yet who's behind the attack. The point is, Maeve and I both think the break-in here, the raid on my home, and now the attack on Schmidt are all linked. I'd like to visit with the people you arrested yesterday. I may be able to discover what they were trying to do."

"Unofficially, of course."

"Of course. I'll bring Gabrielle, if I may?"

"What? Why?"

"I'd prefer to demonstrate, if you want to join us. I'd like to interview those agents as soon as possible. Can you arrange it for me?"

"Expect a car in an hour."

Mark transferred a copy of the video file to Goodwin and went searching for his crew. He discovered them in the lounge, enjoying scones, strawberry jam, and cream again. He put on a disappointed face. "Where's mine?"

Niland pointed at half a scone in the center of the table. "You can have whatever is left."

Mark updated the group while he ate the half scone, liberally smeared with the remnants of the cream and strawberry jam. "Maeve said she'll keep us informed about Schmidt's condition. She's going to run Cerberus US while Schmidt is recovering. Scott and Sera, I need Gabrielle for about an hour this afternoon. A car's coming for the two of us. It'll be here in about forty minutes. The vehicles for our move will also be here soon. Scott, can you organize our exit? Make sure everyone's cleared their room, get all our suitcases loaded?"

"Okay, I can do that."

"I'll handle the account when I return. I'm going to be in two places at once for a while." Mark didn't explain why he needed Gabrielle. He also kept silent about his future involvement with Cerberus UK. There was too much happening and he wanted to organize his thoughts.

"Anything else?"

"No, that's all for now."

Anna said, "Do you want me to come with you two?"

"No, it'll be a quick visit. Reb and you can help clear our rooms so we're all ready to leave when I return."

Scott and Gabrielle reached the lobby as the police vehicle arrived. Mark was a handful of steps behind them. Unsurprisingly, DI Goodwin was a passenger.

There was a whisper in the back of his mind.

Are we going to tell her about all our abilities?

Mark silently replied: *Let's keep most of it private. We can say both of us are able to determine whether a person is telling the truth or not. Otherwise we'll play it by ear. It'll depend on what we find out, what we need to do, okay?*

Yes.

Mark greeted Goodwin. "Good afternoon, Detective Inspector. I wasn't sure you'd be here."

"Well, I'm intrigued. If I can learn something new, I'm open to doing so."

"So am I"

"Me, too," Gabrielle said.

"Where are you holding your prisoners?" Mark asked.

"We've utilized some army barracks. They have a small hospital unit and the military is providing treatment. Our prisoners suffered more or less minor injuries, as you know. SO15 decided to hold them as suspected terrorists, which gives us a lot more flexibility."

"Terrorism actually may be an accurate call. Are they able to speak?"

Goodwin laughed. "Able to, yes. Willing to, perhaps not. Speak to you? I'll be interested to see what happens."

"Did you view the video I sent?"

"Oh yes. Remind me to be extra cautious if I ever pay you a visit. What did you use?"

"I've been field testing an automated weapon system. It's a projectile weapon—think 'rifle', mounted on servos, with a camera unit, all remotely controlled from a laptop or any similar device. It's effective once you know how to use it." He didn't mention he had used an earlier version of the weapon against the mercenaries who had attacked his parents' lab. "I had to be extra careful. Killing people attacking our home might be legal, but I thought it was more prudent to injure them. I haven't had a chance to follow up, to find out what the FBI or the local police did with them. Gabrielle, will you ask Scott later to find out what happened?"

To his surprise, Gabrielle pulled a cell phone out of her jacket pocket and made a call. He had not realized the two children were equipped with phones. He listened while the girl conveyed his message.

"I should have known," he said when she finished her call.

Gabrielle giggled and returned the phone to her pocket. "It's very useful."

"I know. That's why I have one," he replied.

"I have three," Goodwin said. "One for the Met, one for Cerberus, and the third one is personal."

The trip to the barracks didn't take long. The soldier on duty waved them through once he sighted Goodwin's SO15 warrant card and they parked in the rear of the barracks. Goodwin led them into a nearby army building and they passed more military and police guards on the way. The building was set up as a small hospital with detention facilities.

"We have your three attackers here. The senior officer is Parrish. Joseph Parrish. We'll see him first." Goodwin nodded to the guard at the door of a small room and ushered Mark and Gabrielle in ahead of her.

Parrish was handcuffed and wore a leg chain, which prevented him moving away from his bed. He was sitting up, with pillows bracing his back. His jaw was bandaged. There was a water container with a long straw on the table beside his bed. He looked up, recognized Mark and snarled. He tried to talk and the words came out as mumbles.

Mark said, "We understand ICE has disowned you. Your controller's denied all knowledge of your activities. I thought you might like to tell me about it." He moved closer to the man who was mouthing threats. "Mind your language," Mark instructed, stepping aside to reveal Gabrielle. "I don't think what you said was suitable for young ladies."

Gabrielle moved to stand beside Mark. He focused his attention on Parrish. "Don't struggle. We only want to talk with you, to ask some questions. Be quiet."

The ICE agent stopped struggling against his restraints and ceased his attempts to speak.

Mark spoke again, "Parrish, we want to know who ordered you to kill me." Unnoticed, Gabrielle approached closer to the bed and laid her hand on Parrish's arm. The man stilled. Mark stepped closer and placed his hand next to Gabrielle's.

Mark said, "Who ordered you to carry out your attack on me? You knew it was illegal. Why did you accept an illegal order? Do you know who issued the instruction to your controller? Can you guess?" The man appeared resigned. A minute later both Gabrielle and Mark released the agent's arm and stood back.

Mark said, "Thank you for your cooperation. If you'd like to provide Detective Inspector Goodwin with a comprehensive written statement, I'm sure your treatment here will be improved. If you think it's necessary, we can discuss the Witness Protection Program for you. Understand?"

Parrish nodded, subdued. He mumbled through his bandages.

Gabrielle said to Goodwin, "He wants paper and pen. I think he'll prepare a detailed statement for you."

The DI led them out of the small room to an empty office. She sat them both down and looked from one to the other. At last she said, "Alright. Tell me, what just happened?"

Gabrielle looked at the floor.

Mark said, "We have some…attributes, I suppose you'd call them. We're able to soothe someone who's trying to fight us, as you witnessed. We, if we're fortunate, can sometimes read an impression of what the person is thinking." He did not mention he was able to access and transfer whole memories as though they were files.

"I'll be damned. None of the Cerberus people I know can do anything approaching that."

"Gabrielle is the only Cerberus person I know who has this talent. Mine isn't Cerberus-based and is different from her's. I'd like a copy of Parrish's statement, when he's done."

"So what did you discover?"

"It was an ICE operation."

"That was my impression."

"They were instructed by their local manager—their controlling agent who denied everything when you questioned him. This controller gave them the assignment and when they protested, he arranged a videoconference with a senior—very senior, from what I can discern—manager from DHS headquarters in Arlington. He confirmed their instructions."

"Can we get verification, do you think?"

"We should talk to the others. Fortunately, Parrish surreptitiously recorded both meetings and will arrange to have tapes delivered to you. However, they're voice only, no video. We'd like a copy. Maeve's people can run some voice recognition analyses to see if they can identify the speaker. Parrish didn't know his name; he was referred to as the Italian Blade."

"I'll issue an arrest warrant for the local controller, once I have a written statement from Parrish. If I can obtain one more statement to confirm what he says, even better."

"Oh, we'll get more for you. Who's next on the list?"

"Strachan; he's the junior. Let's see how he's faring. He's conscious and able to speak, I understand." She indicated the way to another small room.

Mark led the way in. "Strachan, I understand you want to talk to me?"

The prisoner backed away, his face pale. Mark reached out and touched the agent's hand. Strachan stopped his movements. Gabrielle stepped forward and placed her hand beside Mark's. He asked the same questions he had directed at Parrish. At the end of the short, one-sided interview, he made the same comments about a written statement and witness protection. The prisoner nodded his head.

Goodwin led the way out back to the office. "I'm not telling anyone how this happened. No one would believe me."

While Goodwin was out of the office to deliver pens and paper to her detainees, Mark said, "Well, Gabrielle, what do you think?"

"We almost have enough information for Maeve. She'll be delighted when she hears. I have an image of this man in Arlington but I don't think I can draw his picture."

"Me, too. I think the DI will let us use one of her police artists and we can send a scan of the result to Maeve."

Goodwin returned with a happy expression on her face. "Come on, I want to see how you deal with the third agent. He's a tough bastard."

"Oh, Scarface. I'm surprised he's not more seriously injured. I tried."

"Our surgeon agrees. Now he's awake and complaining. Come and see for yourself."

Mark and Gabrielle followed Goodwin into the next room. Again, there was an armed guard on the door. This patient was also handcuffed and had a restrictive leg chain. He growled at his visitors. "Get the fuck outta my space." He looked startled when he saw and recognized Mark. "You? You're the son of a bitch who cracked my skull open."

Gabrielle walked up to him and said, "You're hurting. Let me remove your pain."

The agent growled again and Mark stepped forward, shielding Gabrielle. He stared at Scarface. Gabrielle was correct—the agent was hurting, but not from his injury.

Mark said, "Relax, buddy. Stay still, now." He reached out and touched the man's arm and got another almost animal-like response. However, the agent didn't move. Gabrielle placed her hand next to Mark's. The agent shook violently, his eyes rolled up, and he fell back, unconscious.

Mark and Gabrielle released the prisoner's arm. Mark turned to Goodwin. "He may not ask you for a pad and pen but he'll be a lot more tractable. We've done all we can for now. Let me know if he causes any more problems. It's

142

unfortunate he got too close to one of your men. I trust he'll recover quickly?"

"How did you know? Yes, my officer's recovering—just superficial injuries. It looked a lot worse." Goodwin led the way out of the patient's room. She turned to Mark when they were out of hearing of the guard. "Now tell me, damn it, what's this all about?"

Mark shrugged. "I told you and that's all I can say. We don't understand the process, either."

She had a doubtful expression. "I'll be interested when you can tell me more."

Mark nodded. Perhaps some time in the future he would do so, if his involvement with Cerberus UK deepened. "Shall we return to the hotel now? The crew is waiting for us."

***

Chapter 21

Anna found Reb on the small balcony off her hotel room. It provided a view of the Tower Bridge and the boats on the Thames. Reb was deep in thought. Anna was almost reluctant to interrupt. She pushed open the sliding door and Reb turned, flinching as her shoulder reminded her she was still healing.

"Aren't you cold out here?" Anna asked. The sun was hidden behind gray clouds and the breeze was razor sharp. She could feel dampness in the air from the London mist.

Reb looked abashed. "I like to watch the river activities. It reminds me—"

"Of being on board *Hammer*?"

"Well, being on a yacht. That yacht has some sad memories for me."

"Really? I thought being at sea was what you liked."

"Oh, it is. That's where I want to be, out at sea, heading to—oh, I don't know—anywhere."

"But you had problems on the yacht?"

"I shouldn't have said…" Her voice faded and her expression showed pain. "I was abused. The Chairman. He was a very nasty person."

"But how—I mean, you're as strong as Mark, almost. And I've seen you practice with those knives."

Reb smiled but it was a sad expression. "Sometimes strength is not the answer. Anyway, you were looking for me?"

"What? Oh yes. I wanted to spend some time with you. Stay there. I'll get my jacket." She returned in seconds, wrapped up against the cold. Reb had moved to one side to allow Anna to sit beside her. She sat and let the seconds stretch into minutes.

"What did you want?" Reb asked at last.

"I suppose girl talk," Anna said. "You know how I feel about your brother?"

"Yes." Reb smiled and this time it lit up her eyes. "I envy you, you know. Your relationship with Mark will grow, I'm sure. Me—I'll head back out to sea on board another yacht. I've contacted the agency I used before, to see if they have any vacancies. I suppose it sounds exciting but it can be dangerous. Or it can be boring. It depends..."

Anna reached out to Reb at the same time Reb reached for her. They held hands, providing each other comfort.

~~~

Andrew Wentworth waited somewhat anxiously for his scheduled meeting, although he had no reasons for his anxiety. He was in a mid-sized coffee shop in a part of DC he had never visited. The environment was comfortable and the coffee acceptable. The constantly changing crowd seemed amenable. He had seated himself at a small table in the corner, where he was able to see both doors into the shop. He sipped his coffee. The voice from the adjacent table startled him.

"Good, you were on time."

Mercante, Wentworth realized, must have arrived early. "I didn't see you there."

"Obviously. Tell me why your people haven't destroyed the New Hampshire evidence?"

"You're being ridiculous," Wentworth replied. "You sent a shitload of mercenaries into New Hampshire, they set fire to and destroyed a house and other buildings, got their vehicles all shot up, plus six are in hospital with serious gunshot wounds, and you expect to see all the evidence removed from our files. The local police, the emergency services, and FBI agents outside my control, all have details of what occurred. As does the hospital where these people are still being treated." Wentworth realized his voice was becoming louder and he reduced its volume. "Midway provided the FBI and the local police with a video of the entire operation, from when they blew the gate to arrival of the emergency services. They have to be the stupidest freelancers, ever."

"Now, now," Mercante said. His smile reminded Wentworth of a snake, a deadly one. "My sources didn't know about the defensive equipment Midway had installed. Devious."

"Dangerous, more likely."

"What can you do?"

"You mean apart from having all fifteen of the mercenaries shot and buried at sea? Nothing." He did not add that Mercante should be included in the sea burial.

"Have you heard anything about Schmidt?"

"He's critical." Realization hit Wentworth. "You didn't—it wasn't you—"

"I can't tell you anything." Mercante shrugged. "I have no idea who was behind the attack. The result's good for us, though."

Wentworth was not convinced. "If you set up some Russian spies who were illegal residents, got them a missile to take out Schmidt, you're a bigger—"

"Don't say it," Mercante growled.

"Damn, it *was* you."

"Improbable, my friend. I had other ideas. Useless now."

"Well, Schmidt might not recover."

"Do you have any updates? Is there any way into his room?"

"No and no. A Cerberus security team is monitoring the ICU and the hospital twenty-four seven. They're top members of Cerberus, military and even some FBI."

"Pity. Well, if you get any ideas, let me know."

Wentworth nodded. He finished his coffee. "I need to go."

"I'll call you if I have any good ideas."

"Sure, sure. Have a good one."

Mercante smiled to himself as he watched the senior FBI agent leave.

~~~

Neither man had paid any attention to the little old lady sitting by herself at another table. She had a large handbag, inside which was sophisticated recording equipment. After both men had left the coffee shop, she, too, left and caught a taxi. She contacted Maeve's analysts; they expressed interest in the tape and asked her to bring it to their office.

~~~

The analysts had conducted their tasks with a thoroughness that matched the urgency Maeve conveyed in her meeting. They had identified the mercenaries who raided the Midway property using the facial images Mark had forwarded. The men were known members of a Georgia militia unit with ties to an extremist religious group called the Southern United Fundamentalists. There was, according to the analysts' data, a link to a Reverend Barker, a man associated with a previous attack on Midway, and who was known to be involved in the leadership of the religious group. The analysts unearthed records suggesting the CIA had used the militia for at least two black operations in South America.

Reports from police and FBI after they had interviewed the militia members simply added confusion.

The analysts had detailed statements forwarded by the British Counter Terrorism Command from the ICE agents now under arrest by the Metropolitan Police. Maeve's team was waiting for the police artist's sketch of the person who had confirmed, by video to London, his instructions to eliminate Midway. They were also running voice analyses to identify the person.

Separately, FBI investigators and DC police had discovered the suspected launch site for the missile that had taken out the helicopter carrying Schmidt and Dempsey. They had found five bodies, subsequently identified as Russians, on the roof of the building. FBI crime scene reconstruction supported the theory the men had been killed by a single person. The killer's weapon had been left at the scene. The approximate time of death of the Russians matched that of the helicopter attack, and the evidence indicated the Russians had fired the missile. The analysts were also coming to the conclusion there was a link of some kind between the attack on the helicopter and the attack on Midway's property.

Two of the senior analysts met with Maeve to discuss the data threads they were exploring. Linda Schöner said, "It's intriguing us. One of the dead Russians at the missile launch site has been identified as Colonel Alexey Grigoryevich, a junior Assistant Air Attaché at the Russian Embassy. The other four were FSB shadows; they were on our watch list."

"The Russians were used. That's why they were shot and the bodies so easy to find."

"We're in agreement. The missile has been tentatively identified as a Russian Strela, either a 20 or 21."

"Do you have any idea how a new version of their top missile got to Washington?"

"Not yet. We're still working on that."

Maeve said, "Details of the Russians haven't been given to the media. The President has placed a hold on the news release. The sensitivity of possible Kremlin involvement is high, given other recent Russian missteps."

"We wondered about that. We suspect Grigoryevich was SVR. They and FSB are political enemies in Russia. It's unusual for them to be working together here. Someone must have applied a lot of pressure to motivate that. We're trying to discover what would cause them to even consider a joint task. FBI agents are interviewing family members of the deceased FSB members to see if they know anything. We've made sure our Cerberus people are doing the interviews."

"We've been back tracking Grigoryevich," said the other analyst, his eyes glowing with excitement. "He was good at covering his trail but we think he was meeting with a senior CIA officer. We've also uncovered a Zurich bank account in Grigoryevich's name, with substantial deposits. He was recently paid a large amount. We're tracing the source. It's almost as though someone has left a small trail of paper to lead us to a possible traitor. The obviousness makes me suspicious but the trail is too interesting to ignore."

"Continue exploring and let me know," Maeve said. "Have you any thoughts on the London hotel raid?"

"Some of the team are convinced this is all driven by Ricardo Mercante," Schöner said. "He's high in the CIA chain of command, about three from the top. A nasty record, when you dig deep. The problem is, he's Agency while the London people are ICE. Our voice analysis gives us a 50 percent probability he was the authorizing officer for the attack in London. The probability might increase once we have the police artist's sketch Midway promised to arrange. We haven't yet linked Mercante to these militia people but we're optimistic. We suspect some Agency people are prepared to attack both Cerberus and Midway, and Mercante may have decided to get down and dirty. Someone wants both and Schmidt and Midway dead and Cerberus eliminated. In any case, for now we must regard Mercante and the Agency, as potential enemies for us, Schmidt, and Midway until this is resolved."

"Can I have hard copies of your reports? I might take a selection with me, tomorrow for my meeting with the President."

"Yes, ma'am. I'll get a full set to you," Linda confirmed.

After her two analysts left her office Maeve sat back in her high-backed chair, deep in thought. Someone was trying to create anti-Russian reactions in the government, and when the White House released news of Russian involvement, the media would go into a feeding frenzy. Someone wanted Schmidt out of the way. He'd accumulated a number of powerful enemies and it wouldn't surprise her if one or more of those enemies had taken action. Cerberus was likely a target, as well. And Midway. Someone would earn a lot of points with the neocons if they took out Schmidt, Cerberus, Midway, and the Russian shadows. It was even possible *she* was a target. The probability of that would only increase if, as she suspected, the President asked her to run Cerberus in the US, given Schmidt's current incapacity.

***

Chapter 22

Mark was running late; he had far too much to do. He and Gabrielle had been driven back to the Tower Hotel by the SO15 driver, and Mark rushed to settle the hotel bill. The crew was waiting in the ten-passenger tour bus ready to travel to the safe house. The interior of the bus was dimly lit and the darkened windows would make their journey private. They wouldn't be able to do much sightseeing—the windows, light rain, and approaching evening gloom would all combine to hide the scenery. A Cerberus security guard was in the front passenger seat; Mark hoped the man's services wouldn't be required. Scott and Sera were seated in the back. Gabrielle sat down next to Reb and Niland while Mark took his seat next to Anna. She grabbed his hand and squeezed it. "We were wondering," she said. She kept hold of his hand. It was a comforting feeling.

"It took a little longer than I anticipated. London traffic—a phrase that's going to stay with us, I'm sure." Mark nodded to the driver. "We're all here, now."

The driver used his radio to call their lead security vehicle and the small convoy set off. Their luggage van was the last vehicle.

The driver handed Mark a thin folder when they stopped at the first traffic light and said, "Sir, the DI said to give you these details. Our destination's near Sparrows Green, East Sussex. It's pretty countryside, in the daytime. It'll take abaht one and a half hours."

Mark thanked the man and turned his attention to the folder. He asked the others, "Did you all get a copy of the property description?" He received a hail of affirmatives. According to the page he was reading, they were going to an old manor house, built some hundreds of years ago. It was three-storied, with six bedrooms on the second floor and a long attic as the third floor. In addition to the main house, there were two cottages and a number of outbuildings. The property had a separate four-car garage. There were thirty-five acres of wooded land, most of it to the rear of the house. According to the small map, some buildings were close to the house while others—barns, from the descriptions—were farther away. They would be difficult to defend, he thought. Although, if Cerberus provided a capable security team, it should not be a problem.

As the small bus moved along with the traffic, Mark reflected on his outstanding tasks. He needed to arrange a session with a police sketch artist to build a picture of the senior ICE agent who had confirmed Parrish's assignment, then send a copy to Maeve's team. He needed briefings on the Cerberus UK organization and its client base, to understand its business operation. Perhaps DI Goodwin will tell him who to contact to obtain the details he sought. He had not received lab results for Reb's DNA and the gunshot residue tests on her parka; the reports may have been overlooked with all the other events impacting Cerberus US. He would contact Maeve's analysts to check the results. On Friday—today was Wednesday—he, Reb, and Anna would visit the three children in London. If they wanted to join him and his crew, their new residence would be crowded. Mark fell asleep counting bedrooms.

Anna woke him as the bus approached their destination. Waves of rain and sleet were sweeping across the front of the vehicle, caught in a late winter storm. The main visible feature was trees bending in the wind. The bus reached the end of a private road and slowed to a stop at a lighted entrance to the manor house. Two people were waiting in the shelter of the front entry. Their reception committee, Mark supposed. Everyone climbed out of the bus, attempting to stretch and avoid the rain at the same time. They followed Mark's lead and headed for the front door.

"Good evening, sir," said the nearest person at the door as Mark entered the house. "My name's Richard. Richard Carroll. This is my wife, Mary. Welcome to Bankton House."

"Pleased to meet you both," Mark stepped away from the doorway, allowing space for the crew to follow him into the house. "My name's Mark Midway. This is Anna." He counted off the rest of the new arrivals. "Reb, Gabrielle, Niland, Scott, and Sera. We have drivers and security."

"Yes, sir. We're pleased to meet all of you. We've two cottages for your men. The buildings each have five bedrooms, small but adequate."

"Ladies, sirs. And children," said Mary. "Please come along. We have a fire going and the heating is on."

They stepped into a large lobby from the entry area. A wide wooden staircase with red carpet runners led to a second floor. Living rooms were located off the lobby and a hallway led farther into the interior of the house. Mary continued, "All the bedrooms are upstairs. These are the living rooms, formal and informal. Here's the dining room. A study and a security office are through there. There are two downstairs bathrooms. The kitchen and other utility rooms are toward the rear. Please explore, at your leisure."

Gabrielle and Niland did not need a second invitation. "Where do you keep the prisoners?" asked Niland. Mary looked bewildered. She recovered rapidly. "Oh, we moved the dungeons to the stables last century. Our problem now is to find miscreants to throw into them. You can be our first prisoner this year, if you like?"

Niland looked doubtful and then his face brightened. "Okay, as long as I can have a long chain and make lots of noise at midnight."

"He'll be your ghost prisoner," Gabrielle said, intrigued in spite of herself.

Mary said, "Get along with you. Go and explore the house. Watch out for the skeleton in the attic."

Reb, Sera, and Anna accompanied the two children on their exploration. The housekeeper turned to Mark. Scott was standing beside him. "Sirs, do you want to explore as well?"

"We'll wait on reports from the current batch of intrepid explorers, I think," Mark replied. "If you have an informal sitting room, we can wait there."

"Certainly. You can use the room through here."

Mark said, "I assume Richard is settling in the drivers and security? If you have a diagram for upstairs, perhaps we can assign rooms, and when our luggage arrives, we can get organized."

Mark and Scott had completed the room assignments by the time the explorers returned. It didn't take long for Anna and Reb to modify their decisions. Scott shrugged. Sera approved results. Mark ignored it all. He went off to explore the house and Scott followed. The windows were alarm-protected and Mark checked the security room, which contained a bank of video screens displaying different parts of the house and grounds. There was a large map of the property with circuitry marked and coded, and someone had drawn and annotated changes and modifications in pencil. He assumed this showed where the cameras and other intruder detection equipment were located, both in and outside the house. He directed Scott's attention to the map.

"What do you think?"

"I'll need to walk the grounds tomorrow with one of the security guys. Afterwards I'll give an opinion."

"Good. I think effective security is going to be our top requirement. The house seems to be comfortable, and the people are helpful and friendly. The security people I've met so far are on their toes."

"I agree."

"Let's check out upstairs. Remind me I need to order some computers."

***

Chapter 23

Whenever Maeve now was driven to the White House in an escorted SUV to meet with the President, her thoughts returned to the occasion when a gang of Russians had kidnapped her on this same journey. They had killed one of her guards, and injured both her driver and a FBI agent, when they attacked her vehicle. The gang leader had later been killed, shot at her command by Mark Midway. She still wondered at Midway's reflexes and accuracy with a handgun. She had given him the signal to proceed and it seemed, within a fraction of a second the Russian was on the floor, dead. This time, she hoped, her trip would be without such a high level of excitement.

She'd checked with the hospital before leaving her office and Schmidt's condition was still categorized as life threatening. Her Cerberus team had managed to place two nurses into the ICU and they were providing her with unofficial updates. His condition had improved but not enough to warrant a change to his status. Specialists were planning to operate on Schmidt later in the day to remove pressure on his brain. The doctors did not expect the process to endanger their patient and Maeve hoped their optimism was warranted.

The entire affair still had inexplicable elements. As her analysts had stated, it was as though someone had left some tiny clues purposefully for them to find and follow. There were multiple layers of intrigue prepared by a master tactician, she suspected. She had taken steps to ensure whoever it was would not succeed with any other attempt on Schmidt's life.

The driver stopped the vehicle at the first security checkpoint at 1600 Pennsylvania Avenue and she handed her pass to the guard. It was returned moments later with a murmured "Thank you, ma'am." The driver continued on to the next checkpoint, where another guard repeated the process. At each checkpoint the guards checked for explosive devices in and underneath the vehicle. At last the second guard waved the vehicle through to the next checkpoint where Maeve alighted, clutching her briefcase, and made her way to the personal security check. She surrendered her briefcase and reclaimed it anxiously after she and it had been subjected to the X-ray machines.

Another guard escorted her to the meeting room. It was smaller than the room where she used to meet with the President when she was Director of the FBI. She seated herself at the small table; it seemed this meeting would be informal, without a large number of attendees. She was not kept waiting for long. She stood as the President entered the room. He was accompanied by the National Security Advisor and their aides.

The President's welcome was as warm as she had previously experienced. "Maeve," he said. "Welcome. It's been too long. In future, don't forget to visit more often, huh? Now, here's the thing. Cerberus needs to continue its operations. Thoughts?"

Maeve relaxed. "We have a challenging operation in place and it would be a major negative to terminate it. We're researching the attack on Schmidt and are finding some interesting trails. It's far too early to report. We know the men who fired the missile were Russians. We think they were killed within minutes of firing the missile. Someone was covering his tracks, eliminating witnesses. Our concern is to discover who was behind the attack."

"Agreed."

"Also, we've managed to get someone in place to recover, at least partially, management of Cerberus UK. Mark Midway."

"Indeed? Well done. I was uncomfortable with the UK organization running who knows where. I know Midway is an independent cuss. Will he cooperate fully with you?"

"Unlikely. There'll be local and national issues he won't share with me or Schmidt, when he recovers. Midway is very independent. However, he'll cooperate and work with us on international matters. He has defined an initiative that we intend to drive forward."

"Which is?"

"He's pointed out that in the US our research was focused on genetic engineering and manipulation, but not on the downstream impacts. The UK research was minimal; they're far more aware of the illegalities than Cerberus US. There has been no research on the medium to long term effects, for what they call pre- or post-engineering."

"Pre- and post—yes, Schmidt informed me. Didn't he undergo the post-process?"

"He did. It may be a factor in his survival of the crash, which may be an example of what we don't know. Midway has proposed we stop pure genetic engineering research and concentrate on understanding the impacts on both pre- and post. We have no idea of how genetically engineered children will mature, or as they mature, what adverse or indeed, positive changes will occur, what their life expectancy is going to be. It's a bad place to be, in a lot of ways. Dr. White—she was the head of research for Cerberus before she fled to China—was only interested in one thing and she pursued her interest aggressively."

"This proposal provides me with a lot of comfort. Midway is going ahead with it?"

"Yes, and so are we. We're going to share efforts and results. I'm placing a hold on other research."

"Very good. What about the Chinese? Can we do anything to inhibit their research? Can we stop this Dr. White?"

"It's difficult. I've a team of analysts addressing the possibilities. We believe Midway intentionally corrupted a lot of her files. She would have been set back by his actions. However, penetrating China has its issues."

"I understand. Keep me informed. I've issued formal statements confirming you're now heading Cerberus US, pending Schmidt's recovery. I must tell you, there were one or two protests. At least one agency wanted to eliminate Cerberus."

"CIA? ICE is closely aligned with them? Perhaps with a tinge of support from the FBI?"

"As usual, you're on top of things."

"We've been encountering some black ops from the Agency and ICE, and there's a possibility of some FBI involvement. It could get nasty. I've included details in my report."

"I'll read it with interest. Now, *pro tem*, Cerberus is yours. Only depart from objectives I agreed with Schmidt if it is absolutely critical for national security or your survival, understand?"

"Yes, sir. Thank you."

"If you wish to initiate any changes, write up a brief for me. I suspect you wrote a number of Schmidt's papers, anyway?"

Maeve smiled. "You can identify our different styles. We both knew you could."

"Make sure I'm informed of Schmidt's progress. Let me know if there's anything I can do. Keep him and yourself safe." He checked his watch. "I've run out of time. Report personally every two weeks. I'll add you to the weekly security meeting as well. You'll attend as an observer."

"Yes, sir." She stood as the President left the small office. The NSA had been quiet during the meeting although he gave a thumbs-up as he left the room. Maeve opened the door to the external corridor and her escort was there, waiting. He led her back to the security checkpoint where her driver and car were waiting. She felt relief and excitement simultaneously. Relief, because the President was encouraging her continued management of Cerberus. Excitement, because she would be able to further develop the scope and activities of the organization. There were a number of topics she wanted to address with her analysts and the Cerberus team. It was going to be a busy day.

~~~

Mark checked the time, surprised most of the morning had fled. He'd spent the day so far exploring the grounds of their new accommodation. It seemed they'd been transported to another time. The lawns were over a hundred years old and reflected tender care across the years. A gardener, wearing a flat cap and an almost shapeless tweed suit, had saluted him with an almost tug of his forelock as he said, "Good marning, sir." The man's accent was so strong Mark had to mentally replay the words before he understood their meaning. He returned the greeting. Scott confirmed later that he, too, was experiencing some culture shock.

"I thought the Brits spoke English," Scott said. "But this is another language."

"What do you think of the security?"

"We've six ex-SAS soldiers on site. They're all Cerberus. Good men, I'd say. Someone's always monitoring the video cameras and detectors, which are relayed to the second cottage. The buildings are scattered, which might be a negative. The main house is solid, built from heavy slabs of sandstone. A number of ground floor windows are narrow and have metal bars embedded in the stonework; it would be difficult to assault those. Upstairs is a different story—the windows are nowhere as well protected."

"Overall?"

"We're safe unless an army attacks us."

"Good. As of today, you're responsible for all security issues. Use Sera as your backup. The security room is yours to command."

"Gee, thanks. While you dine with the local landed gentry, I suppose?" Scott smiled, softening the import of his comment.

"No. At least not today. We might have visitors, though. I want to sift through the senior Cerberus people, see who they are, what they do, perhaps meet with them. I have about a hundred dossiers and they're just the tip. If I see you slacking off, I'll put some on your reading list."

"As I said—gee, thanks. I should've shot you when I had a chance."

As they headed along the path to the house, Anna and Reb came out, looking for them.

Reb said, "Lunchtime, according to the housekeeper. We're going to be spoiled, the way we're being cared for."

Anna added, "We've even a maid to tidy the rooms. Niland and Gabrielle will never want to make their own beds, again."

Mark laughed and said. "I agree. I saw three gardeners. The grounds are impeccable. Scott was complaining he has nothing to do."

"Who has nothing to do?" asked Sera, joining them. "I was sent to find the people who were sent to find the people who should come to lunch when it's lunch time. Come on."

After the meal Mark decided to call Maeve. He wanted to know the result of her meeting with the President and the status of the two lab reports he'd requested. He closed himself off in the study and connected to Maeve.

"Good morning, Mark. I can guess—you want to know what the President said?"

"Exactly."

"The meeting was productive, from my perspective. I'm taking on Schmidt's responsibilities until he recovers. Business as usual, I think, is the President's view. He was pleased to hear of your involvement in Cerberus UK, by the way."

"Excellent. And Schmidt. Is there any update on his condition?"

"No change. He's alive and has the best care we can arrange. We have to be patient."

"One more thing."

"Yes?"

"Schmidt was arranging some lab reports for me. One was a DNA test. The other was a firearm residue test. Do you know whether anyone has the results?"

"I saw the results back from the lab this morning. The DNA test is a no-brainer. You look like twins and the results confirmed it. The other test is also positive. There are traces of residue, months old according to the lab. They says it's probably blowback from firing a shotgun or rifles, perhaps from target practice."

"It's good to know I have a sister. And a relief to hear the residue is aged."

"Reb's definitely your sibling. Parentage for both of you, I realize, is still unknown. We can and will do some searching for you, but I'm certain no one kept those early research records. I'll let you know if my team discovers anything. I'm not holding out for quick results, though."

"Thanks, Maeve." Mark was deep in thought as he ended the call. He left the study, searching for Anna.

***

Chapter 24

Mercante sat back with his feet on the desktop. It was a modest office for a senior Agency manager. On one wall he had rows of photographs, mainly of him with either an important politician, a senior military officer—sometimes foreign—or someone else who had a visible and high profile. Another wall held his university degrees and diplomas, together with his military and professional certifications. The third wall was a window to the outside world, a rarity for an Agency office. The fourth wall which was centered by the doorway, displayed a photograph of the current President and on the other side of the door was a large version of the US flag. The desk was scarred and nondescript. In addition to Mercante's chair, there were two visitor's chairs, and a small couch against the wall with the photographs. Bookcases and filing cabinets intruded into otherwise empty spaces. A heavy-duty shredder stood beside his desk.

Mercante was concerned because some of his plans were failing and this was an entirely new experience for him. He now realized the assessment report he had received on the Midway property contained numerous flaws, some major. For example, Midway and his followers were overseas somewhere, but the report had not mentioned their possible absence. The raid *had* destroyed the property, which was a plus. It was only a partial success, however, and he was disappointed—no, frustrated—at achieving only a fraction of what he desired. It was a shame the reverend's men had been arrested. But they were stupid. They attacked the property in broad daylight, had no exit plan, and their vehicles had been almost demolished by whatever weapon system Midway had installed. The attackers were fortunate Midway had injured only six of them.

He read the target assessment report again, then, angry with its lack of reliable content, threw it on the floor. Not only was there no mention of Midway's absence, there was no mention of any defense system. There were only minor details about the overall security systems.

Mercante had built up a team over the years. Some were direct reports, some indirect, and some not even aware he was pulling their puppet strings. The assessment had been conducted by one of his indirect reports. He reached for the phone and punched in a number. When the call was answered, he sat up straight in his chair, his feet back on the floor.

"Mercante here. One of your people wrote up a TAR for me, a week ago. It was seriously flawed."

"Who did it?"

"What's his name…" Mercante retrieved the document from the floor, turned it the right way up and read the name. "Frederick Abrahams. Crewcut Freddie."

"Abrahams resigned and left almost a month ago. For the last two to three weeks he's been somewhere in Africa helping a Doctors Without Borders team."

Mercante fumed. "Are you certain?"

"Yes, I attended his farewell party."

"Well, we have a larger problem, then. I sent an e-mail to you requesting an informal assessment. You volunteered Abrahams. I sent him an e-mail with the details and cc'd to you. I got a response, and later he sent me the report. What the hell is happening?"

"It implies a security breach somewhere."

"It sure as hell does. I'll check my e-mails for the dates and sequences. Check yours, and let me know what you discover."

"Consider it done. We'll talk later today."

Mercante disconnected the call. He opened his e-mail application and searched his e-mail folders. He was unable to find the communications to and from Abrahams that he so clearly remembered. He checked his deleted e-mails and his inbox again. He could find nothing from Abrahams dated after the end of the previous month.

"Damn," Mercante said. "This is getting ridiculous." He had the printed report. He had an excellent recollection of the exchange of messages. Someone was rigging the books. But how had they known he would e-mail Abrahams after the man had left the Agency? Mercante tried to recall the details when he sent the first e-mail. He'd mentioned to someone he wanted a target assessment report. That person had suggested Abrahams. If only he could remember…

He pushed the thought aside. Perhaps he did have enemies who were exceptionally smart. Or maybe the answers were simple. Midway's property had been vacant; it was likely Midway and his people had left unexpectedly. The weapon was another story, though. How had Midway obtained equipment which was more advanced than what the army had? More importantly, why weren't the details included in the assessment?

He phoned his contact again. "Yeah, it's me. I think you can forget about my questions. Something else has come up that's more critical." He listened. "Okay. When this is over, we should catch up. Thanks."

He planned to investigate and solve the problem on his own. It was safer this way. For him.

~~~

Mercante was not aware his searches had triggered a simple algorithm. The tiny software routine was self-deleting and it disappeared once its mission was completed. Shortly, someone, somewhere, received a brief note providing the mailbox identity and the search keywords.

~~~

Later in the same day, a passenger presented his boarding card to the flight attendant in business class. She read his name and seat details.

"Welcome on board, Mr. McCarr. Your seat's here, by the window. I hope you enjoy your trip with us." She smiled, her white teeth gleaming. "Let me know if you require any assistance. Let me take your overcoat and jacket. I'll hang them up. You'll want them back when we arrive. London's almost as cold as DC."

McCarr surrendered his heavy outer garments after emptying the pockets. London he knew very well. He had chores to do once he arrived; activities that would help keep out the cold. He sat down, fastened his seat belt, and accepted the English newspaper delivered by the flight attendant. He declined the glass of fizzy wine disguised as champagne. He planned to read for a short while, after which he would sleep.

~~~

Mark found Anna and said, "Here's your coat. Let's walk in the gardens."

"But it's raining." She frowned as she looked out the window. Beads of rain were following each other down the glass, racing faster as they joined with others.

"It's not bad. I need some fresh air. Come on, the fire will still be here when you return."

Anna reluctantly accepted her jacket. It was insulated and adequate against most of the cold wind blowing outside. For walking on the muddy ground, it was *de rigeur* to wear wellies, rubber boots properly called wellingtons, that reached up past her knees. Hers were green, decorated with colorful daisies. Anna hung onto Mark as she struggled with the boots. When she stood, he straightened her collar.

"What's wrong?" she asked in a soft voice.

"Outside," he replied.

Anna waited until they were a hundred yards or more away from the house. It was mid-afternoon and the only person in sight was one of the gardeners. The trees were trying to push out green buds and there were promises some would shortly succeed in their annual chore despite the weather. She assumed she and Mark were on video; someone would be watching from the security room. She kept her face down and said, "Now tell me, what's the matter?"

"I spoke with Maeve. The DNA match confirms Reb and I are siblings. The firearm residue test suggested the traces were probably months old."

"I think Reb's been worrying, at least about the DNA. She'll be pleased. I know she's missing her ocean life. I'm not sure she'll wish to stay with us."

"I'm open to suggestions."

"Reb is feeling lost. She sees you and me together, and it emphasizes how alone she is. We had a chat and she offered us her support. Your sister is still recovering from her gunshot wound. She's worried about her three friends in London and more than anything, wants to be back at sea. She's lost in London." Anna looked around. "And here, wherever we are, as nice as it is."

"That's very strange—the last part, I mean. I have no inclination to navigate a small boat, none at all. It's wet enough, here. We'll organize something for her friends. I don't want to rush it; something tells me to be cautious. We need to care for her, make sure she can do whatever she wants."

"I've something else to tell you. Reb hasn't been forthcoming, but she's said enough for me to know she had problems with the Chairman when she was on his yacht."

"What? What kind of problems?"

"Abuse. I don't know anything more."

"Try to find out, in case she needs our help."

"I will. Now just relax. As for Reb...you know, the simplest approach might be to talk to her."

"Hmm." Mark turned and led the way back to the house.

***

Chapter 25

When Mark and Anna returned to the house, Scott said, "An official-looking vehicle's about to stop at the front door. The passenger must be important. A driver and a guard, too, I think. Where do you want to talk to him?"

Mark shrugged. "If someone's driven here to meet with us, we should be courteous. Use the formal sitting room. I'll see what he wants, and if necessary I'll add you or Anna, whoever needs to be in the meeting."

Three minutes later Scott again spoke to Mark, a grin on his face. "I've directed the driver and guard to the kitchen. I'm sure Mrs. Carroll will take care of them. Your visitor is waiting for you. Colonel Evelyn Hudson, British Army."

Mark headed to the room where the officer was waiting. She was dressed in civilian clothes with a military touch: neatly pressed dark green slacks and a lighter green turtleneck sweater. Her brown hair was cut short and she wore minimal makeup. Mark assessed her age to be late forties. She was standing to one side of the room, examining a painting of a group of eighteenth-century cavalry officers. She turned as Mark entered the room.

"Mr. Midway?"

"Yes, ma'am."

"I'm Colonel Evelyn Hudson. Please call me Evelyn." She held out her hand.

"Call me Mark." He shook her hand. "Please sit, Colonel—er—Evelyn."

She sat on the edge of the chair, straight-backed. She gave Mark an appraising look, searching his face, then sighed.

She said, "You're not the Chairman, are you?"

Mark did not hide his bafflement. "Me? No way. Whatever made you think that?"

"You can prove you're not him?"

"Uh, prove a negative? Wait, in this case, I probably can." He mentally reached out to Gabrielle. *Please ask Scott, Anna and Reb to join me in the formal sitting room.*

Gabrielle's whisper affirmed she would carry out his request. Mark continued the conversation with Hudson. "Why do you need this proof?"

"I'll give you the answer when you provide validation."

Reb entered first, followed by Anna and Scott. He felt Gabrielle's presence. He heard her whisper. *She's Cerberus.*

His three friends regarded Mark with curiosity as he carried out introductions. He explained, "The colonel asked me a question and I'd like to hear how each of you would answer it. Evelyn, please repeat your question."

She faced Mark and said, "Can you validate you're not the Chairman?"

Shock and disbelief vied for supremacy on Reb's face, then she started to laugh, the sound bordering on hysteria. Anna took her hand. Scott was silent, speechless for once in his career.

At last Reb recovered control. "The-the Chairman is—was—at least twice Mark's age. And he was cruel, not kind. He died, I think, on board his yacht when pirates sank it in January."

Scott added, "I've known Mark long enough to be certain he's not the Chairman."

"Not only that," Anna said, "any one of us would shoot the Chairman on sight, if he's alive."

Hudson looked at each speaker in turn, then turned back to Mark. "Alright, I'll withdraw the question. Now tell me, if you can, why twenty of my soldiers are AWOL, at the command of someone who claims he is the Chairman of Cerberus. The details I've garnered so far are vague, but your name was also mentioned."

"Tell us more," Mark said.

"I have an operational role and included in my responsibilities are two companies, with about two hundred and fifty young Cerberus recruits. Yes, I'm Cerberus, too."

"I know," Mark said.

Hudson did not hide her surprise. "How would you?"

Mark shrugged. "We can discuss the details, later. I'm not the Chairman, but I will be assuming strategic responsibility for Cerberus UK. Believe me, I haven't ordered or requested members of any military unit to report to me."

"So what the hell is going on?"

"Please tell us why you came here," Anna said.

"One of my captains, an effective and dependable officer, came to me early today and told me we were missing twenty soldiers, ten each from my two companies. One company specializes in target acquisition and surveillance and the other has a mechanized infantry focus. Both are due to deploy to Germany in thirty days as part of a NATO build-up; the Russians are saber-rattling again. I've suppressed details of these absences, to protect my soldiers, but I can't delay beyond twenty-four hours—forty-eight at the utmost. My captain said he heard comments such as 'the Chairman is back,' 'recalled by the Chairman,' and 'it's Midway.' When I heard your name, I checked with a couple of the senior Cerberus management team and they told me you were here. They also told me they thought the Chairman had been killed in some kind of pirate attack. It's all unverifiable, however."

Scott said, "Interesting times."

"Absolutely," Hudson said.

"Reb, please tell the colonel what you know," Mark said.

Reb was silent for a moment, then she proceeded to describe her role on *Hammer* and the yacht's recent travels at the direction of the Chairman. She concluded with a description of the attack off the Spanish coast and her sailboard escape. "I heard shootings and screams before I launched the sailboard. The pirates blew up the yacht and I think they headed out into the Atlantic. I was on the sailboard for twelve hours, until the crew of a small tourist boat rescued me. They took me to Gibraltar." Reb shrugged. "I assumed the Chairman was killed. I have no proof, though." Anna was still holding her hand.

"Hmm. A reasonable assumption. Although the pirates might have taken him prisoner for some purpose we can't guess," said the colonel. She took a deep breath. "Very well. So you're not the Chairman," she said, looking at Mark. "But your name *was* mentioned. Any idea why?"

Anna spoke up. "We—those of us in the younger Cerberus generations—have heard a lot about Mark. To some of us, perhaps all of us, he's somewhat of a hero." She blushed. "It's almost a folklore thing."

"How old are these people, the missing twenty?" Mark asked.

"Very young. Maturity age is eighteen, chrono is twelve. They've completed basic training."

"They were raised under Cerberus care and dropped straight into the military?

"Yes, they've followed the typical process."

"No one checked whether they wanted to be soldiers?"

"No." The word was drawn out.

Gabrielle uncloaked herself. "Lots of us younger Cerberus don't want to be in the military. You won't ever see me do military service."

"Where did—who are you?" Hudson asked.

"Gabrielle is one of our young members. Gabrielle, this is Colonel Evelyn Hudson."

Gabrielle gave an almost curtsy. "I apologize for interrupting," she said. "But I think I know why your soldiers have...gone AWOL. If they're like me or Niland, they'll be highly intelligent and they've been hiding a lot of their abilities. Some, maybe a lot, don't want to be military recruits. I think they're a delegation on their way to talk to Mark."

Hudson studied Gabrielle, who was standing confidently in front of her. "I'd like to have a long talk with you, to learn more about the new generations. In light of what you've told me, I understand your expectation." She turned back to Mark. "I apologize for my earlier assumption." She offered him a business card. "If they arrive here, and I daresay they will, can you let me know? It will take a worry off my mind."

Mark accepted the officer's card. "Of course. We'll do everything we can to safeguard these soldiers. I suppose they should return to their units and use more formal ways to take their leave."

"Yes, thank you. We can work out ways to do so without creating a major issue."

"You realize, as Gabrielle suggested, they'll probably arrive as a delegation for Mark to address. What if your new Cerberus recruits want to do something else? If they want to resign, for example?" Anna asked.

"You would raise that specter, wouldn't you?" Hudson sat back in the chair. She was starting to relax. "I'd like you—Mark—to assist me, to work out how we can give these young people a career that fulfills their needs. I'm unsure how we'd handle two hundred and fifty resignations, though." She turned to Gabrielle. "Do you think all of the younger Cerberus are anti-military? Or would they just like to have a choice?"

Niland appeared in the room. "I wouldn't mind a military career. I think I'd be good in a military role, perhaps in the Navy. But we need a choice."

"Goodness, how many more of you are hiding here?"

Mark chuckled. "I apologize. I hadn't realized Niland was here. We have one more member on our team, whom I'll introduce later. She's in our security room, monitoring external security cameras. The only young children we have with us are Niland and Gabrielle. They and Anna survived a mass killing where we lost a lot of Cerberus children."

"I heard about that," Hudson said.

"Please stay and join us for dinner. I heard your escorts are enjoying some of our housekeeper's cooking." Anna said. "You can talk to Gabrielle and Niland—me too, if you like. I'm probably a little older than your recruits and these two are obviously younger. We'd help you understand a lot about your soldiers and what motivates them."

Hudson considered the request for a moment. "I'd love to."

~~~

Later, after the army officer had left, and they were preparing for bed, Anna said to Mark, "Do you think these young soldiers will come here?"

"I'm certain. Now, what was your comment? Oh, 'He's somewhat of a hero.' And that from the person who shot the murderers of a Cerberus military company and all those children."

Anna blushed again. "You *are* my hero. I thought you knew?"

Mark laughed. "It's only folklore."

Anna dug him in the ribs. "Just you wait," she said.

Mark held her hands. "There is one thing that worries me. The mention of the Chairman. 'The Chairman is back'. If he wasn't killed by those pirates..."

"Reb has doubts. I was holding her hand while she was describing her escape from the pirates and she was scared. She may have thought he was killed when she left the yacht, but she never saw his body."

***

Chapter 26

The man called McCarr—at least his passport carried that name—awoke refreshed after his first night in London. At eight a.m. he was ready to leave the hotel to carry out his self-imposed task, something that would give him leverage, he hoped, and advance him in this game. He had contacted two people he had worked with previously and arranged to meet them at a small pub near their eventual destination. Both men were seated at a table in the restaurant area of the pub when he arrived.

"Dr. Sutter, how are you? And you, Miles? Good to see you both. Have you ordered? No? May I suggest the English breakfast? It's excellent." Sutter, a tired remnant of a man, was dressed in a scruffy three-piece suit. He cross-combed his hair to hide an ever-growing bald patch; the subterfuge was worse than the reality. The second man, Miles, wore an anonymous uniform. His hair was long and unkempt. While he was clean-shaven, some change would need to be applied to the definition of clean.

With little comment, the three men ate their breakfast. It was close to ten a.m. when they left the pub. McCarr said, "Miles, you have the transport I requested?"

"Yes, it's a private ambulance. Anonymous, as you requested. It will accommodate three, er, bodies."

McCarr handed him a card. "Drive to this location. Park nearby. Wait near the front of the building until I signal you. No sirens. We don't want to draw attention to ourselves. Sutter, you can accompany me. I'll drop you back here, when we're finished."

Their destination was an older building south of the Thames. Constructed with red bricks, the building had a discouraged, disused air. The only clue to its possible use were faded letters along the front.

Sutter read the words and nudged McCarr. "Got religion, have you?"

McCarr growled, "It's changed ownership a number of times, I believe." McCarr had parked his rental vehicle in a side street, hoping the lack of a resident's permit would not attract the attention of a parking enforcement officer. He pressed the large button beside the front door and waited patiently. He pressed it again. There were no footsteps or any other noise from within the building. He pressed the button for a third time, holding it down for nearly a minute. No response.

"Are you at the right place?" Dr. Sutter asked.

"Definitely." McCarr produced a set of lock picks and opened the door in seconds. "Quick, come inside."

There, ten feet inside the lobby, was the aspidistra, now upturned and separated from its container. McCarr motioned for his companion to remain where he was standing, just inside the doorway, while he continued farther into the building to check each room. At last, in a room messy with personal belongings and remnants of meals, he discovered the body of the housekeeper. It lay in a small pool of blood that had streamed for a short while from a bullet wound in her chest. The body was no longer warm. McCarr stood, deep in thought, ignoring the small, crumpled figure on the floor. He walked back to the obediently waiting doctor.

"We have to get out of here. Did you touch anything?"

"Certainly not."

"Good." McCarr used his handkerchief to hold the door handle. "Come on. Step out, look as though you belong. If you see Miles, ignore him and walk the other way. He'll understand. I'll be behind you."

There were no bystanders, no passersby, the street was almost empty. McCarr caught sight of Miles walking away at a casual pace. He wiped down the door and the doorbell, replaced his handkerchief, and turned to follow the doctor. He failed to note the small video camera set below a window on the upper story of the building. Nor had he noticed small cameras inside the building.

He caught up with the doctor in three or four paces. "Half the fee, Doc," he said. "I may need you again. I won't know until I discover what happened."

"You have a competitor?"

The doctor's question reflected an astuteness McCarr had not expected. "Perhaps. I'll drop you at the nearest station. You can make your own way from there?"

"Oh, yes, old boy. London is my home."

Later McCarr met with Miles. "Someone was there before me," he explained as he handed the man an envelope. "Here's half your fee. I may need you and your vehicle again, same activity. Try to get a haircut in the meantime."

Miles accepted the envelope, waved his hand in a half salute, and went on his way. McCarr returned to his hotel, deep in thought.

~~~

Earlier that the morning, minutes before eight a.m., a man had approached the building with the faded sign indicating its previous use as a Bible study school. He was slimly built, appeared to be in his fifties, and was smartly dressed in a three-piece, light gray suit. He carried a walking stick and was accompanied by a younger man, wearing a pin-stripe suit, and by a young woman who wore a high-necked pullover and dark slacks. She carried a briefcase. There was a green cross on the outside of the briefcase. The man stepped up to the front door and pressed the doorbell. After a short wait, the door opened, restrained by its security chain. A woman peered out. The man handed her a business card.

"I'm from Cerberus, here to check on the children."

The woman took the card. She fumbled and twisted it until she was able to read the embossed writing. One side of the card was in English while the other side had Chinese characters.

"Chairman?"

"Yes, indeed."

She looked from the card to the man and back to the card. She pushed the door closed and the Chairman heard the rattle of the chain as it was unhooked. He smiled to himself. The woman opened the door wide and the three visitors stepped into the lobby.

"Follow," instructed the woman. They followed.

The woman stopped at a door, knocked, and pushed it open. "Visitors," she said. The noise from inside the room reduced to an almost bearable level.

"What?" asked a voice.

"Visitors." She waved the business card. A hand reached out and took the card. After almost a minute of intense subdued discussion, a young man stepped into the corridor.

"Chairman of Cerberus? Why are you here? What do you want with us?"

"Reb is a friend of mine. She was my navigator on *Hammer,* for years. She told me about you three and your plan to move. I discussed this with Mark, last night. I offered to make my senior researcher available to check you out before you leave here."

The young man shook his head, as though trying to remove the cobwebs of sleep. He turned to speak to people in the room. "Did you hear? He's a friend of Reb's. They want to check us over."

There was a muttered exchange. The young man turned back to the visitors. "Alright. Come on in. Excuse the mess."

The Chairman and the young woman entered the room. The other man remained outside. The room was in disarray.

The young woman placed her briefcase on the edge of a table after pushing away a varied collection of books, clothing, and the remains of a pizza. She removed a small laptop computer from her case and switched it on. As it booted up, she said, "My name's Jane Palmer. As the Chairman said, I'm one of his senior researchers. I'm going to ask each of you some questions. Very basic stuff, the usual things like your name, your weight, height, and so on. I'll also record your temperature and blood pressure. I'll extract a small blood sample, as well." She laid out small containers and three hypodermic needles. She did not mention the process of taking a blood sample was twofold. The hypodermic was designed to simultaneously inject a small measure of a drug that, once it took effect, would ensure the three victims followed the Chairman's instructions without argument. The drug would last for six to eight hours, long enough for the Chairman's plans.

When she finished her task, while the three teenagers sat passively on the settee, Jane gathered up what seemed to be their personal belongings and stuffed them into a lightweight backpack she extracted from her briefcase. She did not pick up the clothes scattered around the room. Either the Chairman would arrange the purchase of new items or the children would not need them. On the way out of the building, the Chairman halted his small group of followers inside the front door. He did not open it. "Henry, go and see the housekeeper. Tell her we're going out for a coffee. You know the rest."

Henry nodded and headed back down the hallway. The Chairman opened the door and directed his young charges out into the street. Jane followed. The subdued children did not mention the camera above the doorway, not did they mention the interior cameras; no one asked about them. The Chairman led the way to an eight-seater vehicle, a Mercedes, parked almost directly outside the building.

"Get in," he directed, opening the rear door. The children climbed in, followed by the researcher. The Chairman opened the front passenger door and got in and waited for Henry. After a minute or two, the young man exited the building and climbed into the driver's seat of the people mover. He nodded at the Chairman, started the vehicle, and edged it out into the morning traffic.

~~~

"Mark," Scott said, "I need you to look at something. Come with me."

Mark followed him into the security room. Scott had taken control of monitoring the security cameras throughout the day. He indicated a disassembled Glock, the components of which he had laid out on a white cloth. "I've been checking our weapons, starting with mine," he said. "I've detected a small problem. They've been sabotaged. Someone's modified the firing pin and I suspect they'll all be the same. It looks to be okay, but it won't impact the cartridge. I checked Sera's Glock; it's had the same treatment. If we depend on these, we'll be dead."

Mark stared at Scott as the implications sank in. Senior members of Cerberus UK, presumably at the direction of DI Goodwin, were setting them up. Scott nodded as though confirming Mark's conclusions.

Mark handed over his Glock. "Check mine. I'll get Anna's and you can check it as well."

***

Chapter 27

Andrew Wentworth's excuse, if anyone had the temerity to ask, was that he was trailing the contacts of a senior Agency manager who may have committed a criminal offense. An offense so serious that he, an FBI Executive Assistant Director, needed to take personal action. The church he sought was north of Atlanta. He was following the directions he had printed out the previous day. For some reason he detested the nagging voice of automated navigation systems.

Wentworth was on a mission, a life and career-threatening mission. Mercante had failed his challenges—Schmidt was still alive and so was Midway. Government and private property had been destroyed, a minor success. Wentworth planned to arrange a follow-up strike. This time there would be no failure. Schmidt was his concern; Midway could wait, for the moment. He braked when he saw the signpost he was seeking. There was a house beside the church, accessible up a long, muddy lane. The house was large, ostentatious rather than imposing, with a mixed architecture of old and new. Part of the house was stone, part was timber. He walked up the stairs to the front entrance and pressed the small, lit button. Somewhere inside he heard the result as his action was transmuted into the heavy chimes of a nonexistent bell. After a moment a woman opened the door, only enough for her to see who was standing in the entryway.

"Yes, sir?"

"I'd like to speak with Reverend Barker. It's important."

"May I tell him who's calling?"

"Just tell him an old friend recommended him to me."

"Yes, sir. Please come in and sit while I go find the reverend."

The door opened wider and Wentworth stepped inside. The interior was as confused as the exterior. There was a cathedral ceiling, reaching up more than twenty feet. The sides of the ceiling structure held a number of small colored glass insets, creating a chaos of colored light beams on the floor leading into the depths of the house. Along the walls, paintings of biblical scenes competed with hunting trophies. Two high-backed chairs were located immediately inside the front door. As uncomfortable as the chairs looked, Wentworth needed to sit. His assessment was correct. The chair was extremely uncomfortable.

Ten minutes passed and he wondered whether he should either remind the person who had opened the door of his presence or retreat to DC. Another five minutes passed. He was about to stand when the woman returned.

"Sir, please come to the reverend's study. He'll join you there shortly."

The decor of the study was also conflicted. There was a lectern holding a large open Bible. Books lined one wall, while the other walls continued the competition of hunting trophies vs. biblical scenes. Several chairs were scattered around the room. Wentworth selected one that he hoped was less uncomfortable than the chair he had just vacated.

He had just sat down when a small man bustled into the room. Wentworth had expected a tubby, overweight person, but Barker must have lost weight on a prison diet. Wentworth stood, shook the proffered hand, and almost looked for a dispenser of disinfectant after his hand was released. The men sat in adjacent chairs. Wentworth extracted a small electronic device from his briefcase and switched it on.

He explained, "It will ensure no one can overhear our conversation." He did not add it also would prevent any electronic recording of the meeting. "Reverend Barker, thank you for allocating some of your valuable time to speak with me. I was recommended by a mutual friends. Well, I knew one of your friends, now deceased, and was recommended by the other."

"Your name, sir?"

"Perhaps for the moment I can remain anonymous? My good friend, the late Senator Boothby, always spoke very favorably of you." The reverend's face brightened at the mention of the senator. Wentworth continued, "Another friend of mine recently had a conversation with you. He was arranging a task in New Hampshire, which I'm sure you'll recall?"

"New Hampshire? Ah, you must mean McCarr?"

"Yes, Robert's a good friend. He's in Europe at the moment, otherwise I would've asked him to phone you in advance."

"I see. I lost some good people. When you stand back and try to let people exercise their discretion, it's disappointing when they fail." He paused. "May I ask what the purpose is of your visit?"

"I've a very good friend I'd like to have someone take care of. He was very badly hurt in an accident. He's someone you may know, and I need to be confident he's treated very well. I'm sure Senator Boothby would also want this, if he was alive today."

"Your friend's name?"

"Schmidt, Archimedes Schmidt. He was a victim of a helicopter accident. He's still in intensive care—he's in critical condition and has scarcely improved."

"Yes, I've heard of him."

Wentworth watched the conflicting emotions on Barker's face.

"That was most unexpected." He stood. "Sir, I've been remiss. Would you join me in a bourbon?"

"Why, yes. Thank you."

"Good, good. If you're a bourbon man, you'll enjoy my favorite—Woodford Reserve." The reverend opened a liquor cabinet and returned with two filled glasses. He handed one to Wentworth. "Your health."

Wentworth returned the salute. The reverend was correct, the bourbon was smooth. He sipped again and placed the glass on the small table beside his chair.

He said, "Schmidt?"

"Yes, Schmidt. I believe I fully understand. I can make arrangements to, uh, care for your friend. How much, may I ask, are you willing to contribute to his well-being?"

Wentworth mentioned a sum. Barker responded with another sum, double the first. Wentworth considered the amount for about thirty seconds. "Deal. I'll arrange to transfer the money tomorrow, if you give me your account details."

Barker wrote details on a slip of paper and handed it to Wentworth.

"What guarantee can you give for success?"

"I'll stake not only my personal reputation," puffed the reverend, "but also my life. For this person, you can rest assured I will do my utmost. If we fail, I'll refund 50 percent. Now, do you have some information for me, perhaps his hospital location?"

~~~

Maeve had used all her persuasive abilities to convince the doctor supervising Schmidt's treatment to allow her to visit.

She had said, "He has no family. I've known him for years. A friendly, familiar voice may be what he needs."

Whether it was her argument or her demeanor that won the day, Maeve was unsure. She had spent an hour in discussion with the doctor, and at last he had agreed, almost begrudgingly. He was aware of the Cerberus process and seemed to blame Maeve for Schmidt's decision to undergo the treatment. Maeve, on the other hand, suspected Schmidt's recovery process was being assisted by his early genetic changes.

She made herself comfortable in the chair set back, a distance away from Schmidt's bed. He was hooked up to a number of monitoring devices. A tube was providing oxygen. A saline drip kept him hydrated. Drugs kept him unconscious. Temperature and blood pressure measurements were displayed above his bed, as were his heartbeat and another five or six indicators, all relayed to an external station where the duty nurses monitored everything.

Maeve opened her laptop; she was unable to sit idly while she had so much work to do. She had promoted her senior analyst and now Linda Schöner managed the entire team of analysts, her responsibilities encompassing everything from data gathering to ensuring data patterns were identified, assessed, and communicated to Maeve. Captain Helen Chouan had accepted responsibility for two MP companies, both now located at Camp Brewer and her promotion to major was pending. The structure was an irregular but expedient solution to the loss of Colonel Dempsey. In addition, Maeve had taken control of all Cerberus teams, again delegating to senior members. She was still familiarizing herself with Schmidt's management structure and finding gaps as she dug deeper.

She yawned. Her laptop was downloading e-mails. The first one was a report from Linda Schöner and the details woke her up. The report contained the current analysis of several data threads the teams were tracking. The first item was a trip by Wentworth. He'd traveled to Georgia and her team tracking him had lost his cell phone signal. The significant item in the report was that the signal had disappeared close to where Reverend Barker lived. Barker also was on her analysts' watch list. He had received a light sentence because of his cooperation with the FBI investigation of Senator Boothby's activities and the raid on the LifeLong laboratory complex. But Maeve was convinced Barker still managed a militia group associated with his church.

The second thread of interest was from Europe. Her team had access to internationally sourced NSA data and continually conducted dynamic data analysis against the massive stream of raw data the agency managed to pipe into its servers. Her team had also tapped into numerous video camera systems. Maeve read the section describing how the team had tracked Midway to an address in London, south of the Thames. Her analysts then had continued to monitor the security system at the location. They reported two sets of visitors, neither of which were aware of the cameras recording their presence.

The first group of visitors removed three teenaged children from the premises. One of the cameras had captured their vehicle's registration plate as it departed and her team was tracking down the owner.

The second set of visitors, timed at two hours later, jarred her into full focus. The man who seemed to be the leader, and who used lock picks to enter the building, was someone the team knew—Ricardo Mercante, a senior CIA manager.

She sat back in the hospital chair, now unaware of its discomfort, her mind racing. Mercante. Well, well. She checked further. In both cases the security system had detected the numbers of the cell phones carried by each visitor. This, she thought, was a sophisticated security system. Maeve fired off a quick response to Linda, directing her to track all the cell phones belonging to the people who had entered the old Bible school. They would also trace calls using NSA data stores; the harvested metadata would be very interesting.

***

Chapter 28

Reb gradually became aware of the stealth coloring Niland and Gabrielle's activities. She observed surreptitiously as they gathered computer equipment and set it up in Gabrielle's bedroom. They spent almost an hour whispering to each other, sometimes dashing out of the bedroom and down the stairs to the security room, rushing back after two or three minutes. All was quiet for another hour or so. She peeked in to see both working intently at computer keyboards, staring at the two monitors they had carried up the stairs.

"What are you doing?" she asked. She sat on a chair near the two industrious workers.

Niland didn't hear her question, Reb was certain.

Gabrielle didn't lift her head. She said, "Chopping some of Mark's programming. Sometimes he's far too long-winded with his code."

"Got it!" Niland exclaimed.

"Show me." Gabrielle leaned over to see the streaming lines of code on Niland's monitor. "You're right. That's an hour of coding I owe you. Come on, load it now."

The children worked for about another twenty minutes. Reb remained in the room but decided not to disturb their concentration; rather, she had realized she would be unable to penetrate their focus.

When they seemed to relax, she said, "Again, may I ask what you're doing?"

Gabrielle spun around in her chair. "We've cracked the security system where your friends are living. They're good programmers, though."

"Why would you want to crack their system?"

"We were just being cautious," Gabrielle explained. "When you visited their place, we recorded their cell phone details."

Reb frowned. "But you weren't there."

"We, ah, placed a small bug in your handbag," Niland confessed. "When you returned here after visiting your friends, we downloaded the numbers. We've been tracking them ever since"

"But why?"

"Intuition," Niland said. "I felt we should keep an eye on your friends, in case they needed our help."

Gabrielle continued. "So, we've been monitoring their phone movements. We've adapted some of Mark's software that tracks cell phone via their registration signals—you know the towers? Your cell phone is registered by each one as you walk or drive around. They keep those records, whether you switch your phone off or not."

Niland said, "This morning, their phones were removed from the building, all at the same time. We tracked them to their destination."

"We found out this morning that the kids had set up a security system and we've worked out how to access their files. Now we can play the videos. Niland's downloading the files now." She turned to Niland. "Start about half an hour earlier so we can see what happened."

Reb, Niland and Gabrielle watched entranced, as the video played. When Reb saw the Chairman she was filled with dread that worsened as the video continued. Gabrielle reached over and held her hand. They watched as the three teens were led from the room. They watched as the young man returned and shot Mrs. Grabski.

"Poor Mrs. Grabski," Reb murmured.

"What's happening?" Niland asked.

"The children were kidnapped," Gabrielle replied. "See how passive they were when they left? They were drugged." She had a wild imagination that occasionally proved to be accurate.

"More than likely, I'm afraid. That man—he's dangerous. Very dangerous."

"You know him?" Her intuition leapt. "He's the Chairman?"

Reb almost was ill. She had hoped in her heart the Chairman had been killed when the pirates destroyed his motor yacht. Once she'd sought refuge with her brother and was under his protection, Reb had hoped the Chairman would cease to haunt her dreams. Now she shuddered.

"Yes," she whispered.

The cameras switched to the street and as the vehicle pulled away, Reb went to stand up and Gabrielle pulled her back down. "Wait, there's more. There's a second file." She kept her hand on Reb's arm.

They watched as the displayed time moved about two hours ahead. Two men approached the building entrance and after trying unsuccessfully to get someone to open the door, one of the men picked the lock. They both entered the building. After a few seconds they both left the building.

"This is very odd," Gabrielle said.

"There were two attempts to kidnap the kids," Niland suggested.

"I—I don't know," Reb said. "You may be right. I've no idea who the other people are, though."

"We need to rescue them," Gabrielle said. "Niland, get the address we tracked for the cell phones. We'll assume the phones and Reb's friends are at the same place." Niland busied himself at his computer. Gabrielle turned to Reb. "We can get one of the drivers to take us into London. Tell everyone we need to do some shopping. Perhaps we can persuade Anna to come with us."

An hour later, Anna, Reb, Gabrielle and Niland were on their way to Oxford Street in central London. They sat in the back seats of one of the small buses. After making sure the driver couldn't hear her, Gabrielle whispered to Anna. "Reb's in shock. We watched a security video this morning and someone kidnapped her friends. Reb thinks it was the Chairman. She thinks he isn't dead. We're going to rescue them."

"You're *what*?" Anna was shocked and almost shouted. "Why do you think you can do that? Why didn't you—"

Gabrielle held her fingers to Anna's lips. "Shh. Keep your voice down. We know what we're doing. We've checked out the location. They're being held in a house on the northern side of Kings Cross Station. It's a small house, one of a block of five. There are three people there—the Chairman, a guard, and a nurse of some kind."

"How are you—does Mark know?"

"No, we wanted to save Reb from having to tell Mark. She didn't know what to do. She's worried he'd be angry with her."

Reb turned to Anna. "I'm so sorry," she whispered.

"Reb's just following our instructions," Niland said.

Anna sat back and looked at each of the children in turn. "I don't know what I should do with you two. How do you plan to do this?"

"Reb will knock on the door and ask for the Chairman," Gabrielle explained. "Her presence should create some consternation and either the Chairman will come to the door, or they'll drag her inside. When Reb enters the house, she needs to make sure the door doesn't lock. We follow and take over. In the meantime, we'll have phoned the police and told them there are three kidnap victims in the house.

They should arrive after we've entered and will rescue us, if we need help."

"Stop. Your plan has so many holes in it. There'll be a security camera and the people inside the house will see Reb. The Chairman will recognize her and they won't open the door. Or his guard might simply shoot her. If they allow her to enter, I don't think she'll have an opportunity to leave the door open. So she'll be inside and we'll be outside. How do we protect Reb?"

Gabrielle sat unmoving, in deep thought. "Why don't we phone the police and say some children have been kidnapped and the victims are being held in the house? We'll tell them about the video at the school house, it would help convince them. And the housekeeper was shot by the Chairman's guard. Her body is evidence."

"Okay. My suggestion. We'll make an anonymous call and report a kidnapping and murder at the school. That will get the police involved. We can follow up with another call telling them the kidnap victims are at the address you discovered. By then the police will have seen the security files; we'll tell them where to look. We'll monitor the Chairman's house until the police arrive. We should be able to rescue the children in the confusion. It's the best I can think of."

Gabrielle hugged Anna. "It's a lot better than my plan and Reb's not at risk. Niland, can you spoof my phone so the call can't be traced? I'll make the call now."

Ten minutes later Gabrielle dialled 999. The call was answered in seconds. She said, with an Estuary English accent, "I-I want to report a crime. Two, actually. There's been a murder and a kidnapping." She gave the address of the old school building. "The housekeeper's dead. She was shot. Three children—teenagers—were taken away, in a blue Mercedes. I have the license plate number." She provided the details. "The house has a security system. You'll be able to see files from the security cameras that show what happened." She paused, listening. "No, I can't give my name. No, I'm sorry. Please hurry." She disconnected the call.

Anna said, "We need to check whether the police take action, but I'm sure they won't ignore a call reporting both a murder and a kidnapping."

"When the driver drops us off, we can catch one of the black cabs to the school house, and check if the police are present," Niland suggested.

"This driver will take us there?" Anna said.

"No." Gabrielle and Niland replied in urgent unison.

"I don't think the driver should know," Gabrielle added.

"Okay. Let's hope this works. Maybe we can get the driver to drop us at Tower Bridge; it'll be quicker. We can tell him we want to do some more sightseeing there."

Gabrielle and Niland nodded. Anna looked at Reb who also nodded. "Good. Gabrielle, tell the driver. Let's hope this all comes together."

There was a coffee shop fifty yards or so from the teenagers' home and Anna and Reb sat at an outdoor table while Gabrielle and Niland went inside to order their coffees. A police vehicle was at the house, so Anna assumed someone had decided to investigate Gabrielle's report. As the children brought out the drinks, an ambulance arrived. Within minutes, two more police cars arrived.

"Part one is working," Anna said as she sipped her coffee. "When we finish our drinks, we should go straight to the other address. Gabrielle can make the second call when we get there. We'll find somewhere to wait without calling attention to ourselves. Drink up."

They found a nearby park that allowed them to sit and watch the house where they suspected Reb's friends were being held. London's fickle weather was cooperating for once and the day continued to be warm and sunny.

Gabrielle made her second call. "This is connected to the murder and kidnapping you're investigating at the old Bible study school. The kidnap victims are being held at a house north of Kings Cross Station." She gave the address. "You'll see the Mercedes they used, parked outside. No, I can't give you my name. No, it's not a hoax. I called you before, about the murder and kidnapping. No, I can't tell you how I know. Please rescue the children." She disconnected.

Everyone waited, their anxiety levels increasing as the minutes dragged past. At last three unmarked sedans and a larger police vehicle, a small van, stopped in front of the Chairman's house. An ambulance followed. "I've counted ten policemen," Gabrielle said. The police did not waste time. Two men carried a heavy battering ram, painted bright red, to the front of the house and within seconds had smashed open the front door. Shortly afterwards, three people in handcuffs were led out of the building and driven off in separate vehicles. Police officers and the ambulance crew accompanied the three teenagers to the ambulance.

"Well," Anna said. "I think the worst is over. Reb, you and I should see if we can talk to the children, don't you think? They'll recognize you and once we've convinced the police we're all friends, we'll arrange to take them to the manor house."

The police were at first reluctant to believe Anna had any right to ask about the welfare of Reb's friends. Anna signaled Gabrielle and then, as a result of her silent influence, the police agreed to let them follow the ambulance to the hospital.

"We want to ensure the victims have recovered from whatever drug their kidnappers used," the police officer—a sergeant—explained to Anna. "After the doctors give us the all-clear and we have the victims' statements, we'll see if they know you. If they confirm you're friends, we'll be a lot happier about allowing you to talk to them. Alright?"

Anna said, "Yes, officer. We understand. We'll get a taxi and follow. When we get the okay, we'll take them home with us."

The sergeant nodded and left to talk to the ambulance driver, who waited in his vehicle until Anna had hailed a cab. She and the others got into the cab and the sergeant gave the cab driver the hospital address. The police sergeant and his driver also followed the ambulance to the hospital.

~~~

Mark was furious when everyone, including Reb's friends, returned to the manor house. It was almost evening and Anna had phoned him with brief details. He had dispatched one of the small buses to collect them all. Mark had blasted Reb and Anna, and told Gabrielle and Niland they were grounded for a year.

"Anyone would think he was our father," complained Gabrielle afterwards. "I don't know why he's so upset. We're old enough to do things."

Later, Mark met with Anna and Reb, out of hearing of all the children. "Reb, you of all people should have known better," Mark said. "You're aware of the danger posed by the Chairman. Both of you knew the risk. But you allowed those two kids to lead you by the nose into a deadly situation, for them, for yourself."

Reb burst into tears and ran for her room. Anna made to follow and Mark held her back. "Leave her," he said. "I want her, and you, to understand the risks you both took."

"You're being far too cruel. She's had a horrible day. You've no idea what her reaction was when she saw the Chairman on the video. Gabrielle told me Reb was physically ill. And to find out her friends had fallen into that evil man's hands—it was too much. You need to show more sympathy toward your sister." She stalked off, leaving Mark alone with his worries.

***

Chapter 29

It was early evening and Scott was about to hand over his security monitoring duties to Sera. He was watching small groups of people enter the grounds, three or four at a time. He counted: twenty individuals, male and female. He guessed these were the young soldiers who had taken leave without official approval. The intruders were easily avoiding the patrolling guards but not the cameras. A thought occurred to him. Maybe they *could* avoid the cameras but wanted to inform Mark they were coming in. Scott asked Sera to alert Mark.

She returned with Mark as the first group was almost at the front of the house. Scott decided to take a major risk. "Sera, open the front door and make sure Anna and Reb know I said to leave it open. Turn off all lights except those leading here. When you come back, leave this door open. We'll see what these guys are up to."

"What the hell are you doing?" Mark said, as he watched the intruders moving closer. The guards had not reacted to the intruders.

"Intuition or a completely wild guess. I think these are the twenty missing Cerberus soldiers. They've come to visit. I'm making make it easy for them. You've got your Glock, in case?" All their weapons were now in good working order.

Mark nodded, his eyes focused on the monitors. "You'd better be right or it'll be a bloodbath in here."

The first group made its way to the security room, recorded all the way by the internal cameras. They entered the room, hands raised, with apprehensive expressions. There were three young men and two young women, their ages ranging probably from nineteen to twenty-one. They were dressed in unbadged military clothing and wore their hair short. As they entered the room, they focused their attention on Mark.

"Mark Midway?" asked one.

"Yes?"

"Sir, we're here to assist you."

"Tell me more."

"We're Cerberus."

"Yes, I know."

"We're army and we're AWOL."

"I know that, too."

The young man did not show any surprise and he continued. "We have information you probably don't know, which is why we're here. The management of Cerberus UK, at least some of the post-process members, is corrupt. There is a group, mostly senior members, planning to take over the operations. We believe they're working with the Chairman. He wasn't killed when his yacht was blown up."

"Really?" Mark raised his eyebrows.

"Yes, sir. We have evidence. Can the rest of us come in before one of those security wankers decides to shoot us?"

"Yes, we'll use one of the front rooms; it has more space. Scott, you and Sera maintain your watch. Pipe sound and video in here so you both can listen."

While Mark was directing Scott, the young spokesman raced to the front door and turned the outside light on and off. He rejoined the group as Mark led them into the larger sitting room. It would be crowded, Mark realized, but it was the best room available. He waited as another fifteen young people streamed into the house. Anna joined the meeting. Mark suspected Gabrielle and Niland were in the room as well, cloaked. He was still angry with them and didn't check for their presence.

When everyone found places to sit and settled down, Mark said, "We're aware you are all AWOL. Colonel Hudson visited us. She's concerned at your behavior." He focused on the young man who had led the small group into the security room. "I'm Mark Midway. Scott and Sera are monitoring on an internal voice and video system. This is Anna. There are others you might meet later. You're the spokesman?"

"Yes, sir. Me and Laura. My name's Thomas. We're all pre-Cerberus."

"And what's your problem?"

"Two things. A lot of us don't fit in the army. They grabbed us as recruits when they thought we were at the right maturity level. They ignored any personal aptitudes or requests to do other things. They see us as fodder for their expansion plans. We want our CO to consider a review. The other thing—as I said, we believe the Chairman is plotting with Cerberus UK management to take control."

"Why do you think there's some plot to take over Cerberus UK?"

"We heard you had accepted the chief executive role, but at least four of the senior management team are in contact with the Chairman. We have tapes of their meetings. These people intend to raid this property; the security goons here are scheduled to withdraw before the raid. The Chairman and the others want access to the Cerberus bank accounts you control, and all your research papers. We've heard you want to focus research on our futures. They only want to keep breeding genetically engineered soldiers."

"How did you gather this intelligence?"

"Sir, all pre-Cerberus work together. There's a team made up of people who've established they're totally unsuitable for army life—they're older than us. They were given pretend jobs by Cerberus, to keep them occupied. They devote most of their spare time to spying on Cerberus operations. They've gathered a lot of data. We can give you access from here."

"What do you expect to gain?"

"A beating around the ears at the least, when Colonel Hudson catches up with us." He gave a wry grin. "We thought the risk was worthwhile. We'd heard a lot about you and wanted to warn you. Then, we thought you might be prepared to intercede for us with the colonel. We want to be able to follow our own career paths, instead of being dumped into an environment that's entirely wrong for our abilities. At this stage of our lives, we should be at university, studying whatever we wish." He shrugged. "We'd be far more valuable to Cerberus if we're able to make valid, informed contributions to society. I'm trying not to sound arrogant but you know a lot of Cerberus children have exceptional abilities."

"I understand your need for a different kind of life; it's something I've been striving for, too. Okay, I'll help you. I'll do my best, if needed, to hold off the colonel's ire. I think she might be sympathetic, anyway."

"Excellent, sir," said Laura. Several faces brightened, giving confirmation to her comment. "We do have a concern though which needs to be addressed. Thomas mentioned the security guards—we think you should get rid of them as soon as you can. Twenty of us will take over the security role."

"Are you armed?"

"Oh, no sir. We're not allowed to carry weapons in public."

Thomas said, "We'll take the weapons from the current team."

"There's enough of us to provide a proper three-watch patrol system. We'll be far more effective," Laura added.

Mark looked at Anna, not sure if she'd forgiven him for his earlier chastisement. He asked, "What do you think?"

"I think we have some young people here whom we should support. If we're going to help them, and if they're going to assist us, I agree we need to disarm the existing security force before we do anything. We'll send them on their way and then we can work through our next steps."

Mark sighed his relief. While he might not be forgiven, at least Anna was not harboring any resentment. He said to Thomas, "Before we do anything, I'd like to see some of the information you've gathered. Can we view what you consider to be the most damning data? You can use my laptop"

Thomas signaled one of his companions, who stepped forward and commandeered Mark's computer. Thomas said, "Ivy is our top computer person. Ivy, please show us the video of the meeting between the DI, the Chairman and Andrew Jeffries. The one where they discussed Mark."

"Dissed Mark, more like," said the young woman as she sat at the desk where Mark had his laptop. "We're using our own storage cloud. Only a few of us know the technical details, and a few more know how to use it. We're adding more computer training for both companies, so we'll all have an opportunity to increase our IT skills. Here's the file. I'll display it on the larger monitor?"

Mark nodded. Ivy took only seconds to download and play the video, which showed a small meeting room from one end. Mark suspected the camera was in a bookcase or similar location. Three people were seated around the table.

DI Goodwin: Midway seems a capable enough person. He's survived a number of personal attacks.

Chairman: He's been lucky.

Jeffries: He defended the Lifelong Complex against a team of mercenaries. Killed seven of them. Wish I had luck like his.

Chairman: Bah.

DI Goodwin: Andrew has a point. The man's not to be dismissed lightly. He has some strong support—Schmidt, Donnelly, and his personal team. Even the two young children. Reb's an unknown.

Chairman: I'll handle her. I know how to keep her quiet. She'll wish she drowned on that sailboard of hers. Midway is a fluke. An aberration. We can handle them all.

DI Goodwin: You might need to temper your over-confidence if you want our assistance.

Chairman: You need to temper your voice if you want a piece of the Cerberus bankroll.

Jeffries: Enough bickering. Chairman, how will you take care of Midway?

Chairman: First, the DI needs to make sure Midway's security team is under our control. Her men must leave when we give them the signal. As soon as possible after that, we'll attack. Bankton House will be exposed, it needs a dozen or more for proper defense. We'll soon overrun this bunch of children. Goodwin, you have people who can take part, take responsibility?

DI Goodwin: Oh yes, I can arrange the resources for the...raid, not attack. We need a pretext, one that will stand up to a degree of scrutiny.

Jeffries: Can we categorize Midway and his entourage as a terrorist group?

DI Goodwin: We'd need some evidence.

Chairman: They can be charged with kidnapping and murder, after I get my hands on the three children who are living in the old school building.

DI Goodwin: Yes, it should work. How will you dispose of these people?

Chairman: The Chinese will purchase the children; while they're from a different batch than Reb, but from the same laboratory, they'll be interested, I'm sure. They can have her, too, after I've finished with her. Midway should be shot while attempting to escape—accidentally, of course—after we get the bank and research details from him. The Cerberus brats? Perhaps they can be shot during the raid.

Jeffries: I think we're headed in the right direction. We'll work out detailed plans. Goodwin, perhaps you and I can prepare something for our next meeting?

The video ended. Mark looked at Anna. "I think we can work with our new friends, don't you?"

Anna said, "Yes, I believe we can."

Two subdued voices said in unison, "So do we. They called us Cerberus brats."

Mark ignored the comments from Niland and Gabrielle. He spoke toward the ceiling, "Scott, can you and Sera come here for a few minutes? I'll send two volunteers in to relieve you. Thomas, can you select two of your people to monitor our cameras?"

Mark waited for the exchange to take place. After he had completed introductions, he said to the visitors, "My proposal is this—Anna, Scott, and Sera will come with me now to the cottages. I'll also take two or three of your best people to help and another two or three to collect and take control of the weapons we recover. Once we have these security people assembled and weaponless, in the larger cottage, we'll send them off. I'll keep one of the vehicles; we need transport. When we've finished dealing with them, Thomas, I'd like you to contact your CO. She wants to know you're all okay."

Thomas said, "We parked an army lorry in a lay-by about half a mile away. It's got our personal gear. We'll use it for our transport if we need it, and if the colonel will let us keep it for a while. We brought some tents, in case you don't have enough accommodation here. Oh, and we tied up two of the security guards. We left them just inside the entrance to the property." He handed over two pistols. "These are their weapons."

Mark organized his team and set off to the nearest cottage. The off-duty men were finishing their evening meal before the shift change. They were taken unawares and only one protested when his weapon was taken. He stopped complaining when Mark waved a Glock under his nose. The three men coming off shift were similarly taken by surprise. Finally the young soldiers retrieved the two men they had earlier captured.

Mark addressed the ten men and two drivers. "We have your weapons. We have your photographs and fingerprints. I don't care if you're all Cerberus—I don't trust your allegiance. I don't want you to return to this property. If I ever see you here again, I'll have you arrested for trespassing. Assuming, that is, you don't get accidentally shot. We have your cell phones; I'll send those to DI Goodwin. Now, I'll give you fifteen minutes to pack and another five minutes to load up two of the vehicles and get out of here. Do you understand?"

The response was subdued. Mark was confident the now ex-security guards would depart on schedule. He asked Scott and Sera to ensure they left the property on schedule.

He signaled Thomas and his companions. "Come with me. You need to contact Colonel Hudson and make sure she understands where you are and what you're doing."

"Yes, sir."

Mark realized the young man was not looking forward to the conversation with his commanding officer. He added, "I'll speak with her first, if you like."

Thomas looked relieved. "Thank you, sir."

~~~

Maeve had developed the habit of reading her e-mails aloud while she sat next to Schmidt's hospital bed. She had no idea whether he understood or was absorbing any of her words. She hoped the steady sound of her voice gave him comfort. The nurse entered and Maeve recognized her as Cerberus. They exchanged polite greetings.

An hour later, close to midnight, as Maeve was preparing to leave, she heard movement. Surprised, she looked up. Schmidt was watching her. She licked her lips. "How do you feel? Can you talk?"

He moved his mouth. At first she was unable to hear anything, but the heard two faint words. "Rotten. Barely." His eyes closed. She kept silent for a few minutes. His eyes opened again. "Keep...reading." At least, she thought it was what he said. Her heart was thumping far too loudly for her to be certain.

Maeve opened up her laptop and read aloud the next e-mail from her team of analysts.

***

Chapter 30

Mercante was baffled. Typically, his plans worked. No, not typically. Always. Without exception. Midway and Schmidt seemed to cast some kind of bad-luck spell over everything he attempted with their names attached. He was perplexed now as to his next move. He couldn't stay in the United Kingdom too long; he had tasks demanding his attention in Langley. His little foray to kidnap three genetically engineered teenagers had gone awry; someone had beaten him to the finish line. Wentworth was not contactable for some unknown reason. He hadn't heard whether Schmidt was recovering or not. Midway was well guarded. Mercante's revenge path was proving impassable.

He had an open ticket for his return and phoned the hotel's concierge desk to arrange his seat on the earliest morning flight back to Washington. He also arranged for a taxi to take him to the airport. Scheduled departure was seven-thirty a.m., and he would be back at his desk early in the afternoon.

The flight was uneventful. Mercante passed through DHS's passport inspection in minutes and strolled through Customs without a pause. He had ordered a limo to meet him and he would go straight to the office. He could shower and change at the Agency's facilities.

His plans had not allowed for the involvement of Maeve Donnelly.

The limo driver was waiting, holding a sign that read McCARR. Mercante nodded to the man and detoured around a small group of anxious people waiting for other passengers. As he did so, the driver stepped up to him and Mercante felt someone approach from behind.

"Mr. Mercante. Or McCarr, it doesn't matter which," a voice murmured from behind. "Please come with us, quietly. We all would prefer this to be without any fuss, don't you agree?"

Mercante said, "I'll make a fuss and you'll both feel the pain."

The man behind jabbed him in the back, an inch above his right kidney. "This is a Beretta. Silenced. A shot here"— the man jabbed again—"will be painful, potentially fatal, depending on how much time elapses before we get you to the hospital, and my driver is known for how slowly he drives. Now, we'd be obliged to assist you to your vehicle, which is waiting for you at the curb. What did you say about a fuss?"

Mercante did not protest further. Beneath his calm facade he was fuming. Another jab, again above his kidney, prevented his rising temper from exploding. For the moment. The curbside vehicle was an SUV. The driver opened the rear door and Mercante entered and sat down. When the driver closed the door, Mercante swore. The door had automatically locked. He slid over and tried the other door—also locked. There was a hefty plastic barrier between him and the front seat. Another barrier prevented him from accessing the rear of the vehicle. He vowed aloud his revenge on anyone within his reach.

The driver and the other man took their places in the SUV. They ignored Mercante's tirade and drove out of the airport. Mercante did not recognize their route; it was neither to the Agency nor to Quantico. He began to worry.

He didn't know who his captors were; he assumed they were law enforcement of some kind. He was silent for a minute or two. At last he managed a question. "Are you freelancers or some official law enforcement idiots who don't know what you're doing?"

"Oh, we're law enforcement," replied the passenger, "and we know what we're doing."

"Identification?"

The passenger laughed. "We'll get to identification in due course, don't you worry. Maybe first you should work on explaining why you're traveling as Robert McCarr."

He ignored the suggestion. "Where are you taking me?"

"I suggest you sit back and enjoy the ride."

~~~

Maeve Donnelly entered the interview room escorted by two young Cerberus agents. Their prisoner was seated, handcuffed, one leg chained to his chair. He sneered, "So you think you're back running the FBI?"

"Not at all, Roberto," Maeve replied. "I have more than enough on my plate with Cerberus. Now, tell me, why were you at an old school building in London?" She signaled to one of the Cerberus agents. "Run the video for me."

There was a video monitor at one end of the interview room. Mercante watched as the file loaded and the video played. He swore under his breath as he saw himself using the lock picks to open the door. The video switched to the interior and followed him from camera to camera along the corridor and into the room where he had discovered the housekeeper's body.

"We should hand this over to the British authorities. It'd curtail at least some of your travels, don't you think?"

"It's a forgery, obviously," said Mercante.

Maeve spoke to the young agent. "This time, the audio file from within the Agency, the one where Mercante met with Wentworth." She waited until the clip ended. Despite gaps due to the quality, there was enough data to raise suspicions.

"Again—"

"Yes, I know, a forgery. You'll be interested to know we received intel from a surprising source—Colonel Alexey Grigoryevich. Yes, he's dead, as you know. Shot by an unknown person after his small team of Russians launched a Strela 21 at Schmidt's helicopter. But he'd arranged to send me two files, in the event of his death. One was effectively a confession, describing how he had been coerced into a situation that he regretted. The second was videos of meetings between himself and someone named Robert McCarr. This McCarr, who looks remarkably like you, was setting up Grigoryevich and providing him with instructions, helicopter flight details, and even a SAM. The video is clear, the quality is excellent. I'll play it, if you want."

"No, thanks. I'm sure it's a forgery, too." Mercante mentally cursed the Russian colonel. He had thought the man was too cowed to take any such action. "Now that this entertainment has concluded, I want to know who you think you are, and by what right you're holding me?"

"Concluded? Not by a long shot. We've a police sketch of a Robert McCarr, supposedly a senior ICE manager, who authorized a black op in London. It failed, by the way, and we have detailed statements from two of the three ICE agents involved. I can see a remarkable resemblance between the sketch and you. We expect to have the Reverend Barker in custody shortly, and, if he lives up to his reputation, he'll be willing to provide us with all the details of his meeting with you. His militia raid on Midway's property, the one you requested and paid for using Agency funds, was a prime example of disastrous planning, don't you think? The more I think about it, the more I think all your recent activities have been disastrous, hmm?"

"Listen, lady, I'm higher on the totem pole than you'll ever be, despite your FBI background. These trumped-up charges will be regarded as the result of professional jealousy. They'll be dismissed by any sensible prosecutor, assuming you're able to get anyone to listen to you."

"Oh, I don't think it will be an issue. The murder of Colonel Dempsey and the attack on General Schmidt clearly fall within the definition of terrorist activities. We've arranged your flight to Gitmo. You leave tomorrow morning. Don't expect a return ticket."

"The Agency will stop you. You can't write me off so easily." He struggled against his restraints. "The Agency looks after its own."

Maeve shrugged. "The President has signed the order. It was raised and approved by the Agency. They've washed their hands of you."

Mercante swore. "I don't believe you, bitch—"

Maeve ignored the appellation. There was a knock on the door and she turned to the closer of the two Cerberus agents. "That should be our man. Let him in, please." She turned back to the prisoner. "You don't need me to introduce you to your Executive Director?"

A final wave of doom crashed over Mercante. The CIA ED stood in the doorway and looked at him for a moment, the way an entomologist might examine a particularly nasty bug. He said, "Mercante, your tenure with the Agency has been terminated. We've approved your transfer to Guantánamo. I trust I'll never see or hear from you again." The man turned and walked away. The Cerberus agent closed the door and resumed his seat at the table.

Maeve looked at Mercante, a small amount of pity seeping into her expression. It disappeared almost before it formed. She said, "There may be things you can tell us, to alleviate the conditions you're going to experience. Your future, to a limited extent, is in your hands." She stood and one of the young agents rushed to open the door. She exited the interview room, followed by the two agents. Mercante cursed Schmidt, Midway, Grigoryevich, and everyone else he had involved in his plans. He did not think to curse himself.

***

Chapter 31

Mark watched the vehicle slow and stop outside the door of the manor house. He looked at Scott who was also focused on the video monitor. "Who do you think—" Mark asked.

"I've no idea. Let me go see." Scott stood, stretched and headed to the door. A young Cerberus soldier sat down in the vacated chair, acting as a relief operator in the security room.

Scott returned in minutes. He said to Mark, "You'll never believe it. It's weird, working for you." He shook his head. "Your visitor is an attaché from the Chinese Embassy in London. He asked specifically for Mark Midway, so I'll leave him in your capable hands. He's in the formal sitting room."

When Mark entered, his visitor was seated. The man looked to be his mid-forties, with a slim build, and his jet-black hair, graying on the edges, was cut short. When he saw Mark, he stood and offered his hand. "Mr. Midway, it's a pleasure to meet you. I've heard so much—oh, forgive me, my name is Yu Jenhai. Please call me Ralph."

"Mark." He shook hands and indicated the chair. "Please make yourself comfortable. I'm intrigued by your visit."

"Thank you. I must admit to a similar feeling."

"Yes?"

"Allow me to explain. I'm the senior trade attaché here in London, with the Embassy of the People's Republic of China. I received an instruction from Beijing a couple of days ago. It seems, and I'm quoting their words, there has been a series of unfortunate events in the United States, involving yourself, an organization called Cerberus, and genetically modified soldiers and children. The latest event affected both you and your sister, I understand?"

"Correct. There's not only the attack on my sister. Our relationship with your government has been fraught; I think the responsibility is more yours than ours. A Chinese killer squad poisoned and shot—assassinated—a company of Cerberus-engineered military police and Cerberus children we were protecting. These killers—Chinese—murdered two-hundred people. At about the same time two Chinese gunmen tried to kill me and they wounded an FBI agent."

"Ah, yes. I have details, but of course, my Government did not know about these events, at the time."

Mark raised his eyebrows at that claim and said, "Indeed? That's not all. We suspect the attack on a motor yacht on which my sister worked was by a Chinese ship. Add the recent shooting by an embassy employee when she was trying to reach me, in New Hampshire. Most of those assailants, except the ship crew and the person who shot my sister, were killed."

The Chinese attaché stood and bowed toward Mark. "Sir, please accept our sincerest apologies. I have been advised these actions were absolutely unauthorized. A rogue element carried out these attacks and murders and the people who authorized them have been...dealt with. My government wishes to make amends even though we realize, of course, it's not possible to bring two-hundred people back to life. We regard their deaths with absolute sorrow." He sat down. "You might know of a Dr. White—she was killed in a car accident four days ago."

Mark was taken aback. The death of Dr. White implied the Chinese were discontinuing their genetic engineering research. He wondered at the change of heart.

"You have proof of Dr. White's death?" he asked.

"Yes. I have been informed her body is on its way to America, together with a full report detailing the accident, our investigation, and results of the autopsy. By now, Ms. Donnelly should be able to confirm the details. We were thorough in our investigation."

"Have you—has your government ceased its research into genetic engineering?"

"I believe so. My briefing did not provide a complete status report. I understand some of Dr. White's research produced some horrifying results, so bad as to cause our rejection of any more research. We have about five-hundred survivors, what I believe Cerberus describes as pre-engineered. We have about the same number of post-engineered. The research laboratory has been closed. My government has completely stopped further research."

"I think Dr. White was careless about the possible results of some of her attempts to build her concept of a super soldier. I'm relieved to hear she is dead, as callous as that may sound."

"I fully understand. Mr. Midway—Mark, I am seeking your assistance despite the events which have taken place. There has been substantial pressure placed on our embassy in Washington to surrender our employee who was involved in this attack on your sister, so he can be subjected to American legal procedures. If we don't agree, the State Department will rescind his accredited status and withdraw from current trade negotiations that are critical to us. They're critical to both countries. We—that is, the People's Republic of China—desires your support, as strange as it may seem to you. We're in your debt. We have taken steps to reduce the burden—Dr. White, for example. Now we are increasing our debt to you. We will have this burden for a long time."

"What do you expect me to do?"

"We want to make amends to both you and your sister. Privately, my government acknowledges our actions have been unwarranted. Totally unauthorized. We offer our formal apologies. If there is any way we can compensate past victims, please advise me of such. At the very least, we wish to offer financial compensation to Mr. Gilmore, and to you, and your sister. Anna and the younger children, too, if you think it is needed. We, in turn, request, most humbly, that you to intercede with your State Department on our behalf."

"I doubt I have much influence with the State Department."

He checked his notes. "I believe if you contact Ms. Maeve Donnelly and request she removes the pressure, it will meet our needs."

"I don't know. Your embassy employee shot my sister and shot at my property. The shooter deserves some punishment, don't you think?"

"The Ambassador here in London, and I, both agree. In some ways I represent a different culture. I spent five years in America as well as studying at Cambridge. I have an understanding of the two cultures, Western and Chinese. Sometimes it makes my life difficult when I can see both sides."

"I assume your government would agree to return this man to China and subject him to some form of legal penalty there?"

"Personally, I think yes. Such action would be preferred to a trial in America, with our employee spending time in an American jail. Your suggestion would remove the potential for considerable loss of face for our people, for our government. Also, we want the trade negotiations to continue. I'm giving you some private information, you realize?"

"Yes, I understand. And I repeat—this man should lose his accreditation, be returned to China, and suffer a penalty similar to what he would receive in an American court, for attempted murder. You can add financial compensation to injured parties. My sister may have other ideas. I'll ask her to meet with you."

The man bowed his head. "Thank you. Your sister is here?"

"Yes, I'll arrange for her to talk with you. Excuse me for a minute."

Mark found Reb in the atrium on the southern side of the house. She appeared relaxed, enjoying the warmth of an early spring sun. She had not fully recovered from the fright of her friends' experiences in London.

"Reb, we've an interesting situation. A visitor is here from the Chinese Embassy in London. He's being apologetic about past events, including the Camp Brewer murders. I think Maeve has been making waves within the State Department and they've been applying pressure on the Chinese. Now their embassy in Washington is under pressure to either submit their man—the guy who shot you—to the American legal system, or the US will cancel his accreditation and withdraw from some critical trade negotiations." Reb sat up and focused on Mark. He recounted the conversation he'd just had with the attaché. "He's in the small living room. Can you come and talk to him?"

"I-I think so. Give me a minute or two to tidy myself. "

Mark waited with their visitor until Reb appeared. He introduced them and said, "I'll let you two discuss everything. Let me know when you finish, okay?"

Mark joined Anna, Niland, and Gabrielle, and briefed them on his visitor. After a short discussion, they concluded there was no reason to demand further compensation for them, as long as the person who shot at Reb was punished. Scott was another matter and needed to be considered.

Ten minutes later Reb found Mark. "I told him I agreed with you. Their embassy is going to pay me for what he called pain and suffering. It's a good amount. He said he'd authorize a payment to Scott and to you too, for property damage. I didn't tell him someone had wrecked our home."

"He probably knows. He seems to have access to good intelligence. He mentioned compensation to me, but you and Scott, you're the ones who suffered."

Reb hugged Mark. "Thank you." She held a tissue to her face and almost ran from the room. Mark returned to his visitor.

"I understand my sister and you have reached an agreement?"

"Yes, we have. I thank you for your forbearance."

"I'll arrange for Scott Gilmore to meet with you, as well."

"Very good. If you can communicate with Ms. Donnelly?"

"I'll contact her today, once you've settled with Scott."

"Excellent. The ambassador will send each of you a letter to confirm, confidentially, of course. No publicity?"

"We don't like publicity."

Mark rejoined the attaché after the man met with Scott and reached a mutually agreeable settlement. He watched as the attaché gathered his papers and laptop and packed them into his briefcase.

Ralph said, "Thank you again, Mark. I assure you, our government will be appreciative." He paused. "There's something else I'd like to mention. We've heard you have persuaded Cerberus to defer its mainstream genetic engineering research in favor of researching the effect on people who have undergone genetic treatment. We—I emphasize this is unofficial—we are hopeful at some stage you can share some of those results with us. We have over a thousand people affected and we don't know what the future holds for them. I understand there might be some history to overcome, but keep the possibility in mind. I'm sure my government would be agreeable to sharing research costs with you. Please feel free to contact me if ever you need to. Here's my card."

***

Chapter 32

Maeve stretched, sighing to herself. The hospital chair was uncomfortable. Most of the nurses now gave her informal updates when she arrived and so far there had not been any significant change in Schmidt's condition. The two Cerberus nurses usually provided additional details, information the doctor normally would restrict and, as a result, she was able to gain better insight into Schmidt's condition and likely recovery. The doctors' major concern was not so much Schmidt's physical condition but rather his mental state. It seemed their patient was not responding as expected and the doctors were unwilling to give a detailed prognosis or expectations for their patient's recovery.

She had moved herself to one side of the room where the lighting was better. It meant, however, she was hidden from anyone entering the room. Maeve was struggling to keep her eyes focused. She had been sitting here for more than two hours and it was almost time for her to leave. The reports were boring and she was only reading them to make sure she was up to date with her analysts' evidence gathering. The case against Wentworth was ironclad and she expected to gain the President's approval within the week for the man's arrest. Her main concern was whether to recommend she make his arrest public or simply ship him straight to

Guantánamo. In a thought she would not voice, she wondered if it'd be better for all concerned if the man resisted arrest, with a fatal conclusion. Schmidt, Maeve mused, would arrange an accident. He always acted as though life was defined in black and white, with hardly any shades of gray.

The slowly opening door caught her attention. The nurses were not yet due to check on Schmidt and none of his vital signs had changed. She felt in her handbag and withdrew her pistol. If she was mistaken, she would apologize. The door swung shut with a soft hiss as the man moved farther into the room. She didn't recognize him. She raised her handgun. The faint click as she released the safety contrasted with the susurration of the monitoring equipment. The man froze.

Maeve placed her handbag on the floor and stood. "Raise your hands above your head," she instructed.

The intruder started to turn, but stilled when Maeve said, "Move one more inch and I'll shoot you in the back of your knee. Your choice."

The man hesitated and then started to raise his hands, slowly. Maeve stepped toward the red emergency button. She didn't know how this man had managed to get past the two guards on duty, one at the nurses' station, the other in front of Schmidt's door. As she reached the button, the man lunged toward her. She fired two shots. The noise was deafening in the confines of the room. The man dropped to the floor, motionless. Blood seeped onto the clinically clean floor. Running footsteps announced the arrival of two nurses and a guard. Maeve maintained her grip on the pistol, still aimed at the man on the floor.

"Maeve," cried the first nurse through the door. "What's happening? We heard—" She stopped when she saw the intruder on the floor and Maeve holding a handgun. The nurse knelt beside the man as the other nurse and the guard crowded into the room. Maeve moved back and gathered her handbag and papers, returning the pistol to its normal location.

"He's one of the guards," said the second nurse.

"He's a dead guard, now," said the first nurse.

Maeve spoke to the other guard who standing behind the nurses. "Notify hospital security and call the police." After he left the room, Maeve addressed the nurses. "This room is a crime scene, so don't touch anything." A doctor hurried into the room and stopped inside the door when he saw the body.

"Anything we can do?" he asked.

The first nurse replied, "He's dead. Two shots to the head. Ms. Donnelly says we shouldn't touch anything because this is a crime scene."

The doctor turned to Maeve. "Are you okay, ma'am? Is there anything we can get you?"

"I could do with a stiff whiskey, but I daresay a glass of water would be better. We should leave the room and close the door. You can monitor Schmidt from your stations. I need to sit down. I'll wait outside his room until the police arrive."

"Yes, ma'am," said the doctor, stepping out into the corridor. The nurses and Maeve followed. There were anxious nurses and orderlies standing around, part-alarmed, part curious as to what had happened. Maeve let the doctor deal with their questions. She pulled the door closed and instructed the Cerberus guard to help her ensure no one entered Schmidt's room until the police arrived.

"They said they'll be here within five minutes," the guard advised.

"Did you know this other man?" asked Maeve.

"No, ma'am. We always have new people joining our part of the operation. He presented his ID when he arrived. He was here to relieve the other guard. He didn't talk much and the nurses' station is too far away for us to have a conversation."

"Thank you." She turned to the ICU nurses, who were still regarding her with concern. "I'm okay. I need a glass of water, though. Perhaps I can sit down here?"

A police sergeant, the first officer to arrive at the scene, was polite once he saw Maeve's ID and heard her story. After reporting back to his base, he turned to Maeve. "The crime scene guys will be here shortly. The medical examiner won't be too far behind them. While we're waiting, I'd like you to give a statement to one of my men. We also need your weapon for forensics."

"Of course, Sergeant." She handed over her gun and the sergeant dropped the weapon into a plastic evidence bag. "I'll be here when you want someone to take my statement."

"Yes, ma'am." The sergeant left to speak to one of his men and Maeve sat back on the chair. It was as uncomfortable as the chair inside Schmidt's room.

The crime scene technicians checked the body when they arrived. The dead man had a small pistol, with a silencer attached, in his right hand. Maeve provided her statement, twice, then she went home.

Her hands were still shaking when she climbed into bed.

~~~

Mark listened to the almost painfully loud diatribe that was focused on him and his decision to dismiss the security team. He held the cell phone away from his ear to ease the pressure. The caller was DI Goodwin. Her security people had briefed her on their removal and she was expressing her reaction. At last Mark interrupted the flow of words. "DI Goodwin. I have a video of you and other members of Cerberus UK planning with the Chairman to launch an attack on us, here at the house. The plan, if I recall correctly, is for me to be shot while attempting to escape." He did not mention the sabotaged Glocks; it was better if the DI didn't realize that little subterfuge had been discovered.

There was silence for a very long minute. She said, "You're wrong—you've been misled—I would never engage in such activities." Goodwin must have been shouting into her cell phone; Scott and Anna who were standing at least six feet away were listening with avid interest.

"I have other recordings that appear to show the planning in progress—identifying the participants, timing, and so forth. You're clearly visible in the videos. So are Jeffries and the Chairman. There are two or three other people I don't know, but we're running facial recognition against a number of databases and I'm sure we'll identify them."

"Listen, you little upstart, Cerberus is ours, not yours." She cursed some more. "We will take control." The call was disconnected with a crash.

Mark shrugged and looked at Scott and Anna.

"Game on, I would say," Scott said. "The lady's not for turning."

"Some of her language was not at all ladylike," Anna said. "I suppose they'll still try to attack us?"

"Definitely. The Chairman's not going to walk away from this."

"So we're all in danger?" Anna asked.

Mark smiled and said, "I think the Chairman is in danger, if I can do anything about it. Let's meet with Thomas and Laura and see what the British Army can do for us."

Scott asked, "Do you know if they've spoken with Colonel Hudson?"

"Yes, she's given them leave to be here."

"Good."

"Can you contact them both, Scott? We'll meet in the larger sitting room. Get someone to relieve you, and Sera should join us. Anna, you and Reb, too."

Mark briefed Thomas and Laura, the two young Cerberus soldiers. "DI Goodwin was irate. She said Cerberus is theirs, not mine. I'm not sure she realizes I don't want to control the organization; I just want to guide what it does. We're in a situation where local law is unlikely to be much help. I've asked Maeve to try to communicate with people in British law enforcement who might be able to help us and so far she's been unsuccessful. My conclusion is we need to protect ourselves. I know you've been updating your CO. Is she still in agreement about you providing assistance here?"

"Yes, sir. As you know, the first call was wild for a minute or two. We've given her updates and she's confirmed her approval of ten days special leave for each of us, so we've got about a week left."

"I'd be surprised if the DI and the Chairman will wait much longer before they attack," said Laura. "Based on all the videos, the Chairman is more than impatient to see this raid finished and successful."

"Scott, what have you and Thomas planned for protecting the house?" Mark asked.

Scott said, "We're assuming a pre-dawn attack as worst case. We've split the team into three shifts, one on watch, one on standby and one sleeping. The soldiers are helping me and Sera with monitoring the cameras. We added motion detectors to detect anything over a hundred pounds and infrared and photoelectric cameras with beam sensors. We're able to run the army lorry behind any vehicles that come down the lane. The soldiers have three men on truck duty. They're also charged with immobilizing the intruders' vehicles."

"What else?"

"It will depend on their approach. We don't expect them to have heavy military equipment. They'll come in and shoot up the place, maybe drop flash bangs, maybe get serious with grenades. Worst case for us would be if they stand off and fire mortars. I think that's unlikely—they'd never get the information they're looking for if they did that. We think they'll opt for the quieter approaches—a surreptitious entry followed by selective shooting of targets.

We have some surprises ready. The worst-case scenario is if they decide to withdraw and destroy everything with some kind of explosive device."

"We can use deadly force to defend our home against invaders," Mark said.

"Yes, I've been checking, too. There are legal cases in support of people defending their homes, even if they kill the attackers."

"We should try to capture these people. Thomas, tell your team to use deadly force only if your lives are threatened."

"Yes, sir," Laura and Thomas replied.

"Scott, do you have anything more?"

"No, not that I can think of. The team seems to have the external needs covered. My approach boils down to: detect the intruders, block their exit, attempt to capture them, kill them if we have to, and avoid getting shot."

Mark looked at Anna and Sera. "Thoughts?"

They both shook their heads. "No," Anna said.

"Good. Laura and Thomas, continue to report to Scott. If you can't find him, look for me or Anna. Okay?"

"Yes, sir."

"Well, that's it. We've a lot of work to do. I need to contact Maeve again."

Mark did not notice the two small intruders who backed quietly out of the room.

***

Chapter 33

Maeve read the report. It was just after sunrise when three black SUVs stopped in front of the house north of Atlanta. Four men raced to the front door. They wore quasi-military clothing and bulletproof protection. One was carrying a heavy battering ram. Four other men hurried to the rear of the property, one of whom also carried a battering ram. Three men, including the person in charge, remained with the vehicles. At precisely six-thirty a.m. the two teams smashed down the front and rear doors of the house and rushed inside.

The noise had alerted the residents. Two—a cook and kitchen maid—hid in the pantry until they were discovered some hours later. By the time the first team had reached the second floor and identified the main bedroom, Reverend Barker's young lady friend had climbed out the window where she slipped on the wet slate and fell fifteen-feet to the ground, breaking her left leg and wrist. She was unconscious for ten minutes and when she recovered, denied any knowledge of the reverend. An addendum to the report supplied the information that a few days later, the young woman was hospitalized for severe pneumonia. The doctors discovered she was pregnant and since she was only thirteen, informed the local authorities.

During the commotion at the house, Barker, learning from prior experience, had taken shelter behind what he had been informed was a bulletproof door protecting his panic room. He also had acquired an UZI SMG for his personal defense. As the invaders entered his bedroom, he poked the small weapon around the edge of the door and fired. He used half a clip and failed to hit anything except the gaudy chandelier above his bed, shattering its crystal components. The response from the four men who had entered the bedroom was loud and sustained. One was armed with an HK MP7A2 which used 4.6 mm cartridges capable of penetrating 20 layers of Kevlar. The other officers carried Glocks. They fired multiple rounds at his bulletproof door. The impacts tore the door from its hinges and it fell back, partly crushing Barker. He struggled to remove himself from under its heavy weight and in so doing, exposed most of his silk pajama-clad body. A second burst of fire hit the reverend, fracturing both femurs, shattering his pelvis and one bullet, smaller caliber, pierced his heart, ending his days of leadership of the Southern United Fundamentalists' church and its militia. No one claimed ownership of the smaller caliber.

Maeve admitted to herself that she gained some pleasure at the conclusion of events. She read the details aloud while visiting with Schmidt, but she still didn't know whether either her voice or the contents of the report penetrated his unconsciousness.

~~~

Gabrielle and Niland vowed to assist in defense of the manor house. They had memories, which for months had given them nightmares, of the attack on Camp Brewer, where over twenty of their companions had been murdered, either shot or poisoned. They and Anna had escaped, rescued by Mark after Anna shot and killed the murderers.

They still had nightmares, even now. At Gabrielle's suggestion, they set off to visit with Reb's three friends, now settled in to the comfort of the manor house, home from their short hospital stay.

They found the teenagers in the boys' bedroom. "We want to protect Mark and Anna, and Reb, of course," Niland said. "Mark has protected us, and I'm sure he'll protect you in the future, too."

"Oh, we don't have any doubts about Mark. We've seen how he takes care of everyone. He's even watching out for the army brats. But what can we do?" Lewis asked. His two friends listened intently to the discussion.

Gabrielle said, "We need to have a better idea of your abilities."

"Oh." There was a long silence as Lewis looked first at Carys and then at Owen.

Gabrielle reached out to Carys and held her hand. She said, "I'll share one of my abilities—I can make people not see me, or anyone I'm with." Both girls disappeared. After four or five seconds Gabrielle and Carys re-appeared and she released the Welsh girl's hand.

"Amaze balls," Lewis said. Carys shook her head in disbelief. Owen seemed too surprised to speak.

Gabrielle stepped toward Lewis and took his hand. "What can you do?" Lewis didn't answer and after a few moments Gabrielle released his hand. She looked at each of the three and turned to Niland. "Did you get that?" she asked.

"Yeah. Interesting. Of course, we knew their programming ability was tops. I'm intrigued to learn Carys can also hide people. So that's almost two of you—well, three, if you include my ability. Lewis has a similar ability to you and Mark. He's able to persuade people to do things without them realizing. It's why he's so bossy," Niland said.

"None of them can do mental transfers, though."

"No. Unless they can hide some of their—I sensed a sudden restriction from Lewis when he realized what you were doing."

"I felt what he did and decided not to force my way in."

"Alright, you two," Lewis said. "Your points are made. Yes, I shut you out; I thought I'd disguised it. You're half our age, and you're stronger, far stronger, than me. Is that how you got Anna and Reb to help rescue us?"

Niland said, "Yeah, but they're difficult to influence. We both needed to work on them."

Lewis asked, "What do you think we can do to help Mark?"

"The house has a long attic with windows overlooking the front and back, but not the sides. We think we can get some firearms and ambush the attackers. Gabrielle and Carys can do their thing; the attackers won't be able to see us," Niland said.

"Or we'll set ourselves up in the grounds, let them go past, and attack them from the rear," Gabrielle mused.

"It'd be too risky. There'd be firearms going off in every direction. Using the attic might work. Can we have a look?" Owen asked.

The room was long, dusty, and dimly lit. Heavy exposed timber beams supported the slate-tiled roof. Gray sheets covered furniture, stored until required, or in some cases, because they were no longer required. Boxes and cabinets contained papers and old documents. Niland, in his earlier exploring, had found some papers dated more than a hundred years earlier. The dust they disturbed made Gabrielle sneeze. She led the way to the front windows, which overlooked the gardens and entry area. The lane leading onto the property was visible, although most of the view was blocked by trees.

"Let's check the other windows," said Lewis. Clambering over stacked boxes and other obstructions, they all trooped to the end of the attic, which overlooked the back of the property. A huge water tank gurgled as they climbed past. Everyone was sneezing from the decades-old dust. They stood around the largest window and looked out at the two cottages and pathways at the rear of the house.

Lewis sat on a crate next to the window. "The problem is, how to identify who is friend or foe, at night? What if it's too dark when the attackers arrive? If it's a rainy night, we won't have a chance."

Gabrielle said, "There must be something we can do?"

Owen said, "If I was attacking, I'd pick a time well after midnight. I'd use stealth to get as close as possible. Another idea is to openly approach, pretending we're the local police. We can identify two strategies to reach the house and we're only guessing. Mark can field twenty Cerberus soldiers, plus him and four other adults, a total of twenty-five. Wouldn't we get in their way?"

Carys said to Gabrielle and Niland, "Owen is always the realist. Sometimes he's disappointing." She smiled to soften her words.

"Well, perhaps you and I can hide Mark and Reb if anyone manages to get into the house," Gabrielle said to Carys. "Niland and Lewis can use their abilities to slow down any attacker who wants to shoot us. Owen—I'm sorry, I didn't see what your abilities are."

"Inventiveness," Owen replied. "Taking wild ideas and trying to make them work. I've been thinking."

Carys and Lewis groaned and Lewis explained, "It usually means lots of work for us while dreamer here"—he nudged Owen—"just keeps dreaming and telling us we've got it wrong."

Owen smiled. "Mark developed an EMP blast program, didn't he?" He looked at Gabrielle.

"Yes," she said. "It blew out all the video and image files on cameras and phones when the police tried to enter our home in New Hampshire. Actually I think it deleted all their files."

"This is what I think we can do," Owen said, and went on to describe his idea. "The scenario is this. We'll construct and program a small device based on Mark's EMP program. It'll appear to affect all cell phones within a forty or fifty yard radius. We'll pirate the components Mark ordered for his EMP processes and use them to build the device. When it's switched on, and a cell phone is carried into its range, the field will appear to cause the battery to short out. We have to show that the battery either catches on fire or it explodes. We can demonstrate that it won't take long for the battery to ignite, maybe fifteen or twenty seconds from when the phone enters the field. Once a phone is infected, the process can't be stopped, although we won't try to demonstrate that."

"So the attackers—assuming they're getting information from someone still here—will think they can't use their cell phones. That will cut down their communications abilities when they're on the grounds. It's a good idea, I agree. What will we do about our phones?" Gabrielle asked.

"Same, same, at least for the test. Turn all of them off. The field is supposed to affect any cell phone that comes close enough. The only way to prevent it is to remove the batteries."

"So we do a test?"

"Yes. We'll tell everyone to keep their phones at least a hundred yards away, maybe farther. We need to place a phone in range of the field before we switch on the equipment."

Lewis added, "We have to act as though we're keeping our test hidden from outsiders. I can rig a small explosive device; I saw some shotgun shells in the large barn that I can utilize."

"We can run the test in the area between the large barn and the cottages. I'll brief the soldiers and get them to sweep across the back of the property to make sure no one's watching. We can set up our test there, using one phone. It should work," Gabrielle said.

Niland asked, "Who's going to sacrifice their cell phone?"

For a long minute, no one answered. At last Gabrielle said, "I'll check with Scott and see if we have any spares. We should try to find a cheap one, though."

Owen cautioned, "We can't tell anyone else. It must look real, and everyone has to believe in it, that's the only way to do this."

"I've had a feeling someone is sending out details about us," Gabrielle said. "If I collect all the phones before the test—to remove the batteries so they don't explode—I can check the call logs. I might discover who's making calls they shouldn't."

"You really are suspicious, aren't you," Lewis said. "Alright, let's do it."

"Amaze balls," said Carys.

"Do you think we set it up in time?" asked Niland.

"Totes. Let's start now. Come on," Gabrielle said. "We can do it."

~~~

Scott was intrigued when Gabrielle explained their project. "So you're planning to use all of Mark's EMP components? I'd better replace them before he discovers they're missing. I've got some cheap pay-as-you-go phones; I'll give you one of those. Be careful. Don't blow up all our cell phones or you'll be very unpopular."

Gabrielle thought for a moment. "I think we should tell Mark. I'll collect all the phones and I'll be responsible for taking out the batteries."

"A good idea," Mark said. He'd entered the security room while Gabrielle was describing the project. "I think your popularity would take a major hit if you destroyed thousands of dollars'—or pounds—worth of phones. Set up your test, let us know when you plan to run it, and I'll make sure everyone hands over their phones. Oh, and you owe me for the EMP equipment."

***

Chapter 34

Mark arranged a meeting with Anna, Reb, Scott, and Sera to review their status; he had also asked Thomas and Laura to join in the discussion. They were all seated in the larger sitting room.

"Review time," Mark said. "Stop me if you want to add anything. I prefer to not expose strangers to our problems, so I've given the two gardeners a week off. They're happy with an unexpected paid vacation. The Carrolls are staying with family in the village so we'll have limited housekeeping support for the next week. Once the threat of attack has gone, they can all return, and their lives and ours will return to normal. Well, ours as close to normal as we can manage."

"I'm sure we can cope," Scott said. "And the gardens won't deteriorate in a week."

Mark nodded and said, "Cerberus UK. It's clear the rebel component is being influenced by the Chairman. Their motives are both power and money-based. They want all the offshore funds, from both the US and UK operations and total control of Cerberus UK. I don't see any way to change their attitudes without handing over control of the bank accounts, which I'm not doing. The Chairman's more difficult to read. I think he sees me as a threat, which is a reasonable conclusion for him to reach. I don't think he's aware the Chinese have withdrawn from genetic engineering research and any plan he has to sell specimens to them is now non-viable. I assume, even if he did know, he wouldn't change his mind. So we're going to be attacked. The two unknowns we have to deal with are when and how. Any thoughts?"

Scott said, "I think your assessment of the Chairman is on the money. Have you considered taking him out? A small team would do it."

"If we knew his location, I might entertain the thought. But we can't find him. Maeve's analysts have been trying to track him after the police released him; she says Goodwin somehow arranged that. He's dropped out of sight and he's good at hiding. The Brits now have warrants out for his re-arrest. The US authorities have arranged Interpol warrants and the Brits will also exercise those if they can. Assuming the local Cerberus people don't derail the process."

"What about the DI and her associates? Do you think it's possible to neutralize them?" asked Anna.

"We're lacking a solid law enforcement backing," Scott said. "I've been in contact with the FBI team at our embassy in London and they think taking independent action in this country will be regarded harshly. The Brits don't like private groups, foreign ones, ignoring their laws. We can defend ourselves without breaking the law, though."

"So we wait until these Cerberus…rebels arrive and attack the property before we can do anything?" Anna asked.

"We've enough people to protect ourselves, at least for now," Scott said. He turned to the two young Cerberus soldiers and asked, "How much longer will you and your team stay with us?"

Thomas and Laura exchanged looks. Thomas said, "We might be able to persuade Colonel Hudson to extend our leave."

Laura said, "Or she can replace us with another group."

"We'd have to talk to her," Thomas said.

"Okay. Do that and let me know what she can arrange."

"Yes, sir," replied Thomas.

"Sir?" Laura asked.

"Yes?"

"What if we withdrew early? I mean, we must assume the Chairman or these Cerberus people are monitoring the property and know we're here. If we left—"

"He'd use the opportunity to attack?"

"Yes, sir."

"You'd be able to leave and return without the Chairman or his watchers knowing?"

"If our CO agrees, we'll arrange for some of our company to arrive and pretend to cart us away. We'll stay behind and hide on the property. They'd never know we were here," Laura said.

"Interesting. Let's try it. Discuss your suggestion with your CO and see what she thinks. If necessary, I'll speak with her, too."

"So we're faced with sitting here, waiting for an attack. We don't know when it will happen and we don't know how many people will be involved," Reb said, picking at her index fingernail.

"Maeve is trying to convince local British authorities to help. She's encountering problems because there are some Cerberus people in senior law enforcement positions, well above DI Goodwin, and we don't know how many support the rebels. She said she'll try to set up a phone call from the White House to Downing Street, which will mean additional Cerberus exposure. I don't know how much is known at those higher levels. It's got the potential to get messy."

"So we'll all be arrested by MI5," Scott said.

"At least. Or arrested and deported. In some ways I want this attack to happen, so we can sort out Cerberus once and for all," Mark said.

"We'll make sure our fortress is secure," Scott said. "Don't forget, we're testing the cell phone battery destruction this afternoon. As a precaution, Gabrielle will collect all cell phones and take responsibility for removing the batteries. The test is scheduled for two-thirty. Thomas, I know you're planning a sweep across the woods at the rear of the property with your team at one-thirty. Make sure you hand over your phones before Gabrielle runs her test. Failure to do so will be painful."

~~~

Maeve reviewed her notes on Wentworth, the FBI EAD for National Security. She was certain he'd had some manner of involvement with Mercante and perhaps was responsible for the most recent attack on Schmidt. It was a pity that she'd killed the hospital intruder instead of knocking him unconscious. Similarly, because her team had killed Reverend Barker, she had no answers to a number of other questions. She was confident Barker had arranged for the attack at the hospital, although she didn't have a link yet between him and Wentworth. There must be a trail; Barker wouldn't act on his own, without payment of some kind.

"Harry, will you find Linda for me?" Maeve said to her assistant. "Ask her to meet me in my office as soon as she can. Topic is offshore banks and Reverend Barker."

"Yes, ma'am."

Within minutes there was a knock on her door and Linda Schöner entered with two of her analysts. Maeve joined them at the small round conference table in the corner of her office.

"This is a top priority task," Maeve said. "I want to know if we can find a financial link between Wentworth and Barker. Let's assume Barker received a fee for sending the killer after Schmidt, possibly paid to the same offshore account used for the payments from Mercante. We know the bank, it's Bermudan, and we have the account details. Try your Treasury contacts. These acticities fit within the scope of the Office of Foreign Assets Control so they should be interested. OFAC has been helpful in the past. Schmidt has friends there; check his contact list. If you can't get anywhere with Treasury, do some other research—*how* is your decision. I don't need to know but I'll protect you, understand?" She knew one of the analysts at the table was an exceptional hacker who explored offshore bank computers with ease.

Linda nodded her head. "Yes, ma'am. We've already contacted OFAC and they were helpful. Marion, you have the details."

Maeve said, "Anticipating me, again."

Marion said, "I visited the OFAC people earlier today. I've friends there and I checked with Schmidt's contacts. They've issued an informal request to the Bermudan bank and expect to have a copy of all Barker's transactions for the last twelve months by first thing tomorrow morning. Unofficially, of course. The Bermuda Monetary Authority would be upset if they were aware of our communications. But the bank knows Barker is dead and they know he's been engaged in terrorist activities, so they seem happy to help."

Maeve said, "I hope we get the material I need." She looked at the other team member. "Well Perez, have you had a look?"

He looked startled. "I'd never—"

Maeve frowned.

Perez continued, "Yes, ma'am. I found three accounts and I have an electronic copy of each. But I'd prefer for us to wait for details from the bank, tomorrow. And to answer your next question, yes, we'll have the information and links you're looking for. Probability is greater than 95 percent."

Maeve sat back in her chair. "Ah, good news. Excellent, well done, all of you. Meet with me in the morning when you have the official materials from OFAC and we'll figure out our next steps."

***

Chapter 35

The next morning Mark watched as three truckloads of young Cerberus soldiers arrived from their base to reclaim their missing fellows. Colonel Hudson had readily agreed to the idea proposed by Laura to seemingly remove the team of soldiers and leave the house and grounds defenseless. Scott had earlier detected a small drone overhead, presumably monitoring the property. After a quick conference, Mark had decided not to destroy the drone until later in the day, so that it would first relay their morning activities.

The soldiers all milled around, creating enough confusion to hide what was happening in the apparent transfer of the twenty Cerberus soldiers. Finally, four trucks, including the vehicle the soldiers had first arrived in, roared off, to all appearances leaving no one behind. But both cottages were full of young people who would not move outside until nightfall. Gabrielle and Niland waved enthusiastically as the departing trucks rolled past the front of the house and the soldiers in the trucks all waved back.

Mark checked in with Scott, who was busy in the security room, while Sera helped monitor their cameras. "There's nothing in sight," Sera said when Mark asked if anything was happening. "All I've seen is one or two crows and a fox. Yesterday it was two foxes. The second one must be hiding somewhere."

"I don't suppose our friends have enlisted the foxes," joked Scott. "Although GoPro's probably designed a harness for one."

Mark shook his head in exaggerated disbelief and went to find Anna. She was with Reb, sitting in the atrium. Both were enjoying the warmth of the springtime sun. He sat next to Anna and said, "I think this is the lull before the storm. My guess is they'll attack us tonight, after midnight."

Reb looked concerned. "I've had a similar premonition; it's given me a headache." She reached for Anna's hand. "It's why Anna's keeping me company." A worried expression disturbed her face. "It's okay, isn't it? For Anna to sit here with me?"

"Of course it is," Mark said. "Both of you relax, take it easy."

"Oh, good. I thought you might want her or something."

Mark stood and patted his sister's shoulder, careful to choose the one that wasn't injured. "Don't be silly. As I said, relax. If you hear some shooting, don't worry. Scott's going to take down that drone later this afternoon."

"They saw the soldiers leave?" asked Anna.

"Yeah, the little subterfuge seemed to work. One of the trucks was behind the second cottage, out of direct view of the drone. There were enough soldiers milling around to confuse *me*, so hopefully the watchers fell for it. Our five little inventors are building their cell phone exploding devices and they plan to install them this evening. Remember, when the devices are switched on, their range will include the house. You'll need to give your phones to Gabrielle. She's in charge of battery removal to make sure you don't get burnt."

~~~

The children were all ecstatic. Their fake test had worked perfectly; the cheap cell phone had exploded into smoke and flames within seconds of its exposure. Gabrielle had collected everyone's cell phones and removed the batteries before running the test and Lewis had done an excellent job with the explosion.

Now the five young people were working in almost complete silence, building the equipment they said was needed to install and run their processes. Mark entered the boys' room and watched while the children worked. Occasionally there would be a muttered curse, or one of the teenagers would say something indecipherable in a soft accent. Gabrielle looked up the second time Lewis said something that sounded odd.

"It's okay, Mark. They're not being rude. But I am learning some interesting new words. Not as many as I learned from the soldiers, though."

When Mark started to protest, Gabrielle laughed. "Don't worry, I won't use them on social occasions."

"Thank you. So how's progress?"

"We'll be finished by six o'clock or so," replied Niland. "The code is functional, we've installed all the motherboards, and we're working on the carrier software you developed to make it work faster. These are the best coders I've ever met."

They all laughed at the seriousness of Niland's statement. Gabrielle said, "So you've worked with lots of coders, have you?"

"Yes—no. I meant I'm the fastest person I know and Lewis and Owen are as fast and Carys is way faster."

"I'm glad you clarified," Mark said. "Otherwise we'd still be confused." Niland looked up, apparently uncertain whether or not Mark was teasing him.

"I see," he said and dipped his head to refocus on his task. "I'm busy. Go away."

~~~

Maeve studied the account statement her team had received from OFAC. She said to Linda Schöner, "It seems straightforward. We can tie Wentworth to this account. The FBI is developing bad habits; their account's clearly being used for black funds. Wentworth's the only one with signing authority. The remittance goes out on this date and shows up here in Barker's offshore account three days later, the same amount less the transfer fee. Did you get a copy of the transfer instructions?"

"Yes, it's underneath the bank statements, there."

"Okay, the transfer form shows both accounts. The signature—any thoughts?"

"We analyzed the handwriting and there's 90 percent probability it's Wentworth's signature. It's not in his real name of course. I think it looks like McCarr."

"The name Mercante was traveling under—another link to our CIA friend. Unless you or your team have reservations, I think it's a wrap."

"We all agree. Legal said it's enough to get search warrants. There are other payments we can investigate, all with the same signature, that might also be enlightening. We obtained copies of the transfer instructions for each."

"Well, we'll be able to take him out of the FBI picture. I'm not sure yet whether he's a candidate for Gitmo. Do you know anyone we can recommend for a promotion? A Cerberus person, of course."

For a moment Linda looked surprised, then a slow smile appeared. "I'm sure we can find one or two strong candidates."

As she tidied the papers that contained evidence marking the end of Wentworth's career, Maeve said, "Not that we would influence the appointment, of course."

Linda's smile grew. "Of course."

~~~

The exodus started after lunch. Scott drew Mark's attention to the monitors displaying feeds from around the property. "Look, the soldiers were supposed to stay hidden until nightfall but they seem to be packing up to leave. There are no vehicles available for them. I don't know what's going on. Do you want me to go check?"

"No, you stay here. I need some fresh air."

Mark reached the nearer cottage as the young Cerberus team was preparing to depart. Each soldier carried a small backpack. They stood to attention when they saw Mark.

He looked for Thomas and Laura but they were not in the group. "What's happening?" he asked the closest soldier. The young man looked embarrassed and stared at the ground.

Another soldier spoke up. "Sir, our CO has been kidnapped by the Chairman, at least we think it's him. The message we got from our base is to stand down or she'll be killed."

So the morning's subterfuge had failed, or else the Chairman was not taking chances.

"Where are Thomas and Laura?"

Another voice muttered, "Go on, tell the man."

"They're restrained, sir. We had to tie them up because they wouldn't agree to stand down. We haven't harmed them, truly. Well, Thomas has a black eye, that's all."

"We'll take them with us," said another voice.

Mark asked, "What about transport out of here?"

"A truck's due to arrive at the front entry in about fifteen minutes. We have to be there to meet it. We're sorry, sir, but our CO looks after us and we need to look after her."

"I understand. Contact the authorities. You can't try to rescue your CO by yourselves."

"Yes, sir. Thank you. We've spoken with our captain. He's contacted army MPs and the local bobbies. We're all hoping she'll be released, you know, unharmed."

"So do I. Okay, if you have to meet with your transport, you'd better hurry. If I can speak to Thomas...?"

"Yes, sir. He's not hurt, really."

Mark walked toward the cottage as Thomas and Laura were pushed through the doorway. Their hands were tied behind their backs. Thomas had the beginning of a black eye. By tomorrow it would be a real shiner, Mark thought.

"Thomas, Laura, I'm sorry for getting you into this predicament." He turned to the other soldiers. "Come on, untie them. You don't need to sink to the level of the Chairman."

Two soldiers rushed to remove the ropes. Thomas shook his arms to remove the stress of being tied-up. "It's alright, sir. Our CO is a real hero to us, as you can tell. I saw our duty differently and we had a slight...argument."

"Thank you, sir," Laura said. "I'm sorry we can't stay to help." She was close to tears.

One of the other soldiers spoke up. "Come on, the truck will be waiting for us. It'll leave if we're too late. Sorry, sir."

"No, carry on. I would have preferred to have your support here, but understand why you need to go. When you see the colonel, please give her my best wishes."

The young soldiers had started heading along the lane toward the front of the manor house. Mark watched them depart. Some of the soldiers turned and waved a half salute. Well, he thought, that was interesting; the Chairman had his share of cunning. He headed back to the house to discuss their situation with Scott.

"More news," Scott said, when Mark entered the security room.

"Good or bad?"

"Mixed. Sera decided she only signed on to be a mother—on paper—for the two kids. In her words, her assignment doesn't include getting shot in some kind of war. She's decided to leave."

Mark was silent for a minute. "Okay. Well, she's correct, the scope of her assignment was to act as a mother. Do we need to drive her anywhere?"

"She's arranged a taxi from the village, for four o'clock. I think she plans on catching a flight out of Gatwick."

"What about you?"

"Me?" Scott laughed. "I'm in for the duration. Life's far too interesting around you to miss out."

"Thanks. And I hear you. I think I'm a magnet for trouble. I'll update Anna and Reb, and talk to the children, so they all know what's happening. You should shoot down the drone. Get rid of it now while you have time."

~~~

Maeve and two of her Cerberus agents met with Wentworth at the FBI offices at Quantico. Maeve had set the agenda, proposing a discussion of the attack on Midway's New Hampshire property, to decide whether there were additional domestic terrorism aspects for the FBI to consider. The EAD welcomed her into a small meeting room containing an oval table and six chairs. A coffee flask and cups were on a sideboard and bottles of water were on the table. A small sign instructed attendees to clear the table when they finished their meeting. Maeve sat and waited as Wentworth selected the chair at the end of the table.

"Welcome, Maeve," Wentworth said.

"Thank you for seeing us, I know you're a busy man." She nodded to one of her team. "We have a number of documents we'd like you to review."

The Cerberus agent handed a folder to the EAD and passed similar folders to Maeve and her fellow agent.

Wentworth opened the folder. The first document was a copy of the bank statement from which funds had been transferred to Barker's account. His face paled though he remained silent.

Maeve said, "We uncovered several documents during our investigation. This first statement represents an FBI black ops account. The second document is a transfer instruction and attached to it is a handwriting analysis by…well, you can see we used FBI experts for the task. The third document is a bank statement reflecting the deposit of funds transferred from the black ops account. This account is linked to the late Reverend Barker. The final documents include a transfer receipt and a bank statement belonging to the person I shot in Schmidt's hospital room, who, we believe, was there to kill Schmidt. Thoughts?"

"Bitch—"

"I meant thoughts regarding the documents."

Wentworth closed the folder and sat back in his chair. "I'll claim these are all forgeries."

"That would be easy to disprove. We're waiting for the National Security Advisor to communicate the President's decision. I'm in favor of prosecuting you. We shipped Mercante off to Gitmo. As an alternative to the publicity a prosecution will attract, you might like to join him there?"

Wentworth opened the folder again and mindlessly flipped through the documents. "If I don't fight this—what can I expect?"

"With full disclosure, of everything you and Mercante were involved in? Including anything else you've been doing, within the FBI?

"Yes."

"Minimum of ten years, in a high security federal prison."

"Very well. You want my resignation, now?"

"Yes. Hand your Bureau ID card to my agents. You won't have an opportunity to return to your office. It's under seal and a team of agents is conducting a thorough search."

***

Chapter 36

Mark found Reb in the atrium; it seemed to be her favorite place. Her greeting was hesitant, which disturbed him. "What's on your mind?" he asked.

"I don't know what to tell you, after hearing about the others leaving you."

"You've started, so you should finish."

Reb spoke in a rush. "You know I've remained in contact with the marine employment agency. They have a position for me. It's a good one. The yacht's based in the Med. It's owned by a champion tennis player. They want me to sign the contract today and fax it back. If I take the job, I'll have to travel to Monaco on Sunday."

"Why are you hesitant, if it's what you want?"

Reb picked at her index fingernail. "It means leaving you and Anna and my friends."

"We all knew you were heading back to a job at sea some time."

"I know. It's…it's just, well, so many are leaving you. But I don't need to go until Sunday."

"Reb, you do what you need to do. No one is going to think less of you." Mark hugged his sister. "Now I need to find Anna."

"She's in the garden, I think."

Anna was in a small greenhouse adjacent to a large vegetable garden, examining the potted plants which the gardeners intended to plant out when the weather warmed.

"Are you taking up gardening?" Mark asked.

Anna looked up and smiled. She reached for his hand. "No, I'm really curious. Gardens and plants haven't been part of my life until now. I think I could enjoy them in future, though."

Mark outlined the events of the last hour with all the departures. "It's an unexpected exodus but I can't fault any of them."

Anna gripped his hand. "What about Scott?"

"He said there's no way he's leaving, he's having too much fun. Or words to that effect. What about you?"

"Me? I'm not leaving you."

"Maybe you should. Temporarily, anyway. I want you to take the children away tonight. It's about two miles to the village. Our map of the grounds shows a footpath through the woods at the back of the property. If you leave after dark, you'd be okay. Then, when the DI and the Chairman raid us, you'll all be safe."

She stepped in closer and hugged him. "I said I'm not going to leave you. I'll arrange for Scott to take the children; he's supposed to be their father, after all. Assuming you can convince them to leave. They're determined to help you take down these people."

"I know. I think they have all their equipment ready to install once it gets dark. It'll be interesting to see what happens when people bring their cell phones within range of the field."

"From what I saw of Gabrielle's test, a battery caught in their system could cause severe injuries, whether it explodes or catches on fire."

Mark said, "That's their intention. They're a bloodthirsty lot, the five of them. Come on, we should talk to Reb and

Scott. Maybe you and Reb...we'll talk about whether or not you should take the children away from here."

They collected Reb on the way to the security room. When Mark made his suggestion, Scott nodded his understanding. Reb looked doubtful but didn't speak.

Mark asked, "Why the face, Reb?"

"I don't think the children will want to leave you. There'd only be you and Scott left to defend yourselves. The house is too big for two people."

"It might be easier, in some ways. If we moved after dark into one of the cottages, the Chairman won't know where we are. We'd be able to engage in a guerrilla action."

"I don't know. I'd never forgive myself if anything happened to either of you."

"My decision. Scott, I think we should do this. Anna and Reb will take the children out of here after dark. After they've set up their equipment, of course. The children will have to accept my decision. Once they've all left, we can consider moving to the far cottage."

~~~

Sera's departure was a subdued event. The taxi arrived just before four o'clock and she rushed her farewells to the small group seeing her off.

"I'm sorry I have to go, but I didn't think we'd be involved in some kind of deadly fight. I'll be back in Boston, if you ever—"

"We understand," Scott said. "Have a safe flight."

Gabrielle and Niland were nowhere to be seen. Anna and Reb waved their goodbyes.

As the taxi drove away, Scott said, "It's for the better." As he turned to re-enter the house, Gabrielle and Niland rushed up. "Has she gone?" asked Niland.

Scott indicated the taxi as it flashed its brake lights at the turn of the lane leading to the main road. "Yes, she's on her way."

"Good," Gabrielle said. Despite inquiring expressions from Reb and Anna, she remained silent. Niland did not comment. They made their way inside and prepared for the evening.

~~~

Mark called a meeting after Sera's departure. He announced he wanted Reb and Anna to take the children to Tunbridge Wells, which seemed to be the closest town where they could find a hotel, although London was only about thirty miles away. Scott would stay behind to assist Mark. Anna reluctantly agreed to accompany Reb. To Anna and Mark's surprise, there were only token objections from the five children. Mark was suspicious at their willingness to leave but was unable to pin down a reason for his unease.

The plan was simple. An hour after sunset, Anna and Reb would lead the children along the path at the back of the property and onto a more frequented footpath to the nearby village. Once there, they would find taxis. Of course, the weather was closing in with another early spring storm that promised to dampen everyone.

~~~

Fifteen minutes after departing the manor house, Gabrielle, who was in the lead, suddenly stopped, bringing the procession to a halt. The rain was starting to make its presence known, and the narrow footpath, where it moved away from the partial shelter of trees, was accumulating small mud puddles. Gabrielle turned to Anna. They could only just see each other, in the dark.

"I'm not leaving Mark and Scott to defend the house."

"We can't go back. We'll be in danger and we'll put the men in danger, too." By this time the others had crowded around Anna and Gabrielle.

"We prepared for this," Lewis said. "We borrowed two of the tents from the army and set them up in the trees near the entrance to the property. They're camouflaged, so no one will see them. We borrowed some sleeping bags, too."

"And we searched the barns and found three shotguns and about sixty shells," added Owen.

"Okay," Anna said. "You'd better explain all this."

"You've got some devious plan in mind," Reb added. "Where are the shotguns?"

"We hid them near the tents. When the attackers arrive, they'll probably leave people guarding their vehicles," Gabrielle said. "We've made sure no one will be using their cell phones, at least when they're near the house. So we can ambush the vehicle guards and the Chairman won't know, 'cause he'll have the battery out of his cell phone and so will anyone with him."

The way Gabrielle mentioned cell phones caught Anna's attention. "Explain about the phones," she directed. She felt almost tangible exchanges between the five children. There was a long moment of silence, and at last Gabrielle nodded.

Owen said, "We rigged the cell phone test. The whole thing is a dummy."

"What—" Reb said.

"We all thought someone was leaking information to the Chairman, so we set a trap," Gabrielle said. "That's why I had everyone hand over their cell phones and pretend I would make sure the batteries were removed. We found the informant when I checked all the call logs."

"An informant?"

"Yeah, it was Sera. Her phone showed calls to UK numbers on a regular basis. She was reporting, at least daily. We traced the numbers. One was to DI Goodwin. We think the other one belongs to the Chairman," Lewis said.

"Does Mark know?"

"Noooo. We planned to let him know in the next half hour. We wanted to make sure the Chairman didn't find out," Gabrielle said. "It was obvious when the subterfuge with the soldiers didn't work—that either the Chairman was taking out insurance by kidnapping Colonel Hudson or someone was reporting to him."

Anna could not hide her shock. "I don't know what to say. You're far more devious than I realized."

Reb said, "Lewis, you should know better—"

"Reb, it was our idea," Niland said, protecting the teenagers. "We persuaded Lewis to assist us. I think we've done the right thing. We've reduced the pressure on Mark and Scott so now they only have to worry about themselves. We found out who the informant was and tricked her into leaking incorrect information. The DI and the Chairman are under the impression their cell phones'll explode if they bring them close to the house, so they'll remove the batteries. They may have radios, but we think it's unlikely, because radios are not secure. Okay, we didn't tell anyone, but it was necessary, to identify the informant." A chorus of agreement from Lewis, Owen, and Carys supported Niland.

"Hmm. I'm not entirely convinced," Anna said. "Remember, if Sera was giving them information, the Chairman may know we're leaving, too."

"Sera left before we decided to leave," Gabrielle said. "I suppose he might have his people watching the house from the main road."

"Okay. Tell us the rest of your plans."

Lewis replied, "We ambush the drivers. They won't protest too much when we threaten them with shotguns. We'll take any weapons they have and immobilize their vehicles. We hid the keys of the cars in the garage and removed the batteries so they can't be used. We'll follow the DI and the Chairman to the house and attack them from the rear. A few shotgun blasts will startle and distract them.

Also, I think we should alert the local police, and get them here."

Anna said to Reb. "What do you think? Should we go along with this crazy plan?"

"It might help Mark and Scott, even though it has some risks. My only reservation is that Mark would be more than upset if the children were injured."

"And we'd be upset if anything happened to Mark and Scott," Gabrielle said. "Mark's our hero and Scott's our remaining parent. He cares for us and we really like him."

Anna said, "Okay. I'm getting soaked standing here in the rain. Let's do it." She turned to Gabrielle. "I hope you can lead us to your tents without getting lost or alerting these people, if they decide to attack tonight?"

"Follow me," instructed Lewis.

***

Chapter 37

Mark and Scott sat in the security room watching the cameras covering the grounds around the house. It was just the two of them and Mark thought the house seemed inordinately lonely. He hoped sending Reb and Anna away with the children would keep them safe. Gabrielle had ceremoniously switched on their cell phone destruction system, which was powered through the garden's lighting system.

Scott said, "Why don't you make yourself a meal, and when you take over from me, I'll do the same?"

Mark wandered off to the kitchen. All the doors and windows were locked. The doors had additional bars that prevented anyone opening them from outside, while the windows, at least at the ground-floor level, were set into stone and were protected by iron bars. Mark thought it would require considerable force for anyone to gain entrance.

He made a sandwich of thick slices of roast beef on a crusty roll, smothering the meat with a horseradish sauce that made his eyes water. He carried the sandwich and a mug of coffee back to the security room. Scott left to make his own sandwich. He returned minutes later, anxious to see if there were any prowlers on the grounds, acknowledging to Mark he also thought the monitoring process was boring.

The buzzing of Mark's cell phone alerted him to the arrival of a text as well as reminding him he'd forgotten to remove the battery. He set his sandwich and drink to one side while he read the text. He burst out laughing.

"Glad you can see the funny side of all this," Scott said.

Mark spluttered. "I'm glad I didn't have a mouthful of roast beef when I read this. The children rigged their battery explosion test; it was all staged. The damn batteries won't explode. It was a trap they set because they were convinced we had a spy. They claim Sera was making regular calls to the DI and to another number that they think belongs to the Chairman."

"What do those Welsh kids say—amaze balls?" Scott shook his head in disbelief.

"They enlisted the help of Lewis and his two siblings. Lewis got his hands on some gunpowder from a shotgun shell and set off a small explosion electronically, to make it seem the phone battery exploded when they turned on the system. They're convinced the DI and the Chairman will believe they can't use their cell phones, which cuts down their ability to communicate. So, we can also assume it was Sera who advised the DI about our little subterfuge with the soldiers."

"I think that's probably also who turned off the fuel line to the standby generator. I checked it late this afternoon and wondered. I turned it back on."

"Glad you caught it. I hadn't thought to check," Mark said, reaching for his sandwich. "Let's hope Reb and Anna can keep the kids safe."

"Maybe it's the other way around. The kids will keep Reb and Anna safe."

Mark finished his sandwich and stretched out on a bunk in the security room. He forced himself to relax. It was ten p.m. and he was scheduled to relieve Scott at midnight. They had decided not to move to the cottage after Scott realized there were numerous external lights triggered by motion detectors and they wanted those lights to activate only if someone entered the grounds. They both expected action sometime before dawn, if it was going to happen at all. Scott had his feet up on the bench in front of the monitors and was munching another sandwich. Mark dozed off.

Mark woke from his restless sleep a little before midnight. He felt cramped and in need of another two or three hours of proper rest. He yawned and rubbed his eyes. Scott was wide-awake, eating yet another sandwich. Mark checked the video display; nothing unusual to see.

"It's far too quiet out there. I haven't even seen the foxes."

"Hmm. They might have been frightened off."

~~~

It was Anna's turn to listen for approaching vehicles. The children had arranged the two tents so that they formed a single shelter. They built a flap system that provided a small space for two people to sit, protected from the rain yet still able to watch the lane leading to the property. An hour before, Reb had rolled herself up in a sleeping bag behind the flap that accessed the larger area and seemed to drop off to sleep without delay. The children were each on an hourly watch, and it was Niland's turn to join Anna. Lewis sat with both of them for a minute before heading off to his sleeping bag.

"It's gone quiet out there," Anna said, in almost a whisper.

"I'm still asleep, I think. Is it really one a.m.?" Niland asked.

"Shh. I think there are vehicles approaching."

The engine sounds were barely audible. Anna thought she could see three black shapes in the darkness, their lights off, making their way slowly toward the entry ramp onto the property. Each vehicle rumbled across the ramp and turned into the space where the soldiers had parked their army truck. The occupants had forgotten to turn off their internal lights and she counted six passengers and three drivers in the seconds before the doors were closed. After a few minutes a number of their visitors set off down the lane leading to the manor house. Anna thought they were carrying weapons. Wind gusts blew streaks of rain across the lane, obscuring details.

"Wake up Reb. Quietly," Anna instructed Niland. "Then all the children. Tell Gabrielle I want to talk to her. No noise."

She continued to watch as two drivers got out of their vehicles and joined the driver in the third vehicle. The interior lights momentarily displayed the men as the two got into the back seat. She could not determine whether they were armed or not.

Reb lifted the flap and sat down beside Anna. "What's happening?"

Anna indicated the vehicles. "Three men in the one on the left. Six people headed to the house. When Gabrielle joins us, we'll see if we can use her abilities to hide us while we take out the drivers."

"Good." Reb yawned. "Not enough sleep. I'm losing my touch. On board a yacht, the watch change should be immediate."

"You only had an hour," Anna said. Gabrielle lifted the tent flap and looked inquiringly at Anna. She rubbed sleep from her eyes.

"Gabrielle, we have visitors. Can you, or both you and Niland, hide Reb, Lewis, and me as we approach the car, the one on the left? I've counted three men, all drivers. I don't think anyone else is there. Some people have headed to the house. We'll follow them once we've dealt with these guys."

Gabrielle rubbed the sleep out of her eyes. Niland stood beside her; he had nodded when Anna requested his support for Gabrielle. The three teens had also crowded into the small area.

"Yes, Anna, we can help you," Gabrielle said, in the middle of a yawn.

"Good. Lewis, get the three shotguns—one for me, one for Reb, and you can take the third. A handful of shells each, too, I think. Carys, you take the remaining shells and bring them with you when we head to the house. Owen, follow us with those ropes so we can tie up the drivers. I want the three of us with shotguns, to approach the vehicle. Gabrielle and Niland, you hide us. When we reach the car, Reb and Lewis, open the doors and aim your shotgun at the person nearest you. Lewis, you take the driver-side door. Reb, you and I will take each of the rear doors. We need to make sure we don't target each other. Okay?"

Reb said, "As long as I can also use my knives."

"If you have to. Now come on."

The small group cautiously approached the vehicle with Anna moving to the far side, leaving Reb and Lewis to approach the near side. Five seconds after they reached the vehicle, the three gun-bearers each opened a door and pushed a shotgun into the face of the nearest person.

"Sit still, the three of you," commanded Anna, her shotgun barrel only inches from the face of the driver. "Only move when I tell you. Otherwise, don't even twitch. You"— she indicated the driver—"get out. I don't advise sudden movements, understand? Close the door. Now stand with your legs apart and place both hands on the top of the vehicle. Lewis, if he moves, shoot him. Gabrielle, search him for weapons. You two, sit still. If anyone tries to reach for a weapon, I'll shoot you. Okay?"

Gabrielle withdrew a pistol from the driver's jacket and threw it toward the hidden tent to be collected later. Anna asked the driver, "Do you have anything else?"

"N-no, I haven't."

As the driver replied, Gabrielle had her hand on his wrist. She said, "He's lying. He has a knife strapped to his left ankle and something called a knuckle-duster in his pants pocket."

Reb said, "A knife fighter, huh? Can I take him? Please?"

"Not now. Maybe later. Gabrielle, step back. Lewis, keep your shotgun aimed at the middle of his back. At three feet, the shot will almost break him in two; he'll never walk again, if he lives. You, driver, reach down and remove your knife, very slowly. Drop it on the ground behind you. Take out your knuckle-duster and do the same thing. Then put your hands behind your back. Owen, tie his hands. We'll finish securing him when we deal with the other two." Anna repeated the process for each of the drivers. Gabrielle collected a total of three pistols and five knives, plus a couple of knuckle-dusters. Anna told the men to lie face down, next to each other. She watched as Reb tied them more tightly.

"I always thought knowing how to tie knots would come in handy," Reb commented. She looked at the three men. "If any of you try to get out of the ropes, you'll choke your companions. If you all lie still, you'll live. I know, it's raining and cold. You should've thought about that, earlier."

Anna gathered up all car keys and instructed Lewis to hide them in the woods. He returned after a few minutes.

"Done," he said with a grin.

"You can make your 999 call now, Gabrielle. Tell them there's been a shooting here at Bankton House and people are either dead or seriously wounded." They waited while Gabrielle made the call, then Anna continued, "I guess it'll take about fifteen minutes for the police and ambulances to reach here. It should give us enough time. Lewis, take control of the drivers' cell phones."

Lewis pocketed the phones while Reb gathered up the firearms the drivers had surrendered, albeit unwillingly. She gave a pistol each to Carys and Owen and kept the third one for herself. A quick search of the vehicles had not revealed any more weapons.

"Okay," Anna said. "Let's head to the house and rescue Mark and Scott. Gabrielle, I want you and Niland to hide us again when we're close. Carys can help if she's strong enough"

~~~

Mark said, "Looks like we've got movement on camera five." He switched the video to the main monitor, which displayed infrared figures in the upper right quadrant of the screen. He counted six dark images against a white backdrop, moving down the lane toward the house.

"Too big for foxes. Unless they have two-legged deer in England, I think we have people visiting."

The group halted. There was some activity but the images were too indistinct for Mark and Scott to determine what was happening. Suddenly the overhead lights in the security room dimmed, almost extinguishing. The security system operated with standby batteries until the backup generator kicked in. Mark counted down the seconds. When he reached thirty, the lights returned to normal. "I didn't really expect them to cut our power. Our backups work. Thirty seconds to switch over is very good. I'm glad you checked the fuel line."

"So am I." Scott laughed. "Look, they started forward when the power went off and now they've stopped. They know the backup system's working. I hope Sera didn't sabotage anything else."

"So do I."

***

Chapter 38

Two people approached the front of the manor house—one carrying what appeared to be a battering ram. They stopped a few feet away from the door. Mark switched the cameras from infrared to full color. He recognized DI Goodwin and thought the second person was Nelson Cobb, who had been in the Cerberus meeting that he had attended. The man carrying the heavy ram stood it on end and waited.

"Midway," announced the DI. "I know you have video cameras and assume you're monitoring our approach. I have a warrant, issued under the Terrorism Act, for your arrest. The warrant includes any and all associates present on these premises."

Mark reached for the microphone and pressed the button for the front door speaker. "Detective Inspector Goodwin. I understand you're a member of SO15, the Special Branch section," he said, "Do you mind raising your head so we can get a clearer image? We've been recording your actions from when you entered the property and would like to obtain a full facial image of each of you. We've offered direct video feeds to both the BBC and BSkyB. We're waiting on a response from the BBC; it's difficult to get management decisions from them after midnight. However, Sky is getting our feed as of now. CNN wants a live feed, which they'll broadcast in America. They're aware of some of my history. Now, you were saying?"

"Damn you, Midway," said the DI. Exasperation colored the timbre of her voice. "I have a warrant for your arrest. Open the door."

"Just a moment, DI. We're splicing in some of our videos of meetings between you and the Chairman. I believe your own police force and Interpol have warrants for the Chairman's arrest? He's here, with you, right?"

"Who? I've never heard of him," DI Goodwin said.

"Some of the videos we're streaming prove you're lying," Mark said. "You said something about a warrant for my arrest. Can you be more explicit? Perhaps identify the charges? Provide some details of the evidence?"

DI Goodwin ignored Mark's comments. "I don't believe you're streaming a video to anyone. Bill, get that door open, now."

"I think you know you won't get far; he'll only damage the woodwork. You need a SWAT team. Or a far more legitimate request to gain entry." He put his hand over the microphone and said to Scott. "Where are the other people? I think the DI's a diversion. Replay the tapes and try to find where they disappeared to, quickly."

Scott was juggling multiple feeds as well as replaying the tapes.

Mark said, "I'll look after the feeds. See if you can find the Chairman."

"Okay. I think this is it. They split up. Two went to the right and two to the left. I can't identify which is the Chairman, yet. They're heading to the sides or the rear of the house. Let me track them. Now that's strange—there are only three people at the rear of the house. Someone's disappeared."

The heavy and regular thump of the battering ram was beginning to penetrate the security room. Then, the noise eased.

"The guy with the sledge hammer must have knocked a hole in the door," Mark said. "Listen, I can hear sirens. This will make life interesting."

~~~

Anna led the way along the lane toward the house. She could hear voices on a loudspeaker but wasn't able to work out what they were saying. Reb said, "I think Mark's talking to Goodwin."

"Yeah, she's at the front door. Look, there are two of them."

It took less than a minute for the group to reach a position within ten feet of the two police officers; they had arrived undetected, hidden by the combined efforts of Gabrielle and Niland.

"Gabrielle, Niland, you can release your shield," Anna whispered to the children. She raised her voice and said, "Detective Inspector, I believe you're trespassing. Stop and surrender your weapons." She aimed the shotgun well above the heads of the officers and pulled the trigger. She pumped a new shell, ready to fire again.

The officers spun around. Goodwin pulled off her glove and reached for her handgun. Her companion had dropped his battering ram and was also reaching for his weapon.

Anna said, "Reb, you've got buckshot in your shotgun. Fire a round at each. Be careful to not aim at their faces."

"With delight," replied Reb. She fired each barrel. "It's the first time I've fired at police officers, though."

She broke the shotgun, ejected the empty shells and dropped two new shells into the twin barrels. "Okay, I'm ready for another burst."

Anna held her arm out, to prevent Reb from firing again. "Well done," she said.

"Years of shooting at sea. I never thought all my target practice would come in handy."

Her shots had hit both officers as they were about to raise their weapons. Their pistols were now on the ground. The buckshot had drawn blood.

"Goodwin, hands above your head. Both of you," instructed Anna. "Turn around. Remove your helmets and jackets. Get on the ground, face down. You know the process."

"You're in a world of trouble, young lady," spluttered Goodwin. Her companion remained silent. They both followed Anna's directions when she motioned with the shotgun. Reb pushed the handguns away and Owen picked them up.

Anna said, "I can hear sirens. The local police must be on their way. This will be difficult for you to explain, DI." She ignored the string of curses from Goodwin as she and Reb handcuffed the prisoners.

"Reb, See if you can get Mark or Scott to open the door."

Reb went to the door and it swung open at her touch. Anna said, "Lewis, you and Owen stand guard here. Take my shotgun. It's loaded with heavier shot. I think it'll be another five minutes or more before the police reach us. Gabrielle and Niland, please shield them when the police arrive; we don't want anyone getting shot at. Other than these two, at least. Come on, Reb. Let's see what's happening inside."

~~~

"Scott, there's movement near the kitchen. We might have missed an entry into the basement. Perhaps our friendly Chairman knows of some hidden access. Let the team in the front door and I'll go see if we have an intruder."

When Mark returned to the security room, he said, "Nothing there—"

He stopped short, halfway into the room. The Chairman was holding a pistol to Scott's head. Scott said, "I thought he was you, returning."

The Chairman said, "Shut up. Give me any trouble at all and your friend here is dead." He examined the monitor display of the front of the house. "What happened? Why are those two still outside?"

Scott shrugged. Mark said, "We captured them. I thought they'd be happier to remain outside."

The Chairman frowned. "I find that hard to believe but I see you've handcuffed them. Now, I want you both, very carefully, to move to the sitting room. The larger one. We can be more relaxed, there."

Mark edged out of the security room, followed by Scott and the Chairman. He raised his voice and asked, "Which sitting room?"

"Don't be a fool," replied the Chairman. "Just lead the way. Now, where are your guests?"

"We're here by ourselves," Scott said.

"We sent the others away. They should be in London by now."

"Don't try to play me for an idiot," the Chairman snarled.

Mark bit back his response. It might be prudent not to make the man lose his temper. The Chairman remained behind Scott, with Mark leading the way. He entered and stood in the middle of the room, waiting for instructions from their captor and for an opportunity to make a move.

The Chairman looked around. "Good, you haven't changed it. I've always liked this room." He chuckled at the surprise on Mark's face. "Who do you think purchased this property? I had to have somewhere decent to stay when I visited Cerberus UK."

"Chairman, or whatever you call yourself, I suggest you put down your weapon. Those sirens are coming closer. The police will take your friends into custody and you'll be next.

I believe there are a number of warrants out for your arrest, Interpol and British."

The Chairman laughed. "Oh. I don't think I'm in danger, here. I have you two subdued. I'll soon have your sister and the others. Three of my men will be in here in a minute. They'll take care of the ladies. Except Reb, of course. She's mine."

Mark ignored the latter comment. He had to keep his temper under control. "Perhaps we can watch TV while we wait? I think Sky has an interesting news program." He didn't wait for the Chairman's permission and reached for the remote, turned on the TV and selected BSkyB."

"Put down the damn remote—what the hell? What's going on? What are you doing?"

"The cameras follow us," Mark explained. "We're live streaming to a couple of news channels. I think they're running a major item on corporate and police corruption. Their audience probably increased after we captured DI Goodwin and her companion. Your face has just been seen by more than five million viewers, and that's at two a.m. When the day begins, you'll be all over the media."

"The hell, I will. You can add your death to the viewers' excitement." The Chairman was white-faced and appeared ready to explode with anger. But then he regained control. "This is a trick of some kind."

There were sounds of scuffles and shots fired from outside the sitting room. Mark said, "I think that's the end of your companions. Too bad. I wanted to meet them."

The scene displayed on the television screen suddenly shifted to a shot of three bodies, unmoving. Mark recognized it as a scene from the kitchen. To his relief, the bodies were all male, total strangers. He indicated the new scene. "They're your men, I assume? They're unlikely to help you, now."

The Chairman made a sound like a wounded animal at bay. He shouted, "Reb, come here or I'll kill Midway, your so-called brother. You and I have unfinished business." In his anger, he fired a shot from his pistol.

~~~

Scott watched in dismay as Mark crumpled to the floor. The scene on TV switched back to the sitting room and showed Mark on the floor and the Chairman with his pistol still aimed at his victim. A few moments later Reb appeared in the doorway.

"You wanted to see me?" she asked in a quiet voice.

"Yes, you bitch. Come here," the Chairman shouted. He caught sight of Anna standing behind Reb. "And you, too." He waved his weapon.

Reb stepped into the room, her hands down by her sides.

Anna asked, "Why should I do as you say?"

"Because if you don't, I'll finish off your little boyfriend." He pointed his pistol at Mark.

Reb threw two knives with utmost force. The first knife pierced the Chairman's throat and cut through the major arteries in his neck. The razor blade of the second, heavier, knife sliced through his spinal column. His weapon fell from his powerless hand. Dark red arterial blood sprayed across the room. The Chairman collapsed, his eyes wide. Reb closed her eyes and slowly sank to the floor. Scott moved to her side. Anna rushed to Mark and held his head trying to stem the blood pouring from his head wound.

A uniformed policeman entered the sitting room and was momentarily speechless when he saw the blood splattered scene. After a moment he asked, "Alright, what's been happening here?" No one answered.

He was pushed out of the way by two emergency personnel. The first one into the room checked Mark's pulse.

"He's alive."

***

Chapter 39

Maeve took her place on the same uncomfortable chair in Schmidt's hospital room. She removed a file and her laptop from her briefcase. The file was from one of her contacts in MI5. The laptop contained e-mails she wanted to read. Two feet away, Schmidt lay in his hospital bed, with monitoring devices still transmitting their messages.

She began to read aloud from the MI5 report. It summarized a confrontation in England between Midway and some rogue elements from Cerberus UK. Somehow, Midway had live-streamed videos of the confrontation to several news channels together with file videos of meetings between the Chairman and the leaders of the breakaway group. She shook her head. It would take some astute political maneuvering before Cerberus UK recovered.

Midway had been right to publicize the attack, she thought, to ensure his own safety, even if it meant major exposure of the UK operation. The genetic engineering aspects had been buried in the subsequent debate as to whether the news channels had transmitted fact or fiction. Of course, British authorities said it was all fiction. The disappearance of Midway and his friends after the TV program had strengthened that notion. It was perhaps unfair, though, of the public to accuse the media of pulling a ratings stunt.

Maeve finished reading the report: Midway was recovering in a private hospital, Reb had joined the crew of a yacht, Anna and Scott were looking after the children. Once Mark was able to travel, they intended to return to the US. Mark's proposed involvement in Cerberus UK was currently unresolved. She would address that when Mark was back in the country.

A rustle of bedclothes caught her attention. She stood and moved closer to Schmidt. Had he moved? As she watched, Schmidt opened his eyes and tried to speak. She moved closer, to hear his faint whisper.

"Who are you?" he asked, a bewildered expression on his face. Without waiting for her answer, he closed his eyes and fell back to sleep.

***

Books by John Hindmarsh

The following pages describe my books and stories and is current as at November, 2014.

Science Fiction
> Glass Complex Trilogy
>> Book 1: Broken Glass
>> Book 2: Fracture Lines (target is December, 2014)
>
> Shen Ark: Departure
> Another Universe - Volume 1

Thrillers
> Mark One
> Mark Two
> Mark Three

Explore further details at http://www.JohnHindmarsh.com

Mark One

Nine men, ex-military, are on a mission to destroy a genetics laboratory and capture a genetically engineered specimen. They are supported by four rogue CIA agents, who have commandeered a test drone and a missile, at a Marine base. The team attacks the genetics laboratory complex before dawn, during a raging blizzard. Within hours, seven of the men are dead, one is severely wounded, and one barely escapes. The drone with its missile has been destroyed. The next morning the four rogue agents are found dead from carbon monoxide poisoning.

Mark Midway does not know his real parents, nor where and when he was born. Two scientists adopted him when he was a young child and his home since has been a genetic research laboratory.

After the attack, Mark flees the laboratory complex, seeking safety and somewhere he can call home. The FBI is on his case and a mysterious organization offers him its assistance. However, he is at risk. There are unknown killers chasing him and he needs to protect himself and his friends.

Mark needs to survive. All he wants is a normal life.

A fast-moving, finely plotted political thriller that will keep you reading.

***

Mark Two

Cerberus is breeding super soldiers and has penetrated the FBI, DHS, CIA, the US Army, and other government departments. Rogue Cerberus soldiers have killed Agency operatives, deleted FBI records, stolen millions from currency transfers to Istanbul, and are creating even more powerful forces inimical to US law enforcement departments.

Archimedes Schmidt and Special Agent MayAnn Freewell go sailing in the Caribbean and when they meet with a Cerberus informer, a sniper assassinates him. The search for Cerberus escalates and Schmidt is recalled to active service and promoted to General.

MayAnn Freewell and Schmidt are sent to Afghanistan where they enlist the support of Special Forces to arrest a rogue Cerberus MP battalion. Schmidt is shot and survives.

Mark Midway is living in Boston under an assumed name when he is witness to a kidnapping. He shoots and kills the kidnappers and saves their victim, an eighteen-year-old daughter of a billionaire. His life goes downhill from that point: he is attacked, kidnapped, and then held prisoner with a group of Cerberus children.

Schmidt discovers his relationships are not as reliable as he thought, fatally so.

Key people in Cerberus are attacked by Chinese agents tasked with establishing a research laboratory so they can join the race to breed super soldiers.

Mark needs to survive. All he wants is a normal life.

Mark Two continues the page-turning momentum of Mark One; it is a fast-moving, finely plotted thriller that will keep you reading.

***

Mark Three

A young woman escapes from a luxury yacht under attack by Chinese pirates in the Mediterranean. American law enforcement agencies collude and conspire to bring about an end to Cerberus, uncaring who gets in their way. Genetically engineered Mark Midway faces deadly assaults by unknown enemies. A military helicopter is brought down over Washington by a Russian missile and General Archimedes Schmidt is in critical condition.

Mark meets his sister and travels to London to rescue three more genetically engineered children. He finds romance, but he and his companions are under attack in both the US and England. Mark knows only one response - fight back.

Mark needs to survive. All he wants is a normal life.

Mark Three is the third book in the Midway series and continues the page-turning pace and excitement of *Mark One* and *Mark Two*.

***

Broken Glass

Book 1 - Glass Complex Trilogy

Steg de Coeur, his family murdered to further an armed takeover of Homeworld by the House of Aluta, flees to space just ahead of corporate mercenaries and warrants issued for his arrest for treason against the Empire. Adventures follow as his ability to link with computers develops, in emulation of the Acolytes who attend the mysterious Glass Complex of Homeworld. Steg purchases a commission in the Imperial Fleet where he aids in the capture of an alien space ship preying on Imperial shipping lanes. He is court-martialed on trumped-up charges and marooned on Hellfire, a desert planet controlled by the House of Aluta. Steg takes over the computer-based mining equipment and creates havoc, eventually escaping with Milnaret of Fain, a pleasure companion. Duels, deaths, enlistment in Imperial Special Forces, and exploration of ancient portals drives the tension.

A deranged and very bitter rival for control of Homeworld attacks Steg with a blaster. Her attack severely injures him as he is about to step through a portal. He disappears and despite a major search by his fellow soldiers, he cannot be found.

The pace of *Broken Glass* is rapid with well developed and solid characters and a compelling storyline.

***

Fracture Lines

Book 2 - Glass Complex Trilogy
Fracture Lines is the long awaited sequel to ***Broken Glass***
and has a target of December 2014 for its release.

Steg de Coeur, severely wounded by a savage attack, is
transported some hundreds of years in his past. To make
matters worse, he not only has lost his memory, but ImpSec
sentence him to death as a spy when he is unable to account
for his presence on board an Imperial Fleet hospital ship. He
is off-loaded from the hospital ship in chains and admitted to
a prison run by the House of Aluta pending his execution.

Steg escapes the prison when a mercenary commander
recruits killers and other criminals who have been sentenced
to death and establishes himself as a potential mercenary
officer. He finally recovers his memory to discover the
mercenaries, lured into a trap, are about to engage three
Xesset starships.

Steg takes over leadership of the mercenary force and
takes the fight to the Xesset. The mercenaries not only must
defeat the Xesset, but they also must take over the freighter
which is shipping armaments to rebels on the main planet in
the Eo 3 system and then defeat the rebels in a planet-bound
battle.

His adventures take him back his proper time and to
Jochum II where ImpSec have taken over the base
established by the Imperial Intelligence Agency. His
challenge is to survive, discover what happened, and escape,
because a Xesset fleet is on its way to Homeworld.

***

Shen Ark: Departure

Dr. Joseph Krowe, a young scientist in London, develops a mind-bending drug—a pharmacological-chemical-nanite [PCN] mix—tests it on himself and almost dies. He tries to market PCN to a nightclub and disasters follow. Dr. Krowe barely survives. Meantime, his drug has initiated an accelerated evolutionary change in rats—New Rats. Their natural enemies—New Cats—also evolve, and a state of war exists between the two. Rats support Dr. Krowe, and he guides and influences them, as they continue to evolve.

The drug also affects some humans.

Freddie and his family befriend Sam, a young Rat who is a member of the Rat royal family, thus commencing a strong relationship between humans and Rats. Freddie—called Engineer by his friends—takes on responsibilities to aid the Rats' plan to purchase a starship from alien refugees—the Shen. His task is to build the bubble warp drive which he designed; the drive, if successful, will allow the starship to travel at faster than light speeds. Engineer experiences violent attacks, love, deaths of family and friends, looming deadlines, and other challenges as he attempts to meet his commitments to support the Rats' dream to travel in space.

Rats are impatient to board their starship and depart Earth.

Humans want the alien technology.

Cats just want to kill Rats.

Shen Ark: Departure is the beginning of a voyage that will follow Rats and a small group of humans as they attempt to achieve their dreams.

*** *

Another Universe - Volume 1

This first volume is a collection of three short stories, totaling about 11,000 words. I intend to release further collections, mainly science fiction, although some fantasy may creep in.

The Mortgage

Sometimes GalFed commercial operations are unsupervised, planets are mined or assets reaped, and there is no guarantee the planet will survive these attentions. *The Mortgage* is a story at the end cycle of one such planet.

Give Peace a Chance

I recently wrote *Shen Ark: Departure*, which tells a story about mutated rats (New Rats), cats (New Cats), other animals and humans, as the Rats prepare for a voyage in a starship. The Rats and Cats of course are bitter enemies.

Rats are impatient to board their starship and depart Earth.

Humans want the alien technology.

Cats just want to kill Rats.

To give you an idea of the relationship between Rats and Cats, here is a very brief excerpt:-

Cedric shivered and hid a rush of fear from his Rats and from himself as he realized the Cats' intense concentration was simply a prelude to their intended attack. These Cats had identified him as the leader of the New Rats, and he was their target. They stared at him with their almost glowing yellow eyes, as though each Cat was imprinting him on some feline prefrontal cortex target acquisition function. He shivered. Those yellow eyes watched his every move.

So the question arises: what would happen if one of the Cats was interested in peace? ***Give Peace a Chance*** is the result.

(*With apologies to John Lennon.)

Grators

Grators is one of a series of short stories about the Fleet hero, Foster Allyil. He claims he was a Colonel in the GalFed Fleet and has a starfighter stashed away—for defensive purposes only, of course. If readers are interested, I may develop his story and adventures into one or more novel length stories; I have unauthorized access to his logbooks and diaries, which should provide me with excellent material.

Occasionally, in stories about the GalFed universe, you might encounter a science fiction in-joke—if these are too obtuse, or indeed too obvious, let me know.

Watch for Volume Two – early 2015.

***

Quantum Zoo

Quantum Zoo is an anthology containing a wonderful collection of exciting, enthralling short stories from a dozen of the best new authors in science fiction and fantasy. From a ghost park to a time-travel penitentiary of murderers to a menagerie of Egyptian deities, Quantum Zoo presents 12 compelling stories involving 12 very different living exhibitions. Including a wonderfully atmospheric tale by Hugo- and Nebula-nominated Bridget McKenna.

I was invited to contribute one of my short stories and I submitted *You'll Be So Happy, My Dear*, which introduces the Xerggianths, aliens inimical to almost all intelligent life. Xergs just want to breed. The story moves almost into horror, although one of the reviewers described it as alien erotica.

Other contributors include Bridget McKenna, R.S. McCoy, A.C. Smyth, Ken Furie, Sarah Stegall, S.E. Batt, Scott Dyson, Morgan Johnson, Frances Stewart, D.J. Gelner, and J.M. Ney-Grimm. Visit their Author Pages on Amazon.

Quantum Zoo was edited by D. J. Gelner and J.M. Ney-Grimm. It was published by Orion Press.

***

Made in the USA
Charleston, SC
14 November 2014